CHARLES UNDERHILL

CAPTAIN FANTOM

ARROW BOOKS

Arrow Books Limited
3 Fitzroy Square, London W1P 6JD

An imprint of the Hutchinson Publishing Group

London Melbourne Sydney Auckland
Wellington Johannesburg and agencies
throughout the world

First published by Hutchinson 1978
Arrow edition 1979

Made and printed in Great Britain
by The Anchor Press Ltd
Tiptree, Essex

ISBN 0 09 919590 9

Contents

For John and Edna
who are not to blame for
either the history
or the morality
though not necessarily
in that order

She was I guessed from her dress and demeanour a daughter of the family, not a servant, and she looked at me with lively interest as I stepped smartly towards her. I had learned from my life in Venice how courtesy disarms even those most suspicious of the assassin, and now I smiled and bowed low, unfastening my breeches as I did so. When I rose, they fell, and my naked poinard was out; but the girl did not see it, for as I rose I caught up her skirts in my arms, flung them over her head and thrust my weapon upwards.

She shrieked beneath her petticoats and jerked violently backwards, taking us both into a large pigeon pie. The crust broke and a cloud of aromatic steam diverted my senses for a moment. But only for a moment. I thrust again. And behind me I heard a door open.

Editor's Preface

THE owner of the Carlo Fantom memoirs wishes to remain anonymous. In the past her family has done the state some service, but as is often the case this has long been forgotten. Unjust and envious taxation has diminished her fortunes but not her pride, and she rejects equally sensationalism and sentiment as means of re-establishing her once-famous name. It is the fact that the Fantom memoirs are not easily traceable to their present source which made her investigate their commercial potential. I was flattered to be asked to look them over. Later I felt privileged also.

The memoirs are written in such a variety of languages that I was able to read only about a third of them for myself, but I soon grasped their interest and value. Naturally I sought elsewhere for references to this strange and fascinating man. All I have been able to find is a very sketchy account of him in the writings of the seventeenth-century biographer and antiquarian, John Aubrey.

I give it here in full:

CAPTAIN CARLO FANTOM, a Croatian, spake thirteen languages; was a Captain under the Earle of Essex. He was very quarrelsome and a great Ravisher. He left the Parliament Party, and went to the King Ch. the first at Oxford, where he was hangd for Ravishing.

Sd. he, I care not for your Cause: I come to fight for your halfe-crowne, and your handsome woemen: my father was a R. Catholic; and so was my grandfather. I have fought for the Christians against the Turkes; and for the Turkes against the Christians.

Sir Robert Pye was his Colonel, who shot at him for not returning a horse that he tooke away before the Regiment. This was donne in a field near Bedford, where the Army then was, as they were marching to the relief of Gainsborough. Many are yet living that sawe it. Capt. Hamden was by: The bullets went through his Buff-coat, and Capt. H sawe his shirt on fire. Capt. Carl. Fantom tooke the Bullets, and sayd he, Sir Rob. Here, take your bullets again. None of the Soldiers would dare to fight with him: they sayd, they would not fight the Devil.

Edmund Wyld, Esq, was very well acquainted with him, and gave him many a Treat, and at last he prevailed with him so far, towards the knowledge of this secret, that Fantom told him, that the Keepers in their Forests did know a certain herb, which they gave to Children, which made them to be shott-free (they call them Hard-men).

In a Booke of Trialls by Duell in foli (writ by Segar, I thinke) before the Combatants fight, they have an Oath administered to them by the Herald; where is inserted (among other things) that they have not about them either Charme or Herb.

Martin Luther in his Commentaries on the First (or second Commandment, I thinke the First) saies that a Hard-man was brought to the Duke of Saxonies Court: he was brought into the great Hall and was commanded to be shott with a Musquet: the bullet drop't downe and he had only a blew Spott on his Skin, where he was struck. Martin Luther was then by, and sawe the Bullet drop-downe.

They say that a silver bullet will kill any Hardman, and can be beaten to death with cudgels. The Elector Palatine, Prince Robert's (Rupert's) Brother, did not believe at all, that any man could make himself hard.

Robert Earl of Essex, General for the Parliament had this Capt. Fantom in high esteeme: for he was an admirable Horse-officer, and taught the Cavalry of the army the way of fighting with Horse: the General saved him from hanging twice for Ravishing; once at Winchester, 2nd at St Albans: and he was not content only to ravish himselfe, but he would make his soldiers doe it too, and he would stand by and look on.

He met (comeing late at night out of the Horse-shoe Tavern in Drury lane) with a Lieuetenant of Col. Rossiter, who had great jingling Spurres on. Qd. he, the noise of your Spurres doe offend me, you must come over the Kennel and give me satisfaction. They drew and parted at each other and the Lieuetenant was runne thorough and died within a hour or two: and 'twas not known, who killed him.

I now set about the work of translation with a will. I was able to deal with the major European tongues myself, but the more obscure languages I had to farm out to professional translators. Curiously, Fantom nowhere writes in English, though he clearly spoke it perfectly. This may have been because the bulk of the memoirs seem actually to have been composed in England and the use of other languages hindered prying eyes. I have thus felt myself free to create an English style for Fantom. Naturally it is based principally on my own, which I hope shares a quality of muscular dignity with Fantom's as evidenced in his French and German. Where frankness was required, I have not hesitated to use it; nor have I shrunk from using neologisms when the mood and tone of the original can best be caught by them.

The owner of the memoirs has accepted absolutely my judgement of how to translate the works. But (and quite properly, I believe) she has retained to herself the right to decide the form and order of their publication.

It is her choice that this first selection should cover a broad sweep of many years. She it is who picked out the thread of coherent narrative which runs through the episodes here presented. My task has merely been to tailor the whole together, and if at times I may have taken more than a translator's licence with certain bridge passages, this is preferable I believe to the frequent intrusion of an editorial presence.

Fantom's memoirs are comprehensive. There is no gap but can be filled in. It is my unselfish hope that the reading public will be eager to hear more and thus restore to the last of an ancient family something of the comforts of life which unjust tribunals and the change of times have taken from her.

Doncaster, 1977 CHARLES UNDERHILL

1623

East Friesland – Brunswick – Munster

I HAD a good war till they fixed Wallenstein.

That was in '33. No. I tell a lie. '34.

I'd had half a dozen very memorable years with him. Fighting the Emperor's wars. Filching the Emperor's wealth. Fucking the Emperor's women.

Oh yes. The Catholic faith got value for money from me.

I was born a Catholic, you understand, and it has always been a great comfort to me to find myself soldiering under the banner of the True Church. Unfortunately it has not always been convenient. After an apprenticeship both with and against the Turks, Uskoks, and Venetians, I started my war service proper with Count Mansfeld in the Evangelical Union's army. Union! We were more like a rampaging mob. But evangelical we certainly were, spreading the word right across Germany. Alas, if the trail of little bastards we left behind us all grew up Protestants, I fear I helped deal the True Church a nasty blow.

Ernst Mansfeld wasn't a bad sort, but his name stank in East Friesland where we were quartered in '23. I was still young, not much past twenty, but I'd learned early that it's not your own deeds that matter but the friends you've got when you're caught. And after a few months' experience of our economic strategy (a subtle combination of plunder, murder and rape), the local burghers about to slit your throat for thieving would slit your belly first if you mentioned Mansfeld's name.

Well, no man of honour could serve under these conditions and, besides, there was no money left to pay us with. So early one morning in late July I packed up my clothes, my arms, and my copy of Xenophon's *Hippike*, saddled up Laura, my Andalusian mare, and with my two other mounts trotting behind, I headed south.

A few days later I found myself on the edge of action once more and I made a few discreet observations before deciding where to offer my services. In fact, there was no competition. On the one side was Christian of Brunswick who was mad, one-armed, destitute, and in retreat. On the other was the much larger army of Maximilian of Bavaria, a well disciplined, well fed and regularly paid body of men. What really tipped the scale, of course, was that this force represented the cause of the True Church.

The general was Tilly, a Belgian but a good soldier in spite of it. His men were mainly Spaniards (too cunning to get killed) and Saxons (too thick to notice it), a good combination. The officers were the usual mixed bunch from just about every nation in Europe. Some of them I knew already, either from fighting with or against them in the past. A professional must go where his talents are best rewarded.

One of these, a grizzled old Scot who claimed to have started his military career fighting for Mary Stuart at Langside, encountered me soon after my arrival in the camp.

'Well noo, Fantom, ye miserable turncoat,' he greeted me.

I laughed, though normally like most rogues I am quick to resent any slur on my honour. The point was that Lauder until a couple of months earlier had been fighting alongside me for the Evangelical Union. He offered to share his quarters with me till I had settled in and made myself familiar with the new set-up. Armies are like monasteries, alike but different, and the novice is well advised to tread carefully for a few days, so I accepted with pleasure.

The army was bivouacked in a good defensive position along the inner bank of a deep curve of the Weser. Water behind, flat countryside ahead, and a small farming settlement, hardly big enough to be called a village, right in the middle. I saw my horses safely picketed, checked that the guard was awake and alert (for my horses were always of the best and naturally a source of some temptation to the raff), and followed Lauder. On our way from the picket line we encountered a fresh-faced young officer whom Lauder greeted in a friendly fashion though the boy's response was off hand to the point of rudeness. I called him a boy because of his clean-shaven girlishly good looking face and pink and white complexion, but in fact he must have been almost of an age with me. I was surprised in view of his youth when Lauder introduced him to me as Colonel D'Amblève. Rank was of little interest to a mercenary like myself. Field officers had too much responsibility, got themselves too well known. I'd fight as hard as the next man for my money, but when the next man decided it was time to go home, I wanted to be with him or, better still, slightly ahead of him without being hauled before a court martial.

But it was still annoying to find myself lower down the ladder than this pretty child. I saluted him civilly enough, however, and when he enquired whence I had come, I assumed this was the usual professional interest and answered without hesitation.

His lips pursed in distaste and he said to Lauder, 'Another of your good example. When the trumpet sounds, I hope you will know which way to face.'

'Our horses are well trained, sir,' said Lauder courteously.

'Your horses will not be distressed by the trumpet I speak of,' said D'Amblève pompously. 'Though you may be. Gentlemen, good day.'

He strode away, vibrating self-righteousness. His scarlet and blue cloak flapped in the wind and his large enamelled silver spurs (worn, I hoped, for ornament not use) tinkled as he walked, making more noise than a flock of Turkish sheep.

I took a step after him, my instincts prompting me to plant the toe of my boot between the cheeks of that tight little arse, but Lauder restrained me.

'He is a Belgian,' he said. 'And second cousin to the General.'

'Ah,' I said. D'Amblève's rank and Lauder's acceptance of his discourtesy were at once explained. Professionally, I shared the old Scot's attitude, of course; but I told myself inwardly, should D'Amblève ever go down in the charge and I be close, then not all the honied words in Castiglione's book of courtesy would coax assistance from me.

Some naughty god must have heard me for two days later this very situation arose. The army was advancing through heavily wooded country and I was scouting ahead with what the English very aptly call the Forlorn Hope, that small advance force whose job it is to start any ambushes the enemy may have laid. In fact, it was rarely as dangerous as it sounded for usually what you encountered was the enemy's Forlorn Hope and after a token skirmish, each group went galloping back to report to the main force.

This time however we ran into a substantial ambuscade. We were riding down a low narrow field bordered by copses of birch and elm when ahead of us and to the left there was the dull crack of a musket. I pulled up instantly, guessing that, as often happened, someone's matchlock had gone off prematurely, and this was confirmed by a rapid rattle of fire from the trees ahead. A few more paces would have brought us opposite the concealed musketeers and our casualties could have been heavy. As it was, two or three of my men were hit and several horses, and while we were still struggling to regain control, from behind the copse to our left appeared a force of enemy cavalry twice as large as our own. I gave the order to withdraw and rapidly set a good example. Orfeo, my Arab gelding, was the best schooled and the fleetest horse in the troop and naturally I was soon well ahead of the bunch. So fast was I going that I almost ran right into a party of our own cavalry headed by the beautiful boy, Colonel D'Amblève.

I did not need to explain the situation as the rest of my men now appeared at the gallop with the enemy close on their heels.

'Still facing the wrong way, Fantom,' said this fresh-faced shit.

I said nothing but let Orfeo pick his way through D'Amblève's horse, not caring to be in the front line when the charge hit us. It wasn't the enemy that bothered me so much as my own men who, unable or unwilling to pull up between their pursuers and their rescuers, hit the latter like a volley of cannon. Horses reared and screamed, riders were unseated, ally shouted abuse at ally, and swords were raised in anger. And the enemy had not yet arrived.

But now they did. Their impetus drove them deep through the already broken ranks of our riders. Numbers were now about equal but the advantage was very much with the enemy and had they been more expertly led, they would quickly have gained the mastery. But they had no idea of tactics other than to stand in their stirrups and hack about wildly; and as most of them were armed with tucks, or even rapiers, both designed for thrusting rather than chopping, this was less than effective. For all that, it was nasty enough, and I let Orfeo walk delicately round the periphery of the combat for a few moments. It's one thing to charge hot blooded into the middle of a fight, another to edge your horse coldly into it. But this was what I was paid for, so I drew the short, heavy, double-edged sword I carried for close quarter work and joined the fray.

Indiscriminate hacking is pretty useless, unless you're desperate to clear a space for yourself, for you are as likely to cut down your friends as your foe. I crouched low against Orfeo's neck and picked my targets carefully. The enemy like ourselves were only lightly armoured. Had they been cuirassiers, I shouldn't have bothered to get mixed up with them. But these men wore only helmets and corselets and occasionally greaves. Their horses were almost completely unprotected, so when I couldn't get the angle I wanted for a thrust through the side where the corslet was hinged, I contented myself with drawing the backhand edge of my sword – which was serrated like a saw – across their horses' bellies or sometimes their hamstrings. It wasn't spectacular fighting but I reckon I inflicted more damage in five minutes than D'Amblève and all his men together. My main concern was whether or not the Protestant musketeers would come up behind their cavalry who would then quickly disengage to let the foot soldiers mow us down with a concentrated volley. I began to think I might be better employed riding for assistance to our main army when suddenly a horse fell close by with a terrible scream. It threshed about for a few moments, its belly ripped open, and the horses round about moved away leaving a small clearing in the middle of the skirmish.

Lying there in a pool of blood, which regretfully I quickly realized came from his dying horse, was D'Amblève. He had managed to injure his left leg in falling – perhaps he had stabbed himself with one of those damned silly spurs – and he was using his sword as a crutch to push himself upright. This is not such a good idea when two very ill-disposed riders are bearing down on you, content to trample you underfoot if their rapier thrusts miss.

D'Amblève saw his danger, brought his sword up to parry the threatened blows and, deprived of his prop, fell flat on his face in his horse's bowels. As a temporary evasive tactic, it worked and both the Protestant blows whistled through empty air. D'Amblève should have feigned dead. It might have meant putting up with a couple of horses walking across him, but discomfort is only relative. Instead he pushed his upper body off the ground, raised his head and looked straight at me.

Annoyed as men become who tread on a beetle then see it scuttle away when they raise their feet, the two Protestants pulled their horses round to finish off the job.

I should have let them get on with it. If I had known the trouble his survival would bring me, I'd have done more – I'd have given them a hand! But he was a brother officer, up to his neck in equine blood and shit, and his only offence had been to be rude to me.

And, of course, he was our commander-in-chief's cousin and apparently of some sentimental value.

So I urged Orfeo forward, waited till the first rider rose out of his saddle, and sank my sword into his groin. Leaving it there, I now drew my pistol – my precious English dog-lock which I could carry into battle primed and cocked with hardly any risk of it going off prematurely and blowing away my balls – rested the butt between Orfeo's ears and fired into the second man's face. I then retrieved my sword, ran the serrated edge quickly across the first rider's neck as he threw back his head to scream, and pulled D'Amblève across the saddle in front of me like a sack of flour.

Orfeo bore us both away from the press and as soon as we were quite clear I tipped the youngster into a ditch where he could lie in safety till the fighting was over. I could have borne him back triumphantly to the main army, I suppose, but to tell the truth he smelt so foully that I felt quite nauseated and I could tell that Orfeo didn't care much for it either.

When I got back to the fight, it was almost finished. The musketeers weren't coming, that was clear, and the Protestant captain had settled for a draw. Both sides had disengaged simultaneously so that neither felt disgraced and the only people still fighting were two unhorsed and disarmed soldiers who were wrestling and punching each other with a vast expense of energy for comparatively small results. Gradually they realized that everyone else was waiting for them and rather sheepishly they stood up, separated and joined their fellows. And that was that. We had seven dead, two seriously wounded and host of minor cuts and scratches. Only two of the dead were my men, which pleased me. I like to be associated with survivors, both under and over me.

I told D'Amblève's sergeant where to find his colonel and took my own men back to report. I made no mention of my part in saving D'Amblève's life, of course. Such things must always come from other sources. It would not have surprised me if the beautiful boy had forgotten to tell anyone, but I did him an injustice. Chivalrous prigs are forced by their own code to acknowledge deeds of valour and debts of honour. I was summoned to the commander's tent that night where Tilly thanked me courteously for the assistance I had given his cousin that day. I made modest noises but Tilly was a professional too, though of a different kind from myself, and he smiled thinly and cut through my play acting.

'Colonel D'Amblève and I are both in your debt,' he said. 'Call on us when you are in most need.'

Yes, the old boy knew that his professionals would always want to be paid in the end.

1624–6

Lower Saxony

SOLDIERING under Tilly was a very different business from soldiering under Mansfeld. For a start you got your money fairly regularly. Don't misunderstand me, there was still plenty of pillaging and all the rest going on, but that was for extras and in your own time. As a well paid and, in a strict military sense, well disciplined force, we moved where tactics demanded, whereas Mansfeld's lot tended to sit on a patch of countryside till they'd sucked it dry then move on in search of fresh suckings.

Mind you, I don't think the peasants very much appreciated the differences between us. I could remember the days only a few years earlier when there was still what the politician's call a climate of confidence. Three or four of you could ride up to some nice isolated farmhouse and get a real welcome with only the minimum of persuasion. Water for the horses, supper with the family, two or three juicy farm lasses who'd have been disappointed if you hadn't given them a good bang on the old farmer's bed. And when that was done, you'd help yourself to the sockful of gold he kept under it and be on your way, no one harmed. The girls were used to having their porridge stirred by everything in breeches, including their own granddads. You brought news of the great world outside, who was up, who was down. It they were Catholics I'd tell 'em the Emperor was triumphant, if Protestants I'd assure them that the Emperor was on the up and up. And as for taking their money, there was sure to be another sock somewhere up the chimney or in the midden. They could keep that. I was never greedy. As long as I could live well, dress well, own good horses, I never cared for the accumulation of wealth. In my trade a private fortune is awkward to transport and difficult to protect, a constant invitation to your improvident fellows to slit your throat some misty night. Well, everyone knew I spent as quickly as I got, so if anyone wanted to catch Carlo Fantom with gold in his purse, he'd have to move like lightning!

But those easy days were long past. Now at the first approach of the soldiery, the locals buried their wealth and headed for the hills so that very often by the time you caught up with them you were too tired to perform. In any case I suffered from a most unfortunate disability which prevented me from restricting my activities to the safety of the general sacking of a town or the remoteness of some peasant's cottage. Most officers of my acquaintance were able to modify their approach according to their company. I have seen men whose bare buttocks I have observed bobbing with the best after a successful assault on a city only a few hours later smirking and bowing and kissing hands and going through all the other long preludes to uncertain cuckoldry which polite society requires of a gentleman. But I could never manage it. I was no pampered jade, bred for the safe carriage of ladies. No, like a well trained cavalry horse when the trumpets sounded, there was no reigning me back. I must charge!

And therein lay my disability, for I never knew when those trumpets would sound. And this, as you may imagine, led me into grave danger. It meant that instead of ignorant peasants whom no one really cared about, I was often led on to ravish a much better class of woman, tradesmen's wives, merchants' daughters, gentlewomen even. Circumstance had made me a social climber and the higher you get, the harder you may fall.

Tilly was both a comfort and a liability in these matters. I had saved the life of the beautiful boy and this counted for a great deal. But he was cursed with religious leanings – I heard that at one stage in his life he had thought of becoming a priest! – and though he had as little control over the behaviour of his men as any general who cannot keep up to date with their wages, yet where he could administer discipline, this he did with great vigour. A case once proved, Tilly was quite happy to let a couple of his men be whipped or branded or occasionally hanged. It kept relations with the civilian populace (at least, that bit of it that mattered) in some kind of balance and it provided an entertainment for bored soldiery.

Well, for the most part I had kept my nose clean, only once or twice having to rely on my special relationship with the general to save an awkward situation. Usually I managed things by myself, either by moving with so great a speed that I escaped identification, or else making some kind of financial arrangement with the man of the house. Most husbands and fathers have their price. Oddly, the former generally come cheaper. But word does tend to get around in a small set-up like an army and I knew that my credit with Tilly was perhaps growing a little thin. But he was a fair man. He would make it quite clear to me when finally it ran out.

That time came one smokily hot June day in a little market town called Zweikirchen in Lower Saxony. There had been a long lull in the fighting and for once we could feel able to enjoy our repose. I was strolling down a narrow street which in winter must have become a river of mud but which presently was baked hard and brown. Something whistled past my head and bounded on the hard surface. It was a ham bone picked clean. As I watched a cur ran past me, seized it in his teeth and ran off quickly, pursued by half a dozen others which seem to have sprung out of the dust. I looked up to see a young woman looking down at me from the second storey of the tall overhanging house I was passing. She had a broad grin on her round jolly face. Whether the ham bone had been aimed at me and if so, with what motive, I did not know. But suddenly the trumpet was sounding and the spurs were being dug deep. I pushed open the house door and boldly walked up the staircase I found facing me. On the second landing I turned left and a moment later was in a large well furnished room with the girl. A table was set for a meal and clearly she had been paring the last pieces of meat off the bone which she had tossed through the window. I say 'clearly' because in her right hand she had a large knife with which she was separating the ribs of a half side of beef. Despite the deprivations of the war, there seemed to be no shortage in this house.

She was I guessed from her dress and demeanour a daughter of the family, not a servant, and she looked at me with lively interest as I stepped smartly towards her. I had learned from my life in Venice how courtesy disarms even those most suspicious of the assassin, and now I smiled and bowed low, unfastening my breeches as I did so. When I rose, they fell, and my naked poinard was out; but the girl did not see it, for as I rose I caught up her skirts in my arms, flung them over her head and thrust my weapon upwards.

She shrieked beneath her petticoats and jerked violently backwards, taking us both into a large pigeon pie. The crust broke and a cloud of aromatic steam diverted my senses for a moment. But only for a moment. I thrust again. And behind me I heard a door open.

What it feels like for the *burgermeister* and his wife of a small German town to bring their pastor into lunch and discover their daughter being ravished across the first course, I do not know. But I do know what it looks and sounds like.

The *burgermeister*, a short fat man in his fifties, with a face as brown and polished as the crust of his pigeon pie, rounded every facial orifice, including his piggy nostrils, into an O of incredulity. His wife equally fat but a foot taller threw back her head and began to scream. The pastor stared at us with lively interest, and, reverting to type, began to pray in Latin.

Reluctantly I abandoned the girl and stood upright. The sight did nothing to reassure them. The girl's screams now mingled with her mother's and she swung the carving knife which she still held in her hand, in an arc which nicked my left ear. I felt it was time to leave.

Trying to draw up my breeches, I turned and made for the staircase. Behind me the girl fell into the pastor's arms (strange choice), her father stood surveying indignantly the damage done to his dinner, and the mother seizing the knife from her daughter's nerveless grip came in pursuit.

My German was good enough to understand the proposals she was screaming after me and I started taking the stairs three at a time which, with my breeches still around my knees, proved too hard a task. I tripped at the first landing and crashed head over heels to the foot of the stairs.

The good Frau was upon me in a flash. I caught her knife arm as the weapon came swinging down at my belly and used her own impetus to bring her crashing down beside me. The breath was knocked out of her and I wrestled her over on her back with the simple intention of rendering her *hors de combat* while I made my escape. But despite everything my weapon was still at the ready, I realized, and her skirts were round her bum. I took careful aim.

When the *burgermeister*, his daughter and the pastor arrived on the first landing a minute later, I did not need to look or listen. Their disbelief was tangible.

But at least, I thought as I stood up and adjusted my dress prior to leaving, I had probably discouraged pursuit.

All might have been well if I had ridden straight back to my quarters and kept out of sight till the army moved on. Complaints of one kind or another poured in every day and no one bothered with identity parades. If they wanted military justice the burghers had to bring the criminal with them. But it never occurred to me to hide. By the time I'd ridden a hundred yards, the business had quite gone from my mind. It nearly always does. I enjoy the performance but I neither gloat nor agonize over the memory.

So my indignation was not at all faked when half an hour later a gang of watch-men armed with staves burst into the *Gasthof* where I was drinking with Lauder and seized me before I could resist. The *burgermeister* was with them, more porcine that ever in his triumphant outrage. It was at this point that I realized he *was* the *burgermeister* and I felt a momentary unease.

Lauder was too canny to offer me any assistance in the face of such odds. Indeed as my offence became clear to him, his face, wrinkled and worn like an old leather purse, assumed an expression of distaste and he said, 'He that committeth fornication sinneth against his own body.'

I knew full well from having listened to him in his cups that this deep respect for the purity of his flesh had only developed as age had rendered other attitudes academic, but his sincerity of tone impressed the Germans and they accepted his suggestion that I be brought before Tilly at once.

I was heartily glad at this in one way. While my captors would scarcely have dared to kill an officer of the League in broad daylight, the *burgermeister* looked capable of putting the boot in with nasty effect if he had got me alone in the local gaol. On the other hand a couple of hours' grace might have given me a chance to set up some kind of alibi.

Tilly listened in grave silence to the complaint while beside him D'Amblève glared at me in pink and white disapproval. But some of the other senior officers present turned away to conceal smiles as the details of the story were revealed. The *burgermeister* saw this too and launched angrily into a powerful plea for justice, reminding Tilly of the agreement reached between the army and the town fathers by which the town offered provisions and shelter in return for a guarantee of good order.

It was a valid argument and Tilly looked at me with an expression which told me the end of my credit was near.

'Captain Fantom,' he said. 'How do you answer these grave charges?'

'Charges, sir? Which charges?' I said casually.

'Do not be frivolous in this company,' advised Tilly acidly.

'I am not frivolous, sir. But do we now dignify with the title of charges what seem to me but malicious assertions? When no evidence or witnesses are produced, surely what we hear is not a *charge* so much as a *slander*.'

'Would you have ladies brought before this company, sir, to confess the shame you have put upon them?' This was the lovely lad, of course, his golden curls shaking with indignation.

Tilly silenced him with a glance.

'*Burgermeister*,' he said, 'can you support these allegations with witnesses? We are loth to bring your wife and daughter here, but justice must be served?'

'No need, your Eminence,' said the *burgermeister* triumphantly. A few minutes later, the bible-clutching pastor was produced, ready and eager to tell all he had seen.

'Hold, sir,' I said as he began. 'First I shall require of you to swear an oath.'

'An oath!' he echoed. 'What form of oath?'

'None that I shall not prove willing to swear myself when my time comes,' I assured him. 'You have your Bible there I see. Place your hand on it and take your oath like a Christian.'

I spoke casually but I was tense inside. My guess and my hope was that this so-called pastor would prove to be one of those anabaptists who spotted Germany like the pox and who believed that the third commandment made the taking of oaths a blasphemy.

There was a long silence then finally, 'No!' he said.

I sighed with relief. When it comes down to it some of these anabaptists can be as subtle as Jesuits with their equivocations, but I'd got myself a nice simple one here. The point was that we were an army of conquest, not of conversion, and as far as Tilly was concerned, though he believed firmly in the cause he fought for, the towns he overran were judged by their degree of co-operation rather than of catholicism. A Protestant *burgermeister* leading his fellows in collaboration was preferable to a Catholic figurehead placed there by the army. But tolerance can only be tolerated so far. Tilly was genuinely disgusted by this display of the Protestant ego and in addition there was enough left of my credit for him to welcome a quick way out.

He rose. The *burgermeister* began to protest but the commander silenced him with a wave of his hand, saying, 'I will not hang my officers where the evidence is not given in the name of God.'

I smiled gratefully and perhaps rather triumphantly, for he looked coldly at me and added, 'Though be assured that where the evidence holds, then any of my men, of no matter what elevation of rank, shall be fittingly punished.'

I had been warned. I went away resolved to learn self-control from my near escape, and indeed for a fortnight or more I did not touch a lady of any quality, no, not even an ordinary burgher's wife, but contented myself with females of the lower orders such as freely follow the army.

Then we marched once more and I was kept in a state of grace by the angel of fatigue who was my constant companion. Tilly saw to this, aided by the beautiful boy. I was given command of a company of foragers and found that I was covering twice as much ground each day as the main force in its advance. Nor could I complain that this expense of energy was not necessary for Mansfeld had passed this way too recently for provender to be easily available. What little food and grain remained the peasants hid, and themselves with it. It was no life for a soldier of spirit and strong affections.

Lauder would smile when he heard my complaints, the expression crossing his face like the glint of rare sunlight on one of his native black lochs.

'It's nae more than ye deserve, ye cock-worshipping Goth,' he said. But he devoured with relish the excellent meals which were the one benefit of my enforced activity. He was an interesting old sod. He had seen everything, sampled everything. I honestly believe there was nothing in the whole gamut of human experience from holiness to depravity which he wasn't acquainted with. Finally, assisted by age, he had settled for comfort. But it had to be comfort in the life which had been his for sixty years. No retired Praetorian's hill farm would suit Lauder.

'When do we fight, Lauder?' I asked.

'Soon,' he said sucking at a chicken leg.

'Well, let's hope we win, but not too decisively,' I said. 'It'd be a shame not to spin this war out a bit.'

He stopped sucking and looked at me in contempt.

'Ye've a brain the size of a sow's balls, Fantom,' he said. 'They'll be fighting this war for the next five hundred years.'

During the next few weeks we had several skirmishes with the enemy and it must be admitted we frequently came off worst. But they were clearly reluctant to meet us, strength against strength. Mansfeld would have had no qualms, but his impetuousness had brought him disaster against Wallenstein at Dessau and he was presently on his way to Hungary with the Emperor's second army in pursuit. The enemy we faced was led by Christian of Denmark and we finally cornered him at Lutter.

It was a close fought fight with the outcome delicately balanced till there occurred one of those amusing little surprises which you only get when you're fighting with mercenaries. Suddenly and quite audibly to us in that part of the field, a whole company of Christian's men announced that they were withdrawing their labour till they got paid. This had us falling about with laughter! It's happened before, of course, for it's a common trick of generals to postpone pay day till after the big fight, knowing full well their labour force and therefore their wage bill will have been considerably reduced. Some rapid negotiations began and we thought things would be quickly settled. But soon it became apparent all was not well. We discovered later that Christian wasn't just holding back, he was flat broke. Charles Stuart had evidently promised him a lot of money but the English Parliament had shown more sense and kept their hands firmly in their pockets.

So there was no cash settlement and to our delight, the disgruntled men began gathering up their weapons and moving out. I tried to get authority to offer them terms with Tilly's army, but unfortunately the nearest I could get to the commander was D'Amblève who listened to my suggestion with disgust and commanded me back to the fighting as though I had been seeking an excuse to avoid it.

As it happened, we managed without their help. In fact when I got back to my station, I found our cavalry had burst through the Danes' emaciated line and were busily killing, among others, the poor devils who had withdrawn.

After that we quickly mopped up the remaining opposition

and in a surprisingly short time found we had moved from the possibility of defeat to a complete victory. God bless King Charles and his Parliament. They had done me a good turn unawares. Though twenty years later in just the same casually ignorant manner, each in turn would cause me a deal of woe.

After the battle the victor enjoys his spoils. Unfortunately we had been around the Bishopric of Hildersheim for so long now that there was little left unspoilt. And to make matter's worse, with Christian's defeat all the local rulers hastily asserted their loyalty to the Emperor and suddenly we were surrounded by allies! Well, at least it meant that Tilly was able to squeeze some cash out of them and pay off some of our wage arrears. But it meant that the ambitious soldier had to ride quite a long way in search of the rewards of virtue!

The army then settled down in quarters for a while awaiting news from Hungary of the Wallenstein–Mansfeld conflict. This Wallenstein was beginning to interest me very much. Naturally I had heard of him when he first raised his army the previous year. Any new centre of employment makes every mercenary's nose twitch. First reports had been good, but I was happy enough where I was at that time and still enjoying the full warmth of Tilly's favour. But that was a guttering flame now and when a couple of Wallenstein's regiments came to reinforce us earlier in the summer, I made it my business to get to know their officers pretty well. And of course I kept a close eye on the way their units handled themselves in the fight.

I was very impressed, and was attracted also by what I learned of Wallenstein himself. He was a Bohemian financier who very early on had recognized that Frederick and his Protestant supporters had as much chance as a straw chastity belt of keeping Ferdinand out. So he got in on the act, first by land speculation (not that there was anything very speculative about buying up confiscated Protestant land at rock bottom prices and reselling it later when things had quietened down!) next by loaning cash to the Emperor who was having to dig deep in his coffers for Tilly's wages, and finally by raising an army at his own expense.

He sounded just my cup of tea. Clever, powerful, with an excellent grasp of warfare and a keen eye for profit; I marked him down in my mind for a rainy day, but at the moment my life looked set fair. One or two innovations on the Swedish lines in the disposition of my troop had worked very well in the recent battle and Tilly complimented me personally and invited me to present him with a written account of my concept of cavalry tactics. Religion apart, he was a real soldier that one, no personal ambition, just a mind dedicated to moulding men into an efficient fighting machine. He would pay heed to the lowliest soldier in his service if he felt that a military advantage might be derived therefrom. To me it was a heaven-sent chance to put myself on his sunny side once more and I took great care in the setting down of my ideas, though scrivening such as this present has always been a labour to me. It took me a week, with interludes for a gentleman's proper exercise of course, and I whistled gaily in pleasure at being finished and in anticipation of being well received as I rode into Lutter one sunny forenoon on my way to Tilly's quarters. Nothing was further from my mind than women (in the particular rather than the general sense, I mean) and I even smiled to myself when I saw this girl and rode on as if I could ignore the trumpets. Then I found I had stopped and was looking back. One part of my mind was saying, still without too much urgency, 'Don't be foolish! The maid is noble. Tilly – soon to be your benefactor once more – has commanded the ultimate punishment for all transgressions in this town. Ride on and be happy!'

But another part was asking, 'Where's she gone?'

She had been a tall slender young woman, richly dressed with russet hair plaited and coiled above her crown. By her side had hobbled an elderly serving woman dressed all in black for even these Saxon clods feel that it is unseemly for ladies of quality to walk in the streets unchaperoned, and at a short distance behind, more sensible protection, had been a young man in livery, with a stave in his hand and a knife at his belt. It was this fellow who showed me the direction to take, for he lingered at a corner to exchange compliments with a wench lugging a keg of cider. The man-at-arms paused to paddle his fingers in her neck and she squealed pleasurably and threatened him with her keg. He laughed, made bold with her once more, then moved out of sight. But his amorous weakness had shown me the way to his lady. How soon will these small vices betray a man!

He had gone through a high arched gate into a small courtyard. Here I left Orfeo loosely tethered, for the sound of the trumpet had not yet overwhelmed all the whispers of caution.

A small blue door stood ajar. Through it I saw the moving green of a breeze-touched pear tree and heard the splash of softly falling water. Carefully I pushed the door wide and stepped through.

I was in a garden. These men of wealth know better than to display their luxury to an envious and covetous public. The little courtyard behind me held no promise of such an Eden as this. The garden though not large was laid out with a skill and taste which must have been imported. Some journeying artist of the soil from Italy perhaps. Or even from England whose climate suits so well all growing things. Except man. Beside the pear tree there were a couple of apples, a nectarine and a low-stooping plum all laden with ripening fruit, while all along the walls ran a torrent of roses. A smooth-razed lawn bore a shell of marble in which knelt a small sea-nymph exquisitely carved so the delicate veins of the stone looked like her own. She held an urn before her, from which ran a stream of water whose sound mingled with the piping of birds.

But I had no eyes for beauties of stone, no matter how soft and round art made their form appear, nor ear for any sound save that of my inner trumpets. Seated on a three-legged joint-stool alongside the fountain was the young woman. Her eyes were closed and she might have been part of some sublimely lovely group sculpted by Michaelangelo.

I wasted little time admiring the scene however. When

battle is inevitable, the wise cavalryman never delays the charge. My weapon was ready primed. I took it from its holster and set off across the lawn at a steady canter.

She had no more defence than a troop of drowsy Frenchmen at first light. And I fear her reveries must have been just as carnal, so easily did I melt into them. It wasn't till her bum subsided into the pool that she began to struggle and scream as though the shock had awoken her. But by then it was too late. The walls had been undermined and all that her struggles did was explode my charge the sooner.

'Servant, ma'am,' I gasped and prepared to withdraw.

Unfortunately at that moment the young man-at-arms appeared on the scene. For a second the sight of his mistress with her behind in the water and her legs splayed wide over the edge of the stone shell had the same affect on him as his daughter in the pigeon pie had on the *burgermeister*. Taking advantage of his momentary petrification, I dashed by him towards the blue door, but the stupid lad with more luck than skill cast his stave between my legs and brought me down. While I lay winded, he leapt on my back and to my great relief began to belabour me with his fists, whereas a mature fighting man would have slit my jugular with his dagger and left me kicking there like a Yuletide goose.

I pushed myself upright with the youth still clinging to my back, then ran backwards with all my strength till we crashed into the pear tree. He screamed, branches cracked, and the hard green fruit showered down on our heads. But still he clung on. Three times I had to repeat the process so that the tree was almost uprooted and not a pear remained on it before I persuaded him to loose his hold.

Had there been time I would have drawn my sword and slit his belly for his impudence, but the garden was full of screaming – the girl's, the youth's and now the newly arrived old chaperone's, and there was no time for luxuries.

I sprinted through the blue door, sprung on to Orfeo who looked as if he would have been disappointed had I approached at a normal pace, and before I could dig in my heels, he was off through the gate.

But as we galloped away I knew I was likely to need more than Orfeo's speed and my own fighting skill to escape this predicament.

In order to avoid dangerous temptation I had found quarters in a small hamlet some miles outside the town, or rather these had been found by Lauder, who always chose to mess apart from his brother officers except in the field. While he was careful to keep on good terms with his superiors, he had in his long career seen too many generals become political victims and he knew that guilt went by association or even proximity. My company he accepted because he reckoned no one was going to accuse him of complicity in my own simple failing. I accepted his because I was fond of the old bastard and besides he had an unerring instinct for comfort. But this particular comfort would almost certainly have to be abandoned, I realized as I headed for home.

After the first mad dash I had pulled Orfeo back to a more sedate pace partly to conserve his energy for what might prove to be a long and wearisome journey, and partly to avoid drawing attention to myself. Not that I had much hope of avoiding identification. Had it been only the girl herself I might have been optimistic. But the chaperone had seen me, and the man-at-arms. And he had probably admired Orfeo in the courtyard before coming into the garden. Their descriptions of me and my horse, plus the fame my affectionate nature had won me throughout the army, would soon point the finger.

I resolved to go into hiding till Lauder could see how the land lay. Tilly would not condemn me unheard and if the army marched in the near future, there would be no reason to condemn me at all. Or so I reasoned as I approached the red tiled farmhouse where I was lodged.

The first sight I saw was Lauder sitting outside the stable smoking a long clay pipe. Beside him neatly packed and stacked were all my belongings. For a moment I thought that somehow news of my mishap must have prevented me here and I drew my pistol and gazed around, fearful of an ambush.

But common sense told me no one could have got here before Orfeo and I addressed myself to Lauder.

'Has that disgusting pipe of yours got us dispossessed at last?' I demanded.

'Your nags are fed and watered,' he replied. 'I'll gie ye a hand.'

'Lauder,' I said dismounting. 'Do you practise the dark arts?'

'No witchcraft,' he said. 'Mon, I knew soon as you said you were for Lutter that there'd be a piece of trouble this day. Are they close behind?'

'On *their* nags?' I said. 'It could come to nothing yet, but I'll ride away for a day or so. What will you tell them if they come?'

He thought for a while as we loaded up my two spare horses, Laura, my sweet natured grey mare, and little Osman, the sturdy black battle pony I had of the Turks. I knew that Lauder would help me as far as he could but he was not about to provide me with an alibi which, if broken, would make him an accessory to my 'crime'.

'I'll tell them you spoke nostalgically of some of your people living in a holy brotherhood in the hills to the south and talked of a pilgrimage there.'

I grinned at this. Croatian mercenaries had a not altogether undeserved reputation for breaking off from the main armies and setting up as independent bandits. The story was hardly an alibi but it might at the least discourage pursuit. Not that I feared anything more than a token search from Tilly, but if the girl's family were rich and powerful enough, they might hire a little gang of cut-throats with promise of payment by results.

So I rode away, not too unhappy, certain that things would blow over in a day or two or certainly by the time the next campaign began. I had no desire at the moment to change my employment. By now Mansfeld and his men were half way across Silesia on their way to Hungary with Wallenstein in pursuit. It was a long way to go for a job. And nearer at hand all that offered itself was the sad remnants of Christian's army and I knew how short of money they were.

I gave it seven days before I rode back down to the farm-house. It was a moonless night with a bit of mist drifting around so I was able to get up to the house without disturbing any watcher. I was, perhaps, being overcautious but I had not survived as a front-line soldier in half a dozen armies by taking even the smallest unnecessary risk. I had even ridden Osman because of his colour and his sure-footedness in the dark. I left him loosely tethered in a grove of ash trees about three hundred yards from the house and covered the remaining ground on foot. I have a well developed sense of presence and I did not 'feel' the house was guarded, nor did I hear anything untoward, save as I prised open a window I thought I heard a distant drumming of hoofbeats. But sound travels far on these still misty nights and we were not so isolated here that no one ever passed. Besides the rider, if it were a rider, was going further away; and now it had faded completely.

I clambered in through the window and went in search of Lauder.

He sat in his bed reading by candle light. He wore a woollen nightcap and a pair of spectacles which he had taken from a monk he had slain while fighting under Mansfeld. For all I knew it was the same monk who had provided the Bible Lauder was studying, and probably the large altar candle which gave him his light. The roads to salvation are strange and winding.

He was as unsurprised as ever by my appearance and I assumed from his composure that all was well. But his first words disillusioned me.

'Fantom,' he said seriously, 'ye are a dead man.'

'What!' I said. 'How so?'

He reached down beneath his Bible and produced a pistol.

'I could have five hundred gold marks just for the pulling of this trigger,' he said.

'Nay,' I said alarmed. 'But read me a passage from your book instead, and you may have six hundred.'

'Faugh!' he snorted in disgust. 'Do ye think I would parley if my intent was to shoot?'

This was true, of course. A soldier of Lauder's experience bent on earning a bounty would not produce his weapon and start talking while I still stood some yards distant in an ill light. No, he would have brought me close to the bedside by some easy welcoming speech and shot me through the belly from point-blank range.

But I was still relieved to see him replace the pistol beneath the Good Book.

'The girl's family have offered this reward?' I exclaimed indignantly. 'The commander will not permit it!'

I believed it too. It is hard to prevent one of the citizenry hiring his own cut-throats to take revenge, but no general worth his salt will permit a civilian to offer a public reward for the killing of one of his officers. The temptation to the troops would be more than they could bear – which, as far as temptation went, was little enough already, in faith.

'No. Not the family,' said Lauder. 'Tilly himself has offered the bounty.'

The shock was so much that I swore in my native language an oath that would have had me in hair-shirts for a fortnight had my childhood confessor heard it. Not that he was likely to do so. Having, as was my childish duty, confessed to him the more than fraternal relationship with my sister which our overcrowded household had encouraged, I at first put it down to the wrath of an all-seeing God when that very same night I was dragged from her arms by our enraged father and beaten till I bled. Later it began to puzzle me that an all-seeing God had apparently not seen *anything* till I confessed to the priest. And when a few weeks later, having recovered from my father's assault, I decided to go into the world in search of my fortune, I went to the priest for a final confession.

'How have you sinned, my son?' he asked.

'Murder,' I said.

That took him aback for a second.

'How many times?' he asked finally.

'Just once,' I said, plunging my sword through the thin curtain that divided us. I left it to God to decide where I hit him and the Almighty opted for the left lung.

All this ran through my mind as I absorbed what Lauder was telling me.

'It's D'Amblève,' he explained. 'He met the girl's family three years ago when he first came to join his cousin. He and the girl are betrothed.'

'Jesus!' I exclaimed and struck my own head in anger. Not at myself, of course, but at D'Amblève. No woman I was betrothed to would be permitted to walk the streets accompanied only by a beldame and a stripling youth! I hate these men who fail in their duty to their ladies.

'He arrived at the lassie's house not long after your ain . . . er . . . visit,' continued Lauder. 'It seems he spoke your name before the least description was offered!'

The unfairness of this added to my anger. The country was full of ruffians, good for nothing but to rob, burn and ravish. This rapid identification without evidence was nothing short of slander.

'And he has poisoned the commander against me!' I burst out.

'Aye,' said Lauder cautiously. 'Ye could say so. It didna help that the girlie tried to kill hersel', at least so they say.'

'What? Because of . . . why so?' I was amazed.

'Well, D'Amblève has said he canna wed her. It's understandable, would ye no' say? She's been packed off to some Saxon nunnery that a cousin of hers is Superior of and it's my belief that one way or inither, she'll bide there for ever.'

'Oh God's turds and scrotum!' I shouted. (This was another half forgotten childhood oath.) 'Will the villainies of this creature D'Amblève never cease?'

For some reason Lauder was amused. He laughed till he coughed and had to take a long pull at a flask of brandy which he produced from under the blanket. I wondered what else the huge Bible concealed.

'The boy has scoured the countryside for ye these past days,' continued Lauder. 'I was able to send him a wee bittee astray and my talk of a band of Croats put off his men, though the reward money has put them on again.'

'But the house is not watched,' I said in surprise. 'At least I saw no one.'

Lauder nodded in agreement with both my statement and my surprise.

'I have looked for myself,' he said, 'and seen no one. Perhaps they reckon ye'll nae dare to return here.'

'Perhaps,' I said. But it bothered me a little. Other matters bothered me more, however. I would have to travel fast and I would have to travel far. My first instinct was to head west. France, Spain, the Netherlands, there was always something going on there. Perhaps I could get a job with the Swede, Gustavus Adolphus, whose reputation as a cavalry tactician was already firmly established. The last alternative was to rejoin Mansfeld. I would be welcome there despite my desertion, I was sure of that. And it would be pleasant to be sure of a welcome. But I didn't fancy his chances against this man Wallenstein, so it looked as if my best hope lay in the west.

These thoughts ran through my mind as I said farewell to Lauder and made my way back to the ash grove where Osman was waiting.

It was my preoccupation with my future which almost robbed me of it. Osman neighed softly as I approached and I took this as a welcome as indeed it would have been from Laura. But Osman was Turkish trained to stand in absolute quiet in such conditions as these and a neigh from him meant that something was disturbing him very much. This struck me just as I was about to step out of the shelter of the trees into the clearing where Osman stood. I froze, pressed hard against a tree to break down my silhouette and quietly drew my pistol.

My night sight was good and I had grown accustomed even to this darkness. I sank cautiously down on all fours and edged my way forward till I could see what was happening.

A man was crouched behind my pony trying to hobble his hind legs. In a trice I grasped what must have happened. D'Amblève with more wit than I gave him credit for had realized that a guard on the house would just frighten me off. Therefore he had probably detailed a couple of his troopers to check from time to time the places near by where I might possibly leave my horse. The hoofbeats I had heard earlier had been those of the man who discovered Osman riding off to tell D'Amblève who must be camped close by. I must have just missed the party he had certainly despatched to cover the house, while up here in the grove I had arrived just as the ambush was being set. Someone, recognizing that a man could with a bit of luck wriggle his way out of almost any trap on such a dark and misty night, had decided that at least I wasn't going anywhere on horseback. Hence the attempt to hobble Osman.

Fortunately the little pony wasn't making things easy and the man cursed as Osman lashed out with his hind legs and caught him a glancing blow on the hip. Someone hissed a command at him from the dark and he abandoned his attempt and limped towards the trees, concealing himself not above six feet from me.

I crouched quite still, doubtful what to do. Now that Osman had reassured himself that the interloper had gone, he was settling down to chew the grass once more and everything was perfectly still. His activities had held the attention of the ambushers before, and the noise had covered my own careless approach. But now the case was altered. It was going to be difficult for me to withdraw without attracting attention. And in any case, I was reluctant to be afoot with the countryside full of mounted pursuers.

But I had to act. Taking a deep, slow breath, I began to retreat an inch at a time. Now fully alert, I sensed the presence of many men, perhaps a dozen, in the grove, and I prayed that I did not back into one of them. I didn't, but what I did back into was a thick briar whose thorns penetrated my leather riding pants with contemptuous ease. I moved forward again. The thorns clung. I kept going very gently, reaching my hand round to pluck the clinging branch free. But it sprang away before I could touch it and the whole bush seemed to shake in warning of my presence. Everywhere I heard the sound of flintlocks being cocked. To lie still or to run for it, that was the question.

Then suddenly from the house came an outburst of shouting, clearly audible at this distance, followed by a single shot. It was, I hope, Lauder letting off his pistol to warn me that the house was being raided. All over the grove the waiting men shifted, someone whispered, another shushed him angrily, and I stood up, measured the distance to where the man kicked by Osman stood, then lept forward and clubbed him with my pistol butt.

He sagged against me half-stunned.

'There he is!' I yelled. 'Fantom's here! Don't let him escape.'

And placing my boot against the man's backside, I propelled him into the clearing. I fired first and heard my ball strike home. He shrieked and while the echoes of my shot still bounced among the trees, the whole grove was lit up by a constellation of musketry. The poor fellow in the open must have been torn apart, but others suffered too, for errant balls rattled among the trees and men shrieked in the darkness.

Osman, unperturbed, continued to munch the herb. I ran swiftly to him, reckoning that all the ambushers' shot must now be exhausted, mounted, and sent him plunging through the trees.

I was wrong. A figure rose before me, a pistol exploded, I felt the ball clip my shoulder as I saw in the hectic glare of the burning powder D'Amblève's face, convulsed with hatred. It made him look older, I thought, as I brought up my own pistol and pressed the trigger with the muzzle at his brow. That would have been the end of our quarrel had it been loaded. But of course I had emptied it into the poor devil who had just died to save me.

So I rode him down instead and continued on my way.

The pursuit took a little time to organize and in any case I had the advantage of having fresh horses waiting for me a few miles away. Balanced against this was the time I had to spend packing my gear, a task made the more irksome by my aching shoulder. Fortunately the flesh had not been pierced nor the bone broken but it was badly bruised and pained a great deal.

Osman had been ridden hard so I gave him the lightest of burdens, piled most of my stuff on Laura, and rode Orfeo. Some cavalrymen will argue that it is demeaning for a battle horse to be made to carry loads, but I study to preserve a horse's health, not its pride, and all my mounts are trained to be pack animals if the occasion demands. They don't mind, except perhaps Orfeo who takes his turn with the others but snorts impatiently and lets me know he's doing me a favour.

Dawn was breaking at our backs as we set off but when we reached the crest of the hill in whose lee we had been sheltering, I knew that I must change my plans. Below in the valley it was still dark and for a mile in either direction I could see a moving line of torches burning holes in the drifting mist. D'Amblève had used his influence or his money to rouse half the army against me and I had no intention of trying to slip through that line with the sun coming up fast in the eastern sky. That way must lie my destiny after all. Mansfeld did not know it, but he had just signed on Carlo Fantom for the second time.

1626–7

Saxony – Silesia

I PRESSED on apace for three or four days. A general pursuit was out of the question. Tilly would be reluctant to release even a small number of men to chase me, knowing that, once separate from the discipline of the main army, they'd be more concerned with practising my so-called crime than punishing it. On the other hand he might permit his cousin to seek personal satisfaction for this slight to the family honour. With a bit of luck, Osman's hoofs might have incapacitated the beautiful boy for a while, but luck is to be relied on only when all else fails. So I rode fast changing horses, direction, and identity at frequent intervals. I'm blessed with the gift of tongues and it was easy for me to leave an inn one morning as a Bavarian merchant and be transformed into a Silesian scholar when I sought shelter in the evening. No one could follow such a trail, I complimented myself, and as if to warn me against complacency Osman shed a shoe that day and I missed my road to Leipzig, ending up benighted in a boggy countryside on what promised to be a ball-crackingly cold autumn night. Fortunately I had a bit of luck as a pair of half naked fellows with clubs jumped out at me and the one I only shot through the shoulder told me of a religious house close by where I might find shelter for the night. He was a poor creature without even sense enough to think of stripping the rags off his fellow, and he was touchingly grateful when I suggested it. As I rode away I felt quite warm at the thought that I'd perhaps helped to save his life. Are we not enjoined in Holy Writ to return good for evil? With such thoughts in mind, you may imagine my disgust at the cold, suspicious welcome I received at the religious house. It was a convent and the Mother Superior later apologized fulsomely, explaining that the long war had left them very suspicious of all strangers. When I explained gently that we were not put on earth to suspect, but to trust, she nodded agreement, but I fear it was my status as a messenger from the Vatican on his way to serve a Bull on the Bishop of Crackow that impressed her, not my argument.

I was somewhat worried lest the trumpets should sound for me that night but having acceded to the Mother Superior's request that I should hear her flock's confession, I rapidly came to the conclusion that I had better double bar the door of my cell, not to keep me in but to keep them out. I doled out penances with a will till the swishing of scourges became audible in the still night. I don't know which were worse – the exotic fantasies of the older nuns or the nostalgic memories of the novices. A soldier's life has something in common with these religious eremites' – close confinement with your own sex, strict discipline, long periods of physical effort and sensuous deprivation – and I know what these can do to a soldier's mind. But at least for him there's the anticipation of relief, and his natural longings don't fill him with a sense of sin.

There was one young girl, the last I heard (they have their rules of precedence even in this) whose confession touched me deeply. She was but yet a postulant, of noble family, and it seemed a young friend of her family presently visiting the convent was pressing his attentions on her. At first I was delighted, thinking this young spark wished to woo her away from her marriage with Christ to a secular wedding. But as it became clear that his intentions were merely to take a soldier's farewell of the lass, giving her something to remember through the long, cold years ahead, I became indignant. On the face of it, it was a simple act of charity. But I had heard the anguish with which the girl spoke.

It occurred to me that in my assumed role of papal envoy, I might be able to save both these youngsters, she from a wasted life in a nunnery, he from his baser self. I do good deeds whenever I can, for I am careful to store up favours in heaven as well as on earth. It may seem a strange good deed to deprive God of a dedicated servant, but I had listened to these servants all night and reckoned there was more value in a happy wife giving thanks each Sunday for a worthy husband.

'Child,' I said. 'Is this slip of Satan still on these holy premises?'

'Yes, Father,' she answered. 'He is in the Stranger House.'

'Go and fetch him here,' I commanded. 'Let none deny you. Say it is at my command.'

Off she went and I came out of the confessional into the tiny chapel where it was situated. It was very cold and I warmed my hands on the candle at the altar till I heard footsteps approach. Then I knelt and spread my arms and kept very still.

Behind me the footsteps entered, hesitated, went still. I kept them waiting for several minutes longer before I crossed myself and rose to my feet. With some difficulty, I lifted the heavy jewel-encrusted crucifix from the altar and, clutching it to my breast, I slowly turned.

'My children,' I said in a solemn, thrilling voice. It was a sublimely moving moment and Nature herself conspired to lend it the majesty of her touch by sending a shaft of moonlight through a narrow side window to flick my face as though with the finger of God. It was impossible for even the hardest heart to remain unmoved.

But I had not reckoned on such a powerful effect as this!

The girl flung back her head and screamed. It was a piercing howl which sent the echoes reeling around that tiny room with a force almost tangible.

The youth by her side cried out in a voice almost as high-pitched and just as anguished.

'Fantom!'

And even before he advanced into the moonlight, I knew what I had done. This was D'Amblève, who, baffled in his pursuit of me, had visited this convent where his former love had sought retreat. I doubt if I'd have recognized the girl's face even if the confessional grille had not concealed it, but clearly my features were imprinted on her mind forever.

The beautiful boy's hand was plucking at where his sword would have been had he not (thank God) removed it out of piety. But piety was not going to deter him from attempting to throttle me bare handed.

I retreated to give him an extra moment to turn back from his blasphemy. Then, as he still advanced, I hit him with the crucifix.

He went down like a mined tower and I made for the girl. She did not try to run but fixed her eyes on me and carried on screaming. Suddenly in my mind's eye I saw her once again seated by the fountain in that green garden with the roses, the pear and the nectarine trees, and for a moment the thought passed through my mind that war was a terrible thing which could turn that beauty into this ugliness.

Then I had her in my arms, but before I could do anything to still those screams, the room was full of nuns and the last thing I wanted was for that girl to stop screaming and start talking.

'Leave her,' I commanded those nuns who seemed keen to offer their aid. Then to the Superior I continued. 'The child is in a state of terror. You take but poor care of your charges here.'

Taken aback, the Mother Superior could only ask, 'But what has happened?'

Recalling that she was the girl's cousin and would probably know the full story, I pointed at the still unconscious D'Amblève and said, 'The girl was praying at the altar after her confession when this piece of lechery came in and, thinking her alone as I had not yet issued from the confessional, he approached her with filthy and disgusting proposals. Which being rejected, he then attempted to take by force what he could not gain by consent. I came forth and remonstrated with him. So strong were his carnal appetites, that he would brook no interference, so he attacked me. But God is not mocked in His own house and I prevailed.'

It was the best I could do in the circumstances. The revival of D'Amblève or the restoration of the girl must be imminent and when that happened I must be off. The beautiful boy would not travel absolutely alone and my masquerade as a papal envoy was in itself sufficient to have me lightly grilled.

'There is much to be answered for here,' I said sternly to the Mother Superior. 'I shall come to your cell in thirty minutes to probe further into your management of this place. Let this felon be put in a fast place and the girl be given a sleeping potion and laid in the Infirmary. The rest meanwhile to their prayers.'

So saying, I strode out of the chapel. If nothing else, I am expert at leaving places at speed and in less than ten minutes I was astride Laura with Orfeo and Osman close behind, riding through the gates of the convent. It wasn't till I got outside that I realized I still had the crucifix. One of the arms was a bit bent from contact with D'Amblève's head, and a couple of gems had fallen from their setting but this didn't bother me as it would be best to sell it piecemeal rather than run the risk of recognition.

Now I abandoned all my former twists and tricks and concentrated on speed, following the line taken by the two armies deep into Silesia. It wasn't a comfortable journey. The weather got worse and food and shelter became increasingly hard to find. But I kept up a steady progress and finally one dark, clammy evening I found myself approaching (or so my navigational calculations told me) the borders of Hungary.

I was a little down in spirits that evening. For a couple of days I had had no one for company save ignorant peasants, surly and brutish, and I yearned for contact once more with the lively well-travelled world of the professional soldier. But it looked as if I was doomed to another night of reluctant hospitality and uncomfortable shelter. The farm I arrived at looked larger and more prosperous than the hovels I'd been sleeping in, but the brute who possessed it was of the same breed as before. He took my money readily enough, but merely grunted in reply to my efforts at conversation, while his sluttish wife served me a sludge of oatmeal probably rejected by his pigs, and his uncountable brood of children watched, rat-eyed, from the shadows.

As always in such circumstances, I slept with my horses for our mutual protection. Left unguarded, they would certainly be stolen and *I* would certainly have my throat cut, so we guarded each other.

But it was not from my host that the danger came.

I have learned to sleep through the crowing of cocks and the awful hullabaloo with which the bird kingdom in general finds it necessary to greet the dawn. But when it is accompanied by the rattle of hoofs and the shouting of military orders, then I wake quickly enough.

It was first light and when I rushed to the stable door and peered through one of the many cracks which had been pouring draughts of cold air over me all night, what I saw was a familiar but not altogether comforting sight. A force of about twenty mounted soldiers had descended on the farmhouse and the farmer's family in states of dress ranging from total nudity to full cover were being pushed and pulled out into the cold morning air. With an efficiency born of long practice, small groups of men were rounding up animals and poultry and lugging fat sacks out of the granary. As I watched, two carts came lumbering into view in the distance.

This was, I recognized, a military foraging party. Had I not commanded many such myself and used just such tactics? Arrive at a farm at dawn so that news of your intent is unlikely to have preceded you; leave the carts a little way behind so their noise does not betray your approach; get everyone out of the house, then go through it with a fine tooth comb, for while the farmer's provisions may belong to the army, his personal wealth belongs to him who can find it.

But I had little time to reflect on the morality of the exercise for, as I anticipated, having emptied the granary, half a dozen soldiers were now making towards the stable.

My predicament was extreme. Whose men they were hardly bothered me at all. Wallenstein's or Mansfeld's, or perhaps belonging to Bethlen Gabor, the Protestant prince of Transylvania, it was all one; their behaviour pattern was unlikely to be different. Once they saw my horses, they would take them, and if they saw me, they would probably kill me.

Yet I was loth to sneak away and lose all I possessed without a fight.

My only hope was to parley with their officer. I checked my pistol which had been lying, loaded and cocked, within easy reach of my hand all night, drew my sword and stood against the wall, close by the door. As I anticipated, the focus of all eyes when the ramshackle door was drawn open was my trio of lovely horses. Such a prize as this had not been anticipated and they crowded forward eagerly to get a closer look.

This was the dangerous part. There is no way for a single man with a one-shot pistol to hold off six if they wish to take him. Five must get through, and though usually five-to-one is odds too short when a man's life is at stake, it only takes one impetuous fool to destroy the deadlock.

I made sure all of this group were in the barn, then stepped out behind them and said in my best voice of command, 'Hold!'

Their chatter ceased and they turned swiftly, stopping when they saw the pistol. I did not give them time to start thinking, but said, 'You with the red beard. Call your captain. Quickly!'

Feeling that if he was the object of my special attention, he must also be the object of my aim, redbeard opened his mouth and, after a nervous cough, called: 'Captain! Captain! Here in the barn!'

In the silence that followed I heard footsteps approaching from the house. I kept my eyes fixed firmly on the men grouped round my horses. A word of warning now could make things very sticky. No one spoke but something about their very silence and awkward demeanour must have warned the approaching officer, for he stopped outside the door and said, 'Yes? What is it?'

My heart jumped for I thought I recognized the voice.

'Rydberg? Is that you?' I called in Swedish.

'Yes,' came the cautious answer. 'Who speaks?'

'Carlo Fantom,' I answered in relief. 'We were at Munster together, do you not recall?'

I stepped out to face the tall, thin-faced Swede whom I had

known vaguely in my early days with Mansfeld's army and I hoped his memory was at least as good as mine.

For a moment I thought I was going to be unlucky. He regarded me with a puzzled air for several seconds, then slowly recognition broke and he raised his right hand and said 'No!'

I didn't understand the gesture or the denial till I looked round and saw that one of the soldiers had taken advantage of my distraction to come up behind me, sword levelled for the kill. I swear the man looked actively disappointed. I didn't blame him. Dead, I could not reasonably dispute ownership of the horses.

'What are you doing here, Fantom?' asked Rydberg.

'The same as you is my plan. I've been riding in search of Mansfeld.'

A smile ran across his thin lips.

'Have you? Then you will have far to ride. Or, knowing you, Fantom, perhaps not so far.'

'What do you mean?' I asked, puzzled and alarmed.

'Mansfeld's dead.'

'Oh God.'

My surprise was complete. Some men have a vitality which it seems must have immortal springs. Mansfeld dead was as unthinkable as the Pope growing tits and turning whore.

'In battle,' I said. It wasn't a question, but an inescapable conclusion. Rydberg shook his head.

'No. Disease. Wallenstein's army took up such a strong position that there was nothing for Gabor to do but seek a truce. One of the conditions was that Mansfeld left Hungary for ever. He was on his way to Venice when he fell ill.'

'Shit,' I said. After my initial unselfish shock, awareness of the change this caused in my own circumstances began to seep in.

'You fight with Gabor now?' I asked cautiously.

'No! Gabor is finished. He has few men and less money. The Turks won't help him any more. No, there's only one source of employment for a professional soldier in the East now.'

Wallenstein.

And Wallenstein was no good for me. He and Tilly must work in concert if their two armies were to secure all Germany for the True Faith. And if a Croatian cavalry captain's head helped to keep his fellow general happy, I could see no reason why Wallenstein would not send it gift-wrapped.

Of course, I was probably over-dramatizing the situation. These were stirring times, what the historians call an era of transition. All over Europe the transitions were going on, from Protestantism to Catholicism, from rich man to poor man, from hope to despair, from virgin to whore, from life to death. My own escapades, what were they worth in the eyes of history? Nothing. Perhaps a couple of hundred words in some daft old man's tatty notes which somehow survived the kindling box and the nail in the bog wall. Even D'Amblève after his stupid rage had worn off must surely get back to the normal course of his life. Hurt pride could be a deep wound. I would strike south and see what I could pick up in Italy. Not Venice; no; I had spent a year in the service of the serene republic when I was only a youth and my precocious behaviour might still be recalled there. Perhaps I'd be better off with the Turks currently rattling their swords in the direction of Persia. I'd fought with them before and made a few good contacts.

But I must confess I felt very down. To have come all this way for nothing was a sad blow. My money would not last for ever, but more importantly I was missing the company and security of an army. A man alone must live on his nerves.

'Well, Rydberg,' I said, 'I hope you have left enough for breakfast here. I have paid for my lodging and I'm sure Wallenstein would not have you rob an honest soldier.'

'You're right,' he said. 'Indeed he will do more. He will provide your breakfast in his camp. Come, saddle up. I think we have taken our due here.'

He turned away and I opened my mouth to explain that my plans were other, but when I glanced round at the soldiers who stood behind me, I realized I was wrong.

I shrugged philosophically. In Rydberg's place I would

have done the same if I had come across a lone mercenary whose current loyalties were uncertain. I might be some kind of scout, though for whom at this present juncture God alone knew. Anyway, it was no use worrying about it. It looked as if I was going to see Wallenstein after all.

One thing I noticed before we set off from the plundered farm. Rydberg walked up to the surly lout of a farmer who was still shivering in his shirt tails surrounded by his revolting brood, courteously saluted him and handed him a piece of paper. The man looked at it stupidly, turning it round in his hands in a manner which clearly indicated his illiteracy. Rydberg spoke to him patiently for a moment, then mounted his horse and we all set out after the laden carts.

'What was that about?' I enquired curiously.

'It was a requisition order,' said Rydberg. 'Wallenstein is a strict disciplinarian. He permits no looting.'

'Ah,' I said, puzzled. 'You mean the paper is exchangeable against money from the paymaster?'

'Oh no,' said Rydberg seriously. 'But the farmer knows now that his goods have not been looted but legally requisitioned.'

I laughed out loud for five minutes and then settled down to a steady chuckling for the next half hour. This Wallenstein I had to meet.

It was in fact several days before I had the opportunity. The General was away from camp when I arrived and when he returned the following day he naturally had many more things to concern him than the fate of a wandering mercenary. I was treated well and entertained as Rydberg's guest rather than his prisoner, the only limit to my freedom being that strict orders were given to the picket guards that I was on no account to be allowed to ride my horses. Rydberg was no fool. He knew I wasn't going anywhere without my precious mounts. Or if I did, it would be admission of guilt and he would have lost a spy but gained the three best horses in Central Europe.

I had no real objection to the arrangement. My entertainment was luxurious, and not just by comparison with the rough living I had experienced during the past few weeks. These men knew how to look after themselves. Seldom if ever have I encountered such splendour of dress, such excellence of victuals, such cultivation of behaviour, in a campaigning army. I felt very much a country cousin at first and it wasn't till I had parted with a few gold pieces and accoutred myself in a blue and green suit of soft velvet with a dark navy cloak trimmed with ermine, that I began to feel at home. I also took into my employ a local youth called Bela who despite his tender years had all the makings of a first class scoundrel. His attractions for me were that he knew his way around the camp and the countryside, could lay his hands on the best wine and food at quick notice (and at a price) and in addition he was very knowledgeable about horses and could be trusted to check the health of Orfeo and the others when I was unable to pay my own evening visit. He was also a very pretty boy. Not that this interested me – I have tried a boy now and then by way of change and experiment but it was never the same – but it did mean he had access to some high ranking officers, and indeed Bela told me that Wallenstein was to see me the following day, several hours before Rydberg knew.

Rydberg's revelation was the more dramatic however, for it was coupled with another piece of information. After telling me that Wallenstein would see me at noon, he asked me casually if I was acquainted with Colonel D'Amblève. My hand went to my sword but I released it instantly. Other men might adopt such an oblique approach, but Rydberg like most Scandinavian officers of my acquaintance while being ruthless in the execution of his duty was totally free from malice.

'I know the name,' I replied. 'Why?'

'The poor wretch was found in the forest. He had been robbed, stripped almost naked and beaten.'

'Is he dead?' I asked hopefully.

'No, but he was like to die. Fortunately some papers remained by the body and the sergeant who found him could read enough French to make out that he was a well-born gentleman whose safety might be worth a reward. So he dressed his wounds and brought him to the camp.'

This was a singular example of how out of place and dangerous learning is among the lower ranks. Had I the charge of an army, I would soon whip all claims to education out of my men. A soldier's life is fighting, drinking and fornicating. I would as soon see the plague rife in a barracks as a book.

I sent Bela to find out more about D'Amblève's condition and prospects. He returned a little later saying that the newcomer had recovered consciousness for a moment, but the chirurgeon had then started to bleed him and he had fainted away once more. I cheered up at this news. Army chirurgeons can usually be relied upon to complete what the enemy has begun.

I toyed with the idea of visiting the sick man myself and seeking the occasion to help him on his way, but Bela's description of the room where he lay made me doubt if I could bring it off. The sergeant who had discovered D'Amblève had remained in close attendance to ensure that his claim to reward would be firmly established at the first sign of recovery, and even the renowned discipline of Wallenstein's army wouldn't keep him standing by as I slipped a knife between the lovely boy's ribs.

In any case, nature and the medical profession would probably do the job for me, I thought. But later that evening Bela, to whom I had given a watching brief, came with the news that D'Amblève after passing through a period of crisis in which the priest had taken over from the doctor was now much more comfortable, had woken long enough to take a little nourishment and was now in a deep sleep.

This was bad news. I questioned Bela closely and as far as I could make out, D'Amblève had not mentioned me. Again I wondered if I were not being unnecessarily fearful, but the sight of two private soldiers hanged that morning for assault and robbery and left dangling as a reminder to the rest of the army, approved me in my decision to take all precautions. Campaigns are planned on paper but they only succeed if the plans are as various as chance and changing conditions will have them be. I sat up late into the night, then drank a bottle of Tokay to still my too active mind and went to bed.

The following morning the news from the sick room was worse. D'Amblève was eating well, both the doctor and the priest were modestly accepting the plaudits of their fellows, and the blasted book-learned sergeant was going round all the Belgian and French officers in the army making sure they knew of D'Amblève's survival and his part in it. For a moment I was tempted to take whatever mount I could lay my hands on and ride off to find the Turks. But that was a course perhaps as dangerous as remaining and to tell the truth I was much impressed with what I had seen of the conditions and organization of Wallenstein's army and was reluctant to part company with it. A professional soldier could be happy here – but only if he had his leader's confidence. I was in desperate need of Wallenstein's support on two counts – as my normal insurance against the malicious accusations of jealous husbands and, of more immediate import, to save my neck from Tilly's sentence.

Without boasting, I think I can safely say I've never had much difficulty in getting on with the men at the top. I can sum up a man pretty quickly, but I don't just rely on intuition. No, if I can manage it, I get a bit of background information first, and in Wallenstein's case, I'd had plenty of time to do my research. Basically he was a financier, fighting (to start with anyway) as much for profit as principle. This would have suited me very well, but other snippets of information did not quite fit with this picture of a cold cash-man. He was unstable, subject to fits of wild rage. Well, that didn't bother me. A man out of his own control could generally be fitted into someone else's. In addition he was one of those superstitious wretches who believe in the influence of the stars. As above, so below! Jesus, if that holds, then the skies should be dripping blood! But I was pleased to hear of it in Wallenstein. A man who clings to childish superstitions is like a man who enters a wrestling match with his parts hanging out. Seize them and you have him at your mercy.

But the final bit of information pleased me less. He was, so my informants told me, cruel, treacherous (so far, so good), and a man of unnatural and immutable chastity. This was a real facer. I mean, when it comes down to it, most men don't really rate sexual assault on a woman as a very important crime – not unless it happens to be *their* woman. Otherwise it's generally reckoned that the man can't be *altogether* at fault nor the woman *altogether* innocent. Even Tilly, that monk in armour, had learnt from his religious upbringing to be saddened rather than outraged by the weakness of flesh. But Wallenstein was a convert and there's nothing like a strict Protestant upbringing for putting the fear of cock into a man.

On the other hand he clearly wanted to run the most powerful army in Europe and you couldn't do that with a gang of stitched-up eunuchs.

So I prepared myself as best I could for my audience. He held his court (the only term for it!) in the local Rathaus, a huge barn of a place with a stone-flagged floor and high wattled walls round which ran a rickety and deep-shadowed gallery. The whole place was a study in lights and shades, sun falling in a sharp wedge through narrow windows, jewels shining on skin made brown by much campaigning in hard weather, eyes gleaming watchfully from each dark corner and in the middle, seated on a high backed chair like a bishop's throne, Wallenstein himself dressed from head to toe in black and deep grey, with a sash of dazzling scarlet running across his chest like a sabre-cut.

He was an ugly bastard with a Jew's nose and a lower lip you could have stood a wine bottle on. Had he been a horse, I'd have paid high for him, for such a face would have been worth much in a charge.

'You're late,' murmured Rydberg.

'Barely an hour,' I answered. 'How should so great a man notice?' But he did.

'Fantom,' said Wallenstein as if the name tasted of horse shit. 'I like my officers to be punctual.'

'I am not yet one of your officers, sire,' I said. 'And besides it was not . . . apt.'

'What do you mean, sir?' he demanded keenly.

'My star-readings gave this as a better hour for this audience, sire,' I answered.

He now began to study me closely and I saw the significance of my clothing and ornament beginning to dawn on him. I was wearing a tunic of gold embroidered with a design of an archer slaying a wolf with a crow flying above him. Bruno the heretic says this is a potent image of the sun, and on my hands I wore several rings of gold set with diamonds and topazes which are also alleged to be solar talismans. I had fixed on the Sun as the planet whose influence I wanted to attract because the grimoires say that this is most efficacious in gaining the support of powerful people. An hour earlier and Mars would have been more influential – good for operations connected with military matters, and therefore better perhaps for Wallenstein. The thought had not escaped him.

'So,' he said. 'Your stars say this is a more auspicious hour for you. But not for *me* perhaps. You did not think to consult *my* stars.'

'Sire,' I said calmly. 'I am presently in no man's employ, so I may reasonably put my own interest first. Once employed, however, I will protect to the utmost the well being of him who pays me.'

He laughed now and though there was little of humour in the noise, I took it as a signal to launch upon my *curriculum vitae*, or at least those parts which bore examination. I presented him with the dissertation on cavalry tactics I was taking to Tilly when I was so unfortunately side-tracked at Lutter, and I boasted what was true, that I could take a gang of yokels, who knew just enough of a horse to yoke it with its arse nearest the plough, and within six weeks train them to charge down experienced infantry. Next I spoke in the dozen languages I knew, to demonstrate my usefulness in commanding a disparate army of mercenaries. And all this I interlarded with admiring comments on the organization, reputation, discipline and splendour of his superb force. I was irresistible. The trouble was that Wallenstein did not seem to be listening. His head moved slowly from side to side, his great nose raised as though scenting danger. I felt suddenly uneasy. Then as I finished speaking, a movement in the shadowy heights of the gallery to the left of and behind Wallenstein caught my eye. With a great cry of 'Beware!' I leapt forward and flung myself at the General so that his chair toppled sideways to the ground and I lay athwart him, shielding him with my body.

There was an explosion, something struck me full in the middle of my back knocking the breath out of me, men shouted commands, mailed feet rattled over the stone flags, doors opened and banged shut.

With difficulty, aided by Wallenstein's attendants from above and the man himself from below, I rose to my feet. Something fell to the floor as I did so and rolled among the open-mouthed onlookers. It was a pistol ball.

There was a smell of burning cloth and an aide stepped forward with a cup of wine which he poured over my back to quench the sparks remaining from the hot ball.

'My lord,' I gasped. 'Are you hurt?'

'I think not,' said Wallenstein as he rose to his feet. 'And you, Captain Fantom, were you not hit?'

'Hit but not wounded sire,' I said. 'Work for my tailor rather than my surgeon.'

A murmur ran round the spectators and they passed the ball from one to the other, examining it closely and conversing in whispers.

'It seems your stars are conjoint for my good rather than your own,' said Wallenstein. 'I have been saved from death while you have just spoilt a good suit of clothes. What say you to that, Captain Fantom?'

'Your good is my good, sire,' I said. 'With you dead, where should I find employment? And where would Europe find safety?'

That did it. Finally he laughed with something like real amusement.

'I will no further defy the stars,' he said. 'Captain Fantom, you shall have our commission.'

Suddenly the shouting which had died away was renewed outside and the sound of marching feet approached. The entrance door burst open and a little knot of soldiers entered half carrying, half dragging in their midst a terrified figure whom I recognized at once. It was my servant, Bela.

His eyes searched for and found mine, then opened beseechingly wide. I glared back at him in terrible wrath, and indeed if ever a man had cause to be angry with his servant, it was I.

It was bad enough that the fool, who had been told to fire well clear, should have hit me on the back. (Thank heaven I had prepared the charge myself to couple maximum noise with minimum muzzle speed!) But that he should have let himself be caught was absolutely criminal.

Worse, I could tell from his expression that I could expect no loyalty from this source. These Hungarians have no more sense of duty than an English Protestant.

'Is this the knave who fired the shot?' demanded Wallenstein sternly.

'Yes, sir,' answered the sergeant of the detail. He looked proud of himself as though he had done something clever. Myself, I felt the fellow should have been flogged for dereliction of duty in bringing back his prisoner alive. I could only hope that Wallenstein would act with suitable swiftness and order an instant execution before Bela recovered his powers of speech.

But the General was a cunning bastard and clearly wanted to discover if this had been a one-man job or whether there was a wider conspiracy against his life.

'Bring the wretch forward,' he commanded the sergeant.

Fortunately he spoke in Slovak, a violent-sounding tongue, and Bela must have interpreted this as his death sentence, for as the sergeant attempted to push him forward he wriggled free, dodged desperately among the soldiers for a moment, then deciding in his selfishness that I was his only hope of survival, ran towards me with his arms outstretched.

Quickly I stepped before the chair in which Wallenstein had reseated himself.

'What!' I cried. 'Will you try your villainy again?'

And, drawing my little ornamental dagger which I keep sharp as a razor, I received him into my arms and slit his throat.

My new clothes were ruined. Behind they were burned through to the thick leather jerkin I had fortunately put on next to my skin that morning; and now in front I was stained with blood from my chest to my knees.

I kicked Bela's body away from me and Rydberg stepped forward to examine the corpse.

'Is not this Bela, your servant?' he asked. For someone so malicefree, he managed to turn the knife with disturbing accuracy.

'Nay,' I said. 'No servant of mine. I have used the boy on errands in the few days I have been here, but nothing more.'

And turning to Wallenstein, I added sternly, 'If it is the same youth, then you should know, sire, that I used him no longer when I learned that he was suspected of selling himself in sodomy, aye, and with officers of your own guard, my lord.'

There was an uneasy stirring amongst these assembled in the room.

Wallenstein raised his voice.

'Then he died mercifully at your hands, Captain Fantom. For those taken in these unnatural practices should roast slowly on a griddle to let them taste a while in this life what they shall certainly know for ever in the next.'

It was good mainstream Christian thinking and everyone present voiced approval. I have always found it useful whenever possible in moments of stress to harness to my support those doctrines of faith, political as well as religious, which no man will publicly contradict.

Well, I had done it. Wallenstein had hired me; not difficult as I was well worth the hiring; but he was also under an obligation. It had been a narrow squeak though! I would have disposed of Bela eventually – only a fool lets a rogue run free with knowledge that can kill him – but having to do it publicly might set some nasty minds working. My crack about buggery being rife among Wallenstein's officers had won me no friends and some malicious bastard could easily start wondering aloud at the inefficiency of an assassin whose pistol was so poorly primed, it couldn't send a ball through a man's skin at forty feet.

The next day I was summoned to Wallenstein's presence again and my heart sank when I found him playing with a pistol ball, tossing it into the air and catching it, while he stared at me reflectively. We were alone and I rapidly got as close to him as I dared, resolved that at the first sign of his guard being summoned, I would have my dagger at his throat.

'Captain Fantom,' he said in a voice which my imagination filled with menace. 'Take off your doublet.'

I obeyed. Why not? He could have had me killed in my quarters if he wanted, so there must be some hope still.

'To the skin, to the skin,' he said impatiently as I stood before him wearing only my soft leather vest. This I removed also and the General rose and walked slowly round me. I stood stock still wondering what he had in mind till at the third circumambulation he touched my back, just between the shoulder blades. Involuntarily I started and his hand grasped my shoulder tightly, his nails digging into my skin.

'What, Captain? Think you that I am as those who bought hellfire in the lewd embraces of your dead servant?'

'Nay, sire,' I protested.

'Nay! Then it must be something other that makes you start from my touch. Some secret perhaps? Something to be kept hidden?'

The bastard knows, I thought. He's playing with me. Well, it'll cost him his life.

And I let my hand move down to the little dagger that hung on my thigh, the same that had cut Bela's windpipe.

'Here the ball struck,' he said from behind me in a low

voice. 'Here where naught but a tiny bruise shows on your skin. How to explain this, eh?'

'I cannot, sire,' I said.

'Will not, you mean! But you underestimate me, sir. I know all your secret!'

Silently sliding the dagger from its sheath, I turned to kill him.

'Do not deny it, Captain. You are shot-free. A hard-man!'

'What?' I said. It was uncharacteristic of me to delay. Once you've decided to strike, then quickest is best. But Wallenstein did not look like a man about to order my neck stretched. No. His face was alight with triumph and his eyes shone madly, but not at the anticipation of violence. Rather he looked like some simple priest who has got carried away by his own preaching.

'You are a Croatian, Captain? Aye, I knew it, I knew it.' Tis not a property of the herb *solus*, you understand that? Nay, 'tis derived as are all strengths and essences from the conjunction of the planets at the time of germination and the time of gathering. I recalled a hint of it in my books. See here, see here.'

He led me to his desk and pointed at passages he had marked in the tomes which lay open there. I read swiftly and began to smile inwardly as I let my dagger slip back into its sheath.

'There are many instances. See, a report from Lithuania. Another from Venice. Two such were known at the court of Charlemagne. And the heretic Luther saw a hard-man shot without harm by the Duke of Saxony. 'Tis a liar and a slanderer in matters religious, but in this I believe we may take his word.'

There's nothing like being selective in what you believe!

I had been lucky, I realized. These superstitious men are always eager to uncover evidence to support them in their folly! I had been shot without harm. A reasonable man would say the fault lay in the pistol – a suspicious man might have made a great deal more of it. But the superstitious man had decided that the reason must lie in my skin!

I had heard stories in my childhood of this marvellous herb which toughened a man's skin till bullets could not pierce it! But I had put these stories away with others that told of giants and unicorns and horses with wings.

'So, so. You do not deny it, Captain. But tell me, have you supplies of this herb? May it be cultivated in my gardens? With an army of hard-men, a regiment, even, who would withstand my advance?'

It was time to play things down.

'I fear my lord it is not possible,' I said.

'Not possible?'

'No. Even when I was a child, the herb was hard to find. It is a delicate growth easily bruised by the gentlest winds and quickly choked by the sparsest grasses. Many attempted to take seeds and plant them, but none succeeded. It is as if a greater gardener than any here below has reserved this plant for his peculiar care.'

'So, so. Well, that holds. Aye, such a treasure would be grossly devalued were it rife. Still, I have you, Captain Fantom. One is better than none. Good, good.'

He looked at me with possessive pride. I smiled modestly.

'Now,' he said. 'Now.'

And going to his desk, he took a pistol from a drawer. I watched uneasily as he walked to a spot some twenty feet away, then turned his eyes still agleam with that crazy enthusiasm.

'Now, a test,' he said. 'You do not mind?'

And the star-crazed turd pointed the bloody pistol at me and pulled the trigger!

Thank God it was a wheel-lock which must have been lying ready spanned too long, for the spring had gone stiff and did not work. Wallenstein looked at it with an anger which matched my relief.

'Sire,' I said. 'Spare your powder. The test is a fair one but it is long since I was able to find any of this herb and each shot I receive lessens the strength of what I have taken in the past.'

'So, so,' he said. 'Ah yes. The metal, Saturn drawing up strength from the earth. So it is written.'

The explanation may have fitted with his half-witted beliefs, but he still looked disappointed for all that and I was mightily relieved when a door opened and an equerry entered. He was well-trained in diplomacy, not one muscle of his face expressing surprise at finding the General with a pistol standing in front of a half-naked man. They talked aside for a moment, then with a curt command from Wallenstein – 'Wait!' – they left the room.

I quickly dressed and after checking which of the doors from the room opened, which were locked, I sat at the desk and browsed through the books thereon. Dull tomes, full of magical nonsense, but if the General held them in regard, then it was best to make their acquaintance.

It was more than half an hour before the same poker-faced officer returned and invited me to follow him. Perhaps it was those damned books I'd been reading but as I left the room I had a presentiment that my troubles were not over.

How right I was! The equerry led me to the high vaulted council chamber where my first dramatic meeting with Wallenstein had taken place. The room was crowded. The General sat in his throne-like chair.

And by his side, reclining on a litter, was D'Amblève, the beautiful boy.

I felt a small pang of pity for the lad, so pale and haggard he looked. His beauty was for the moment all gone and might never return, for his face had been much battered and his nose broken. He looked like a sickly child preserved to this life by doting parents against the will of God.

Only his eyes which shone with feverish hate at the sight of me showed him to be a man.

Here we go again, I thought. Another Fantom trial. There should be a special law book for these!

But I felt quietly confident. Had I not saved the General's life? And was I not a precious scientific object in his sight?

His opening words came as a shock, so harsh and stern they were.

'Captain Fantom, you have deceived us. You are no

properly discharged officer, but a deserter, under sentence of death for a vile crime against a fellow officer.'

I should have thought that my crime, if it were a crime, could hardly be said to be against D'Amblève, but this was no time for such nit-picking.

'These are lies, sire,' I said. 'Who speaks them?'

D'Amblève started to say something, but Wallenstein halted him.

'How may you deny these charges, sir?' he demanded.

'I am no deserter, General,' I answered. 'I fought with distinction at the battle of Lutter and received General Tilly's own commendation. The army being then in quarters, awaiting news of your own glorious campaign, I was at liberty to take my *congé* whenever it pleased me, according to old custom, which all here present will agree.'

They did. Professional officers who took their pay during peace and left the army before a battle deserved contumely and condemnation; but once you had fought, you were your own master.

'As for being condemned,' I continued, 'if this is so, it has been done in my absence without benefit of trial, which I take for a great injustice.'

'You could hardly be tried if you had disappeared,' said Wallenstein sardonically. 'Why did you flee this great benefit?'

'I knew I stood accused, sire,' I said, '*falsely* accused, but by one standing so high in the favour of those who would judge me that I left to prevent a taint of unjust dealing from falling on a man I loved.'

'Speak clear, Captain,' ordered Wallenstein. 'You mean General Tilly would pervert justice to favour his cousin?'

This was difficult. I suppose there are circumstances when honest plain speaking is beneficial but I have seen too many men tied to stakes on top of piles of brushwood to favour such outspokeness.

'Sire,' I said. 'I know the General Tilly to be an honest and upright man. But he is a *man* for all that. I know his cousin to be a pleasant amiable boy who might yet do well. But he is a *boy* for all that. And when an honest man makes a boy of seventeen a Colonel of Horse, I admire his family virtues but I do not hang around to let the one be my accuser and the other be my judge when my life is at stake!'

It was as extreme as I dared to put it, perhaps too extreme. I had knocked six years off D'Amblève's age, but his was the only voice which would dispute this and that would be against the evidence of everyone's eyes. I could tell by the reactions of those present that I had made a good case. Professional soldiers distrust promotion on any grounds other than merit.

But it was Wallenstein whose word would kill or save me. This was no godless democracy! I looked him boldly in the face wearing my best expression of fearless honesty.

He looked like the Egyptian dog-god, Sirius, about to dispense a judgement. Then he grinned. Just a momentary twitch of the mouth showing canine teeth. And there was no humour in it. What it said was, I see right through you, Fantom you bastard, but I'll play along.

He spoke.

'Colonel D'Amblève, you are welcome to my camp. But I must warn you that while he is under my command, Captain Fantom is subject only to the disciplines which *I* shall enforce, and any attack on his person by you or your agents shall be regarded as an attack on me. Let all men know that officers of my army shall be answerable to myself and my duly appointed courts alone. We are a just force fighting in a just cause. More even-handed justice will not be found outside these limits. Gentlemen, to your duties.'

And that was that. He had made a decision which was tremendously popular with the men who served him for it confirmed their status as the true rulers of wherever they happened to be.

And he had told me simply that the minute I attempted to leave *his* service, I was a dead man.

I went back to my quarters well satisfied to be in the service of such a General.

1627–34

Saxony – Sweden – Bohemia

THE next few years were among the happiest of my life. I soon became such a firmly established favourite with Wallenstein that even the threat of D'Amblève's presence was reduced to a mere petty irritation. Indeed, I could have forgotten it altogether for, having recovered his health and most of his looks, the once-more beautiful boy seemed to have decided to let sleeping dogs lie; and besides he was much used for liaison between our army and Tilly's so he was often gone from us for long periods. But I never underestimate the hurts I have put on a man. Entirely free from malice myself, I have been too often its victim ever to take food from a hand I've bitten. So I kept my eyes open and my pistol primed, and the curs that hung around the camp gathered hopefully whenever I dined for they knew it was my custom to toss a few tit-bits to any attendant dogs before setting to myself. Paranoiac this might sound, but a favourite boarhound of Rydberg's had convulsions after two or three mouthfuls of a hare pie from my table one night. Perhaps the creature had been taken with a poison bait as is frequently used by these stupid German peasants, but after that I took still greater care and carried with me a small flask of salt and mustard dissolved in sour wine to use as an emetic in case of need.

My only other care was that I was perhaps too close to Wallenstein. A commander's favour is a fine thing – while he commands. But greatness breeds envy, and envy conspires downfalls and the downfall of a great man often plunges his associates to the depths also. Any doubts that may have remained about Wallenstein's notion of his personal role in the future of Europe disappeared after the peace of Lübeck in 1629 when, instead of reducing his armies, he increased them. I'd quickly spotted that Wallenstein was something more than a financier with a lust for profit and a talent for soldiering. He was a visionary, which is to say, in plain words, a natural, and therefore dangerous for all good sane men to be around. When I heard him talking of his plans for bringing the whole of Germany completely under the domination of the Emperor, I listened carefully but said nothing. When I heard him blaming the opposition of priests and prelates for thwarting his plans, I edged my way quietly to the door. And when I heard him speak wistfully of the rich plunder that awaited the first army to sack Rome in modern times, I retired to my quarters and thought seriously about my future.

Then a few months later at Ratisbon the Electors put pressure on Ferdinand to get rid of Wallenstein and to everyone's surprise, the general resigned without protest or demonstration. At first sight, this was the best time for me to go, but in fact it threw me closer to Wallenstein than ever before. D'Amblève was still lurking with my death warrant signed by Tilly in his pouch. I learned later that he had at least six copies of this monstrous document made so that one would be handy should the opportunity to use it ever arise. With Wallenstein a private citizen once more, there was nothing to prevent my arrest and summary execution. But private though he now was, Wallenstein still had plenty of personal power, enough to keep those in his immediate vicinity safe. So I retired with him first to his own duchy of Mecklenburg, which since he acquired it had been the only area of Germany where soldiers were not permitted to enter, and afterwards to Bohemia where he waited quietly for more than a year till the rising tide of Protestant victories should wash him back to command again. My presence he acknowledged with an ironical smile and a small speech of gratitude at my loyalty.

This period of comparative peace and rest fell nicely for me in one respect. Laura had been covered by a stallion which broke loose from the picket line one night, and was in foal. Fortunately the beast had been a fine animal, a Lippizaner his owner claimed, with the high action of the Neapolitan line. Luxuries such as breeding (of horses, I mean) are rarely permitted by the soldier's full life, but now I was able to personally supervise the birth and first schooling of Laura's foal. He was a grey like his father and gave promise of great excellence.

At the end of '31, this peaceful interlude ended. Wallenstein was put back in command, allegedly on a temporary basis. But when in April the following year poor old Tilly was killed at the Passage of the Lech, he was once more undisputed commander of all the League's forces.

Tilly's death did me a power of good too, for now D'Amblève could use his warrants to wipe his arse. No one was going to act on a dead man's name. So I decided to stay with Wallenstein while the pickings were good, but with the mental reservation that there was nothing to stop me moving on if the climate changed.

You may be wondering all this while that my affectionate nature had not caused any more trouble for me, but strangely it was very infrequently now that I heard the trumpets sound. Do not mistake me. There were willing dames enough on the fringes of such a military court as Wallenstein kept and I never lacked company when I fancied it. But the urgent undeniable need which exploded in me from time to time had been dormant almost since the incident of D'Amblève's betrothed. I often thought of that girl and hoped she had come to her senses and left those awful nuns. I thought of those confessions I heard in Silesia and shuddered. Seeking refuge in these convents from sexual attack is like quenching your thirst in the Dead Sea. Pray God the girl, who should be grateful to me for saving her from D'Amblève, had returned to her green garden with the fountain and the roses and the nectarine trees.

So on the whole I was now behaving as an honourable gentleman should, paying for his pleasures when they could not be obtained by fulsome flattery and empty promises. The nearest I came to that upsurge of passion which had so often threatened my life was as we lay at Lützen in Saxony, safe as we thought behind the system of ditches and entrenchments which Wallenstein, following his old custom, had created for our defence. It was a cold November morning and the fog that shrouded all things had clinging to it that smell of damp and decay which pervades an English church beyond all remedy of hissop or incense. I shuddered and felt cold and thought suddenly of my childhood. Then through the filthy air a trumpet sounded a tune which seemed to draw the grey vapour into streamers and tentacles as though the dully droned notes would make themselves visible as well as heard. And soon the Swedish troops took up the burden, singing the German fornicator's doggerel, 'Ein Fester Burg'. As they sang louder and ever louder the mist swirled and curled and on a rudden rose, sucked up into the cold sun of any icy blue winter's sky, and we saw the army of Gustavus Adolphus, King of Sweden, lined up for attack. That music and that sight suddenly filled me with a desire to fight and slay as irresistible as my lust for women when the trumpets sound. Our orders were to await the attack behind our trenches, but for me there could be no waiting. I spurred Osman forward and followed by those of my troop who were foolhardy enough to do more than wonder at my madness, we lept over our own fortifications and flew at the enemy. I remember little of the first part of the battle. Osman must have saved my life a dozen times for my own aim was to plunge as deep as possible into the enemy and bathe in their blood, tactics which must have killed me if my mount had not kept his wits when I lost mine. How a horse can recognize friend from foe I do not know. Perhaps these animals do communicate at a basic level. Be that as it may, when pain and fatigue finally brought me back to awareness, I found that Osman had borne me firmly into the midst of a regiment of our own cuirassiers where a lightly armoured cavalry man could feel as secure as anywhere on that bloody field. But even here, so strongly did the Swedes attack that sharp wedges of enemy cavalry pierced our ranks and though they died for their temerity, they wore down the irresistible impetus which a regiment of heavily armoured cavalry can develop. Before me suddenly I saw two of these foolhardy Swedes; one was a pale-faced lad of seventeen or so who with a courage which gave the lie to his colour was attempting to bear away his comrade, an older man nobly featured who strangely wore no armour and had been grievously wounded for his neglect. There was no escape for them so thick hemmed in were they, and one of the cuirassiers, an English lieutenant, enquired courteously the identity of the wounded man. The youth stared up at him with wild eyes but answered nothing. But the wounded man opened his mouth from which blood trickled thickly and said, 'I was the King of Sweden.'

The youth tried to raise him up and he shrieked in agony while the cuirassiers, pressing closer to see his face as news of his capture spread, threatened to stifle him with horseflesh.

His reputation was great, the noblest general in Europe so they called him. I knew nothing of this personally, but he was a man to respect and oppose on the open field, not to watch shrieking his way to death in the midst of his enemies. So I took out my dog-lock, placed the muzzle on his brow and blew his brains out.

As I covered his head with his blue and gold cloak, I heard a roar of rage behind me. Turning I saw D'Amblève attempting to force a way through the cuirassiers. He had come from Wallenstein bearing orders for the regiment and having heard the troopers murmuring Gustavus's name, had arrived just in time to see me administer the *coup de grâce*. Perhaps I should have tried to explain my act but to me D'Amblève was now nothing but an impotent upstart, so I turned Osman away and threaded my way through the cuirassiers at a speed his inferior horsemanship could not hope to match.

Perhaps I should not have killed the King. Certainly I did it with nothing in my heart but pity, and often the death of a particularly well loved leader will so shatter his army's morale that defeat becomes inevitable. Unfortunately this was not the Swedes' reaction. As the news spread (and the word was that he had been taken, then foully murdered) their anger grew to such proportions that they fought like madmen and though the struggle raged long, the result was never in doubt. Not in my mind anyway. An army of even the best professionals will in the end do no more than give value for money. Well, Wallenstein's men did that, and perhaps a bit more. But capitalism and the profit motive can never resist the fiery energies of righteous wrath, all other things being equal that is. The Swedes were as good soldiers as we were. And for a while they didn't care if they lived or died. Opposing men like that isn't war, it's suicide. Not caring about life is the ultimate weapon. If Wallenstein could somehow have produced a regiment of big naked Saxon lasses, all mounted astride black stallions, and so reminded those Swedes of the realities beyond the battlefield, then the result might have been different.

But he couldn't. I fought till I saw the battle was lost. Then I broke my rule and fought on, though nothing was to be gained. Why I should have felt any loyalty to Wallenstein, who showed it to none, I cannot imagine. And I paid a heavy price. As I heard the retreat sounded and inwardly voiced thanks, Osman gave a little cough and knelt down so slowly that I was able to step out of my stirrups like a lady from a well-trained hack. Seeing me safe alighted, he closed his eyes and rolled over on his side. A musket ball had taken him square in the throat, and as I watched he died. He was the bravest of little horses, sure-footed as a cat, and he loved a new-baked pan-loaf above all things. I had had him from a yearling and owed him many lives. I walked back from the battlefield not caring if another shot should pay for all, but something of his loving watchfulness must have remained for no harm came near me.

So ended the battle of Lützen. The invincible Wallenstein was defeated. The immortal Gustavus was dead. And Orfeo and Laura whinnied plaintively as I watched with them all night till they understood that Osman was not going to return.

Some things did not change, however. D'Amblève, those

stupid spurs of his jangling like his brains, went stalking round the camp complaining of my behaviour to any who would listen. It seemed his sense of honour had been offended by my act of mercy to Gustavus and the idiot boy wanted me arrested on a charge of regicide. Fortunately the king's body was still with us and when the chirurgeon reported on his wounds (three at least of which would certainly have been fatal) and when the cuirassiers who were present described the scene, it was agreed that nothing but praise was owed to me. D'Amblève was so filled with fury that for a while I became very uneasy. A man in such a state of mind as his will sink to any act of treachery and after a day or two of constant trepidation I took the only course possible and hired an assassin. Unfortunately before he could carry out his task the beautiful boy had left the camp in a fit of pique and taken himself off to Vienna, presumably to attach himself to the Emperor who was still theoretically Wallenstein's boss. I sent for the assassin (a renegade Bavarian monk who specialized in driving broad tapestry needles into the heads of his sleeping victims so that the murder went often undetected) and gave him a handsome retainer in case D'Amblève should return, and then set about considering my own future once more.

Perhaps the time was near when I too should seek a new master. Near, I finally decided, but not yet arrived. Wallenstein had lost a battle but he still had the nucleus of the greatest army in Europe and the wherewithal to build it up once more. There was no other paymaster as reliable for me to transfer my services to.

I was shortsighted, I suppose. But I have never claimed to be a politician. All I saw was a man with a huge and powerful army, and what force on earth could withstand that? Perhaps if I'd stayed with the man all the time, I would have seen how things were shaping. But when he asked me to act as his personal envoy in secret missions across the face of Europe I saw no reason to refuse. Even then, the reasons he gave should have made me suspect his judgement. My command of languages and speed of movement were gifts enough to explain his choice, but to them he added trustworthiness – and without his customary ironic inflexion. It was wishful thinking, I reckon. When I saw the odd selection of people I was required to bear messages to, I realized he needed someone to trust. The Electors of Saxony and Brandenburg were bad enough, Bernhard of Weimar was worse, but to find myself bearing offers of alliance to Oxenstjerna the Swedish Chancellor, ruling there till Gustavus's daughter should come of age, was beyond my silly understanding.

One thing I insisted on in all these envoyages was that I should be a mere bearer of despatches, not a plenipotentiary. Captain Fantom, mercenary, was nobody's enemy, unless you paid him. But Ambassador Fantom would have provided a good target for all sorts of people. So I delivered my messages and hung around until answers were forthcoming. I was well looked after, never having to share a chamber with more than two others, and as for entertainment, well, finding that in civilian quarters is the soldier's oldest art.

One incident however reminded me that I was still somebody's enemy, even as plain Carlo Fantom. The infant queen, Christina, had a nurse, a woman of mature years, solid and thickening at the waist though still with a head of tight-plaited ash-blonde hair which would have done credit to a blushful virgin. I glimpsed her one evening through a half open door closely guarded by a pair of heavyweight pikemen as she conveyed the young queen to bed. Instantly I heard the trumpets sound but at the first note I turned and ran to my chamber for to have attempted her there and then would have meant instant death. But with the full fanfare blaring in my ears all I could hope for was postponement and after an hour pacing up and down bent almost double much to the consternation of my room-mate, a sympathetic young Frenchman in Stockholm on God knows what mission from Richelieu, I set off in search of the nurse, Ingrid's room.

I found it easily, having an instinct in such matters. She was resting on her bed, for a royal nurse must get what sleep she can and be prepared for many an untimely summons. Such an untimely summons as she received now was one she could hardly have been expecting, yet in truth she seemed un-put-out by it. And when, having finished, I rose to make my escape, she seized me in arms like a Hanoverian's quarters and flung me on my back, where I lay breathless and watched her bolt her door.

An hour later I was praying that the infant queen would awake and start crying so that Ingrid might be sent for. But suddenly there came an interruption of another kind, the sounds of shouting and pistol shots and running feet.

I rose and dressed swiftly while Ingrid pulled on her nightgown and rushed off to be at the side of her royal charge. I left the chamber with more circumspection. Pistols in the night in a royal palace spell danger, especially to foreigners, and when I found my room full of palace guards, my first instinct was to run. But others came up behind me at that moment and there was no way of escape.

In fact at second glance the situation looked rather more hopeful. Three men in dark clothes were being held, disarmed, against one wall. Across the bed with blood gushing from three bullet holes in his torso and with his face and throat mutilated by slashing sword cuts lay the Frenchman. His eyes were open but he was looking at sights beyond the vision of mortal man.

What he had done or known to make him the victim of such a ferocious attack I did not know or want to know. I gratefully complimented myself on my own lowly status as a simple errand boy. But my complacent mood was soon shattered as Oxenstjerna himself arrived and the guards and the prisoners (whom he seemed to know) began to explain matters.

'Having learned today that the assassin of our dearly loved king, Gustavus, was in our country, what was there to do?' demanded the ringleader of the murderers who I later found out to be Count Iwan of Sura, a minor Swedish nobleman and leader of a fanatically right-wing group. 'No patriot with this knowledge could refrain from action. There he lies, the murderer, Fantom. Judge me he who dares!'

He drew himself up and stared with proud challenge at

each man in that room. When it came to my turn, I gave him an appreciative wink. But for his impulsiveness I would certainly have got a bellyful of shot and ended my days on a Swedish bed beyond resuscitation even by the intricate medicines of nurse Ingrid.

The Chancellor asked a few sharp questions. It appeared that someone, a German it sounded like, had sought out this nobleman to put the finger on me. It might have been mere coincidence that I had been recognized by some blabbermouth Kraut who had been at Lützen, but I doubted it. I smelt D'Amblève behind this.

Oxenstjerna now took me aside and said he felt it best if I departed without delay or ceremony. His despatches for Wallenstein were ready and though he, like most reasonable men, accepted that a king riding armourless and almost alone into the midst of the enemy was likely to be killed, these rumours of foul play might inflame other fools to desperate deeds. I had the feeling that he was delighted to have got his hands on Count Iwan. I was a complication he wanted out of the way so that the Count could be prosecuted for murder of the totally innocent Frenchman.

I made no demur but left at once. If the threat of assassination were not enough to send me on my way, the sight of Ingrid nursing the infant princess and looking my way with hungry eyes certainly was. Thank God the heir to the throne was not a boy, I thought. The poor little sod would have been ruined before he reached manhood!

I rode south to Malmo, preferring to trust myself to the treacherous Baltic as little as possible and landed in Schleswig with a great sense of relief, partly because Sweden was behind me and partly because I have small taste for sailing. Even less fond of the sea was Orfeo though he felt it beneath his dignity to admit to fear. Laura I had left behind with her foal Petrarch, who was still too young I felt for such a hard trip as this. I had bought on my way north a two-year-old stallion whom I called Luke. Mouse-dun in colour, standing scarcely fifteen hands, he seemed a cross between a Halfinger and a Norwegian Fjord, with a good admixture of

God knows what else! Something about his short broad head had reminded me of Osman and his deep chest and strong quarters gave promise of great endurance. If he proved to have half the qualities of Osman, who had been equally indifferent to heights, depths, rock, sand, mud or oceans, he would be a bargain. But he would need a great deal of work before he was fit for even the simplest of military duties and I had left him stabled at Schleswig. When I went to pick him up, I found him in a sorry state. The rogue whose stables he was resting in replied insolently when I accused him of neglecting his duties, so I gave him his own left ear as a fee, and rode slowly back to rejoin Wallenstein's army which I discovered massacring Swedish troops in Silesia. So much for my mission! But that was politics and I have never let myself be troubled by politics. It's like falling in love with a whore; you die betrayed or poxed. No, there were other matters to trouble me more than who our enemy was.

First, D'Amblève was back. Almost the first sound I heard was the tintinnabulation of those ridiculous spurs he still affected, and when we encountered he regarded me with a kind of sneering triumph that filled me with foreboding. Discreet enquiries revealed that my renegade monk had been found in a ditch, surrounded by his own guts. But disposal of a mere assassin could not wholly account for D'Amblève's feline self-satisfaction.

But worse than D'Amblève's presence was the appearance of Wallenstein. I think he'd finally gone so far round the twist that recovery was not possible. Physically he was bent and emaciated so that those big bones of his cheeks and his nose stuck our like buttresses on a gutted church. His lips were a vivid red against his dull grey skin and I suspect he used some kind of colouring, like a vain beldame. Everywhere he went he was accompanied by astrologers and he would hardly piss without consulting them. His temper was always short, but now he flew into fits of crazy rage at trifles and ordered men executed for trivial or imaginary offences. He had become obsessed with noise. The cobbled streets around his quarters were covered in straw to muffle the passage of wagons, cocks were strangled if they crowed within earshot, and even distinguished visitors would find themselves threatened or sometimes even beaten into silence if they spoke too loud for his comfort. The only good thing about all this was that he particularly abominated the jingling of spurs and would allow none of his officers in earshot who wore them. This cut D'Amblève off from his company as the fool refused to discard the monstrosities he wore, though perhaps this very refusal should have given me more cause for fear.

I saw Wallenstein just long enough to be given another mission and I accepted the chance of getting away from his court again with some relief. This time I was sent 'recruiting'. In fact, what I was really doing was touting commissions about the country with orders to sell them to whoever had money. Wallenstein's once limitless coffers were growing empty and he was willing to sell indiscriminately what he had once bestowed only after the greatest deliberation. I didn't like the job, but at least it got me out of the way again, so I saddled up once more and rode off.

My wanderings across the face of Germany during the next months are of little interest here. I didn't do much good but I didn't do much harm either and I enjoyed myself where I could. News from Bohemia was rare and confused. Had I had all my horses with me, I might have given way to the temptation to cut loose and drift down into Spain and France to see which was offering the best terms for soldiers in the war that must surely come between them. Anyway, horses apart, I suppose I owed Wallenstein some loyalty and, more importantly he owed me a great deal of money, so I turned back in November and having spent Christmas in Lebus where I converted half a dozen Protestant virgins, I headed south early in January. It was a journey I made without enthusiasm and even Orfeo who had so long obeyed me unquestioningly seemed to take each step under protest. He was, I suddenly realized, an old horse now and I owed him better than a long trek in the middle of winter. Luke was with me too, full of energy and amiable curiosity. He was the most willing of animals, though far from the brightest, and I would have been better off with Petrarch who under my careful tuition was maturing every day. But Laura had been unwell when the time came for me to leave Pilsen and had seemed so distressed when I made preparation to saddle Petrarch that I had decided to leave them together.

I rode slowly, sheltering whenever the weather was bad, which was frequent. I had no incentive to hurry. Only a fool rides apace with bad news, and my news for Wallenstein was that no one was rallying to his banner any more. I realized just how right 'no one' had been when I reached Prague in February and discovered that the Emperor had issued a proclamation dismissing Wallenstein from his command.

Confused news was coming out of Pilsen. Wallenstein was going mad, executing all who opposed him, forcing his officers to sign declarations of loyalty daily. I discounted most of what I heard, but this still left enough to worry me. Again I thought of cutting my losses and declaring for the Emperor. But Wallenstein wasn't finished yet and it would be stupid to transfer my loyalties prematurely. I was owed money. Also (and this again was the deciding factor) Laura and Petrarch were at Pilsen. So off I went.

I reached Pilsen on 23 February to discover that Wallenstein with about a thousand men had fled to Eger where all loyal officers were commanded to join him. This was the beginning of the end, I could feel it in my bones, but again reasons presented themselves to follow. First, he had money. Everything of value they could lay their hands on had been removed. Rumour put the cash alone in excess of a hundred thousand gulden.

Secondly Petrarch had been taken.

Laura I found abandoned in her stable. Her condition had worsened. She was coughing hollowly and her breathing was noisy and full of pain. I spent the following day with her and by the end of it, I knew there was no hope. To lose such friends as Laura and Osman both in the same year was almost more than I could bear. These poets who write of lovers' pangs are self-deluding fools. They weep because they are rejected or betrayed. I wept because I was faced with absolute trust.

That night I shot her and buried her in the iron earth, and the following morning I set out after Wallenstein and his fleeing men.

I arrived at the Fortress of Eger late in the afternoon of 25 February. I was greeted politely but coldly by the two Scottish officers who commanded the fort, Gordon and Leslie, but this frosty Scots welcome was warmed for me by the discovery in their mess of the one good soul (including all the Stuarts) to come out of that ball-freezing country.

'Lauder!' I cried. 'Why in the name of divine justice aren't you dead?'

He regarded me without surprise.

'I'm like you, Fantom,' he answered. 'The Almighty doesn't want us and the de'il reckons we're mair use to him here on earth than stinking up his fires.'

I could see that this light use of the divinity did not please Leslie and Gordon who had a hard Protestant cast of feature, but an Irish colonel called Butler whom I knew vaguely took them aside and Lauder accompanied me to the stables where I now sought Petrarch.

Lauder, it turned out, had been serving with Colonel Butler whose regiment had been on its way to Prague when they fell in with Wallenstein's force marching to Eger.

'Well met!' I said. 'I'm almost as glad to see you as I will be my horse. Petrarch! Petrarch!'

I heard an answering whinny and a few moments later was examining my young horse.

'He has been well cared for anyway,' I said. 'I'm not yet sure whether I should thank or shoot whoever took him. But tell me, Lauder, what's the news? If you have been here two days, why, you must know everything that's worth knowing!'

Lauder looked at me oddly and seemed uncertain how to answer.

'Come, man,' I said. 'What's so startling that you cannot tell me?'

This time he would have spoken but a sound was now heard which sent my hand to my sword and set me stepping back into a dark corner away from the light of the lantern.

It was the jingling of spurs.

'Captain Fantom!' said D'Amblève. 'Good evening to you, sir.'

He smiled at me as he spoke. Thirty now, he still kept his boyish beauty.

'I see you've found your horse. I'm glad, and glad too that you have arrived in time for the banquet tonight.'

'You took my horse?' I said.

'For safe keeping only,' he protested. 'I knew you would rejoin your master eventually. Have you seen him yet?'

'Not yet.'

'Then I would suggest you do so. News of your arrival has been given to him and I can guess how eagerly he looks for his hard-man.'

There could be some truth in this and I had no desire to offend Wallenstein in his present uncertain mood.

As I moved away, Lauder made to accompany me, but D'Amblève held out his arm in restraint.

'A word with you, Captain Lauder,' he said. 'Till later, Fantom. We'll meet at the banquet.'

As I made my way to Wallenstein's quarters, I mused on what new attempt on my life the lovely lad was plotting. I could see no other explanation of his good mood.

But when I saw Wallenstein, all other thoughts went out of my head. Bent, feverish, shaking, he looked a very picture of desperation. I smelt disaster in that room. I did not need his battalion of soothsayers to work it out for me.

He spoke with an optimism that was worse than despair.

'Arnim is coming,' he assured me. 'And Bernhard. And Oxenstjerna himself will move when the time is ripe. Your embassies have not been in vain, no, no. I saw in the sky the other night a falling star of great brightness which fell far, far, from behind the moon at its zenith down beyond Ursus

Major. At first I took it for my own self falling, but when I had a horoscope cast, it was revealed it was not me, but the Emperor. You note he falls in the North. Well, is it not obvious that here are signified the Swedes?'

I nodded agreement though I was distressed to hear the former champion of the True Faith so dependent upon the goodwill of heretics.

He fell now into a reverie from which I awoke him by asking if he would attend the banquet.

'No, no,' he said. 'I am not well for such things. But you must be hungry, Fantom, hard-man though you be. Hard-man! Ah! Had I but a regiment of such as you! A platoon even. The sky would have blazed with falling stars! Still, I have one. Yes, it is enough, I think. One may still be enough.'

He nodded and smiled. It was the nearest to a real smile I think that I ever saw on those painted lips. Then he embraced me and turned away to his desk which was littered with open tomes. I had no doubt of their subject matter.

Poor old bastard! I thought as I made ready for the banquet. I was in a mood for merriment now as an antidote to that old sick man, stinking of death. I was glad he wasn't attending. Even at his brightest and best, he was a poor head of a festal board.

I went back to check my horses and also to get a feel of the geography of this place. I had been here before during the campaigns, but it is best to make sure that things remain as they have been. Talking to Petrarch kept me longer than I intended and I feared I might be late for the feast.

Then as I made my way to the banqueting hall, I met Lauder again. I had a feeling he was lurking on purpose to meet me.

'What, are you not hungry, you old shagbag?' I asked impatiently for I could hear the rattle of dishes and smell roasting meat.

'Ye'll tak a dram wi' me,' said Lauder peremptorily.

'A thousand!' I answered pulling loose from his grip. 'But let's join the others while the best wine remains.'

'Hold,' said Lauder and began talking rapidly in a low

voice but what he said I did not catch for at the end of the stone-flagged passage in which we stood I caught a glimpse of the most desirable woman I had ever seen. A lesser man might have fallen on his knees and worshipped but the music that sounded in my ears was not the solemn notes of the church organ.

'Who is that creature?' I demanded.

Lauder turned and looked.

'That is Mistress Gordon,' he said. 'The custodian's wife.'

The memory of that stern Scottish face interrupted the trumpets for a moment. There was a dreadful merciless righteousness there. To screw that man's wife in his own castle was the act of a suicidal madman. I tried to take command of myself, but the woman had disappeared now and I found my feet taking me irresistibly in pursuit.

'Stay,' said Lauder, coming alongside me. I looked at him angrily, expecting useless words of warning, threats, exhortations.

Instead he said simply, 'I'll show you her chamber.'

This was no moment to question an act of friendship, however unexpected. I followed him with explosive impatience till he stopped and pointed silently at a door. I grasped his hand for a second – I could spare no longer – then I flung open the door and rushed in.

She had her back to me and before she could turn, I had my arms under her shoulders and my hands locked behind her neck in a grip I had learned of the Turkish wrestlers. But she was surprisingly strong. She staggered but did not go down. Indeed she countered by twisting her hip into my belly and trying to throw me with a half-buttock. For a couple of seconds we spun like a top, then I changed my grip to a simple armlock with my knee in the small of her back. She was shrieking most lustily now, but such was the din from the distant banquet that her cries passed unnoticed. She now tried to back heel me in the groin. She knew where the danger lay, that one. I could not afford the best of three falls. A quick submission was what I needed. So I released my hold. Her own momentum carried her forward on to the bed. I leapt on top, knocking the breath from her body and took her from behind.

So strong was my passion for this exquisite creature that my ordnance scarcely came to bear on her citadel before it was sending forth its victory salvo. I rose hastily, recognizing my danger now. She lay face down still, her pimply red buttocks flexing gently. She looked less attractive than before. Strange how beauty fades, I mused. But this was no time for philosophy. The important thing was that she had not seen me and though I must always be suspect in such a case as this, yet if I could mingle with the revellers unnoticed, I might still escape detection.

In any case, I assured myself as I left the room, she will probably not speak out. Gordon would avenge the honour done to his name, but he also looked the type who would put away a defiled wife.

So it was with a fair amount of confidence that I made my way to the banqueting chamber.

The sounds of revelry seemed to have died down, as if the last great outburst had exhausted the feasters. I hoped I had not missed the fun.

Then I reached the door and saw what I had missed.

The huge table was weighed down with good things, haunches of venison, roast fowl, steaming pies, flagons of wine.

And human bodies. Blood, brains and severed limbs were strewn across the board. The air steamed and stank. Not a man sitting at that table but was dead. Some had arisen and turned and taken their death wounds in the front. But most had died as they ate or drank. I saw men I had served and fought beside with their heads resting on their platters, the unchewed food jammed in their teeth like the apple in the boar's mouth at the centre of the table.

There were still living men in that room, standing with bloody weapons, looking at each other wildly and with the first signs of shame as the fury of their action died away. Leslie and Gordon were there, and Colonel Butler, too. I wished they'd had twenty wives apiece so I could have ravished them all. And two other faces I recognized. Lauder, impassive as ever, but with his sword also a quickly darkening red. And D'Amblève who looked around in a kind of whey-faced hysteria like a novitiate priest who has been carried away and screwed his first nun. Suddenly I understood what lay behind the uncharacteristic reactions of both of them to my arrival.

I backed away quietly. Nothing but death waited in that room for me. All Wallenstein's closest associates lay on or under that table. Everyone except me – and Wallenstein himself! I turned and ran swiftly to the General's room. He might still be unharmed and I had not yet been paid. But I arrived just in time to see a group of soldiers led by a fiery Irishman called Devereux break down the door and as I turned and fled, Wallenstein's death cry followed me down the corridor.

1635–40
Saxony – Brunswick – Holland

The Winter Queen rubbed wintergreen
Upon her snowy breast.
Alas! said she. *And woe is me!*
I cannot reach the rest.

Said Carlo Fantom, *I'm your man!*
I'll work with might and main.
And when I've rubbed from bum to bubb
I'll rub your bubbs again!

No need to go on. Who does not know the scurrilous ballad made on my sojourn at The Hague '39 to '40? I had lived more like a brigand than a soldier after my flight from Eger. But then after Wallenstein's death the war degenerated to such an extent that throughout Germany most soldiers were behaving far worse than brigands.

I joined up with one of the bands of Croats which infested the Saxon forests, living off the local peasants and any travellers who were foolish enough to travel without heavy escort. They were a rough crew and back in our native land would have been nought but peasants themselves, but I felt a need to hear my own tongue spoken and to be awhile among deceits and treacheries I could understand. To my surprise they recognized my name and indeed I was held as a kind of hero among them, my deeds, military and amatory, redounding to the national credit. The tale of how I had interposed my body between Wallenstein and the ball from Bela's pistol was well known to them and caused them so much amusement that I suspected they had somehow learned or guessed it was a put-up job. But gradually it emerged that they were amused because their simplicity had brought them to the same conclusion as Wallenstein's super-subtlety. They thought I was a hard-man. Of course their knowledge derived not from books and commentaries by other learned half wits, but from stories whispered to credulous and dirty ears in their stinking, smoke-filled huts.

At their drunken revels some of the band wanted me to demonstrate my hardness by letting myself be used for musket practice, but I refused, saying that so long had I been away from the forests of Croatia that my supplies of the herb had run out and I feared its effects may have waned.

Later that night while the rest lay in drunken sleep, their leader, a hairy rogue called Josip, took me to his tent and showed me a large box full of dried leaves of what he claimed was this very herb. He offered to share his stock with me saying there was supply here for several years. In face of such generosity from one Croat to another there was nothing I could be but extremely suspicious. Why, I asked him, did he not share his herbs with the others and then make them invincible in battle? To which he answered that shared between thirty and forty, the stock would soon be used up, and discord would break out if they knew he possessed the herb but was not sharing it. Hard-men may still be slain either by use of a silver bullet or by being beaten to death with cudgels, neither of which fates he fancied. But, he went on, he was willing to share with me for only a small part of the great store of booty it was well known I had acquired during my German campaigns.

I retired to my tent much disturbed. As I have said before, a soldier of fortune may be thought to be anything except rich. There was no way of convincing Josip that I owned only my horses, my clothes and weapons, and the few gold pieces in my purse, so I had made vague promises and left him content. But this would not last for long. I had nearly paid the price for not heeding warning signs in the recent past. I was not going to be caught again.

Quickly I put my gear together. The camp was unguarded that night, so plentiful had the supply of alcohol been. When they could not find any to steal, they brewed some filth of their own from the resin of pine trees and drank vast quantities, ignoring the two most frequent side-effects which were blindness and insanity.

Only one man was sober enough to be disturbed by my departure and that was Josip. It seemed safest to take a Turkish farewell so I drew my short horseback sword and began to approach his tent. But after a few steps I hesitated and remembered what he had said to me in our friendly talk. He was a villainous and superstitious old rogue but I was an officer and a gentleman and should behave with the intelligence and panache expected of my rank.

So I put away my sword, picked up a stout billet of wood lying near the fire and went in search of Josip.

Whether his skin would have resisted bullet or sword I could not say, but he had been right when he told me even hard-men could be beaten to death with cudgels.

Pausing only to help myself to what little coin he kept in his tent and, as an afterthought, taking up the box in which he kept his supply of the dried herb, I packed this and my other equipment on Petrarch and Luke, mounted Orfeo, and departed into the forest.

I lived hard for some weeks thereafter for I did not care to hang around for long and I was moving through country devastated by the passage of at least half a dozen armies in the past couple of years. Josip's herb came in very useful for when all other victuals failed, I discovered that the dried leaves, after a long infusion in boiling water, produced a refreshing and sustaining liquid, not unlike this new oriental herb, tea, which I had once tasted at Wallenstein's court.

Eventually I took service with first one, then another general, insisting always on a short term contract and refusing to take any oath of allegiance or sign any paper which would commit me beyond the financial agreement. He who never swears can never be forsworn. It was plain to all those who had eyes to see that Germany was a ruined land. It had had twenty years of war. Now it wanted twenty years of peace to make it worth plundering once more.

My last engagement on German soil was at Vlotho on the Weser. Everything had changed for the worse. There was a new Emperor now, a miserable canting fellow who made the memory of Wallenstein and his ambitions seem almost pleasant even to his enemies. I was serving him in a force commanded by Hatzfeld, one of Wallenstein's old colonels, a pleasant enough sinner but he knew a good deal less about warfare than Orfeo! D'Amblève had flourished as a result of his treachery, he told me. But of Lauder he had no news.

Well, I have never cared to be governed by incompetents, so I was thinking of moving on when news came of a small expeditionary force led by Charles Lewis, the Elector Palatine, son of the old Winter King, who was making an effort to recapture some of his father's former territories. I say this force was led by Charles Lewis, but in the event it appeared he led from behind and when the imperial force swallowed up the intruders, Charles escaped, leaving his young brother, Rupert, who had been in the van, to be captured. This boy (for he was scarcely eighteen) was a fiery termagant and seemed to think there was something honourable in fighting to the death for he refused to surrender even when all his followers had either fled or laid down their arms. I pulled out my pistol for I had no thought to go near that flailing sword, took aim and fired. His horse sank beneath him, its skull shattered and the lad banged his head on a stone and lay stunned till we had disarmed him and bound his head.

I saw him once more before I moved on. He was in slightly more subdued mood and, having by now discovered his identity and intending myself to visit Holland where his mother stayed, I civilly offered to bear a message. An introduction to a Queen, particularly one who is the King of England's sister and a widow of renowned beauty, is worth a few civilities even to a boisterous pup. He accepted my offer, gave me missives and before I left he said with more maturity and humour than I gave him credit for, 'Fantom, I must thank you it seems for saving me from an honourable death. But I shall not forget, you owe me a good horse.'

I bowed and left, smiling. It had indeed been a good horse, and had it not reared as I shot, the prince would now have been lying in his honourable grave and my fine stable would have been increased to four.

At The Hague I was made most welcome by all the young prince's family except for his elder brother, the new Elector Palatine. He was a pompous, self-centred young shit who obviously felt that the world owed him at least one kingdom. But his mother, Elizabeth, she was a woman for whom kingdoms would be well lost. I saw her for the first time alone, which was well for my head. Having heard that I bore tidings of her captured son, she summoned me to her private chamber. As soon as I entered I knew I was lost. Quickly I went down on my knees before her and fixed my eyes on the hem of her skirt.

'Sir, you have news of my son?' she said eagerly.

'Madame,' I stuttered.

'Sir, speak and tell me. Is he well?'

'Madame,' was all I could say.

'What does this mean?' she asked, alarmed. 'What tidings keep you bowed down? Sir, I pray, rise up and let me know what it is you bring me. Let it be good news and you shall have of me what you will.'

'Madame,' I said looking up into that lovely face. 'Your son is well and happy and sends most loving greetings.'

So saying, I tipped her chair backwards and set to.

It's at moments like this that true royalty shows itself. She was surprised, one might say taken aback. But she was not a woman to complain about a bargain whose terms she herself had stated.

When I had finished she said, ' 'Fore God, sir, I trust you have no messages for me from any other of my children.'

I remained in The Hague for more than a year till the Queen dropped some broad hints that I ought to move on. There's always a constant buzz of scandalous rumour in such a place, and though after I had run my sword through a couple of noble bellies no one dared spread the filth openly, yet ballads and broadsheets are not so easily repressed. In any case, a mere writer is below the notice of a gentleman.

On the Queen's recommendation and following my own inclination I decided to cross the sea to England. I had a fancy to see that small but famous country and it would make a change to be somewhere where I was not known save through a royal relation's personal commendation. I delayed my departure as long as possible for sentimental reasons. Orfeo was happily retired now, a great favourite with the children at court, and it would have been an unkindness to take him on his travels once more. Yet I was reluctant to take my leave of so old a friend. The Queen had presented me with a young mare so that my family remained at three, the minimum number necessary for a true riding man. Athene, I called her, for she had a wisdom and grace beyond her years. Compared with my other young horse, Luke, whose eagerness to please and wild enthusiasm in action would always leave him some way short of being perfectly reliable, Athene from the start seemed to listen to what I said to her and act on it in a shorter time than any other beast I had ever schooled. I was basically a follower of Fiaschi and the School of Naples but I had studied later German techniques (Lohneysen in particular) and added some methods of my own. An Englishman called Cavendish seemed to be a man who knew something of the horse's mind and this was another reason for visiting that country. But still I delayed and Orfeo grew older and Athene more perfect day by day.

But in the end, I had to make a move. Orfeo had been guaranteed a comfortable and honoured retirement till summoned to his last charge. I said goodbye to him as a soldier must, with complete finality and no promises of return. He knew what I was doing and ran round his paddock at the high trot as though to show me he was still fit for anything. But he knew as well as I did that it was past, and I gave him a handful of Rhenish sugar and so took my leave. Next to the Queen, to whom I also said goodbye as a soldier must. She thanked me again for my kindness to her younger son, though in a sense it was Prince Rupert who was driving me away. There had been strong rumours that soon he was to be released, when he would return to the Hague. His elder brother was a cold fish, too concerned with his own affairs to be much bothered by what his mother got up to. But Rupert was another beast altogether. From reports that reached us from time to time, it seemed that his long imprisonment had done little to dampen his fieriness and I had no desire to test his reaction if, as would surely happen, my enemies set out to besmirch my name. I have always made it my rule to avoid if possible killing persons of consequence. The sensitivity of some families to such natural accidents is more than a reasonable man would believe possible. Forgive and forget has always been my motto.

This fellow D'Amblève, for instance, wouldn't it seem reasonable that by now, fifteen years after that unfortunate business at Lutter, he would have settled down with some nice horsey Belgian girl to breed another generation of good-looking, god-fearing shits? Or, better still, have got his head blown off on some obscure battlefield? I certainly thought so. There had been one or two attempts on my life since the Swedish business, but I could not attribute them directly to the beautiful boy and for two or three years now I had given him scarcely any conscious thought; but the human mind is like an Aeolian harp – when the wind blows, it plays music we had forgotten we knew. What memories are brought back by what trifles! A gleam of light on the water, the smell of new baked pastry, the tinkling of a fountain. The jingling of spurs. I was in the stable when I heard them, saddling and loading my animals prior to departure. A stable yard is no unusual place to hear spurs, but at this sound the hair bristled on my neck. There was only a single tinkle, but the silence that followed was even more significant. A casual horseman would have no cause to become so silent. Quickly I finished tightening Petrarch's girth and took out of its saddle-rest a new weapon I had acquired after watching the Dutch wild-fowlers on their stinking marshes. It was a form of their *donderbus*, having a shoulder stock, but with a barrel no longer than a pistol's. Loaded with very fine shot which was thrown wide by the short barrel, it was ideal for slaughtering birds but except at very close quarters unlikely to be fatal to man. On the other hand as long as you knew vaguely where your target lay, it was hard to miss.

My preparations were finished. I peered through a crack in the door into the yard. It was very dark. I have grown into the habit when the choice is mine of making my departures at night. The ways are clearer and there are fewer eyes to mark your going. Now however I could have wished for the blaze of noon. But the mind very often is light enough and only one part of the yard offered any protection for an ambush if I discounted the stalls themselves. I felt I could. It would take a brave or stupid man to put himself beside a strange horse when his intent was to blaze away with a brace of pistols, and D'Amblève's assassins would be neither brave nor stupid, just professional. So they had to be in the blacksmith's shop which stood, open-fronted, to the right of the gate. His fire was out and from my viewpoint the shop was nothing but a blacker hole in the wall of blackness. But that's where they were, I would stake my life on it. In fact, I *was* staking my life on it.

Whistling a casual tune (I realized it was 'The Winter Queen' after a moment, but did not change) I blew out the lantern, opened the stable door and led my horses out, Petrarch first with the *donderbus* resting across his saddle, the other two following nose-to-tail as I had trained them. I had thought of making a straightforward dash for it but while I doubted if their marksmanship would be good enough to knock me off a fast moving horse, the animals themselves were much more vulnerable, especially if their armament in any way resembled mine. Also in their situation the first thing I would have done was stretch a couple of thin cords across the gateway, one at knee-height (the horses') and one at neck-height (mine).

Carefully keeping Petrarch to my right I closed my eyes for a few paces so that when I opened them again the darkness had turned into an arrangement of greys. I could see no impediment to my passage through the gate and as yet there had been no sign of movement in the blacksmith's shop. Perhaps I had been wrong, but I had to carry on as I had planned. If they were there, they would prefer a clear shot at me, but they weren't about to let a horse's body save me from attack. Another couple of yards towards the gate and the hail of bullets would surely come.

'Whoa, boy,' I said in a loud voice to Petrarch. 'Time to ride.'

He halted. I put my foot in the stirrup, I sensed movement in the shop as they craned forward in anticipation of my body rising into plain view above the saddle; I levelled my *donderbus* and pulled the trigger.

The flash and explosion would have done justice to a battery of cannon. Petrarch stood still as a rock, but Luke forgot his lessons and reared up with a piercing neigh which almost drowned the screams coming from the shop. There was no time to reprimand him.

'On!' I yelled into Petrarch's ear, and still with only one foot in the stirrup, I was whirled out through the gate and along the cobbled street. Luke, as though eager to make up for his lapse, ran so close behind that I came near to kicking him as I finally flung my leg over and attained the saddle. And bringing up the rear with the unconcern of a riding school horse came Athene.

My flight had been instinctive, but now I dropped the reins onto Petrarch's neck and let him decelerate to a sedate walk. There was little chance of pursuit. In the flash from my shot I had seen and recognized the inmates of the blacksmith's shop. One had been the blacksmith himself, a blackbearded bull of a man. His leather breeches had been round his knees and he was applying himself enthusiastically to a young woman propped up against his anvil. She looked very like the stable-master's wife, but I might have been mistaken. Certainly she was totally unlike the blacksmith's wife.

I laughed to myself as I approached the harbour. So it had not been D'Amblève. But better safe than sorry, and lechery must expect its reward. God had given the majority of men free will. Only a few of us had he predestined to suffer.

The thought saddened me for a while but I soon recovered when the shipmaster welcomed me aboard with assurances of favourable winds and a smooth passage. I was on my way to England, land of parliamentary democracy, which meant that surely any man of wit and spirit could make a fortune there. I was tired of wars and tyrants; I was growing too old for the discomforts of campaigning and the intrigues of palaces alike. I wanted a patch of land, a few neighbours to cheat, good horses to ride and a string of ready dames to keep me on the strait and narrow whenever those wild trumpets sounded. England had finished its civil wars a hundred years ago. Now even the wild Scots had no quarrel with a Stuart on the throne. There I would surely find comfort and peace and a place to rest my head.

1640–2

England : London – Edgehill

It was bitter cold and the small fire I had nursed into life did no more than burn the palms of my hands. I was thoroughly pissed off and did not even raise my head when I heard someone stumbling around in the frost-lined undergrowth which filled this dreadful wood. A ball in the back of my neck would have been welcome relief.

'Fantom? Fantom? Is that you?'

'Bugger off, Robin,' I answered surlily but he came forward nonetheless.

'It's a chill night,' he observed as he sat on the fur-covered stool I vacated. I was in a foul mood but knew that there were limits to the unmannerliness a soldier in the field should offer his commander-in-chief.

Essex took a glowing twig from the fire and lit a pipe as I stamped my feet and wrapped my arm round myself in an effort to get warm. He was my senior by many years but did not seem to feel the cold. Perhaps there was something in this godliness after all.

'Carlo,' he said after two or three contented puffs. 'You are too hasty.'

'Not for myself, my Lord,' I answered. 'Were I hasty in defence of my own honour, Sir William Balfour would be out of the cold this night.'

'No more of that,' Essex said sternly. 'We may leave that kind of vanity to the popinjays who mislead the King. It is God's honour we must study to preserve.'

'My Lord,' I said humbly, thinking, Jesus Christ! how did I come to get stuck with this canting old Puritan and his killjoy friends? Balfour with whom I had quarrelled so fiercely was in some ways the best of the lot. A rabid Protestant certainly, but a professional soldier also, and a man of experience and guile. It was our common ground rather than our differences which had made us fall out. Essex had asked my opinion on some matter concerning the disposition of our cavalry in the imminent battle. I had given it and Balfour had contradicted me, on grounds good enough I acknowledged, but in terms which had angered me so that instead of being diplomatically silent, I had laughingly wondered whether the lieutenant's lodgings in the Tower of London were a good place to study modern cavalry tactics.

'Aye, sir,' he had snarled. 'And it is a good place to put foreign fools with their Papist notions.'

I had left the meeting in anger and moved my bivouac apart from the central encampment, like a spoiled brat sulking in a corner. But Balfour was the occasion rather than the root of my anger. I had hung back as long as I could from joining this campaign. It was not for this that I had crossed the seas to England. Chance had turned me into the most unlikely friend a man could think of for the Earl of Essex, and when war had become certain, his offer of preferment had seemed too good for a man of my calling to refuse. But it had been my mind that accepted it, not my heart.

I had prospered in England and legitimately too. Papers I had had of King Charles's sister on parting, mainly letters of recommendation and introduction, had established me as a gentleman of standing in London. I had put aside enough of my wealth to keep me well for a time, while the bulk of my money I had invested in a scheme for sinking mines in the Malvern hills beneath which lay (according to the prospectus) rich deposits of silver and lead. I know nothing of such matters but I had been introduced to Mr Thomas Bushell, the main proposer of the scheme, and after listening to him for an hour, I was convinced that there was a fortune to be made here. Not that I rushed in without doing some checking first! I have lived too long in a world of roguery to be conned by a charming tongue. But this Bushell, it appeared, had been seal-bearer to that most renowned of scientists, Francis Bacon, and more recently had looked after the Royal mines in Wales and been made Master of the Mint. He was universally marvelled at for his ingenuity in mechanical contrivances and his knowledge of engineering. With Bushell in control, I had no doubts but that soon I would become wealthy beyond lust.

Speaking of lust, I had had some fears that my sad disability might upset my new-found social standing, particularly in times of peace. But I need not have worried. True, the trumpets sounded three or four times in my first few weeks, but to my amazement my outbursts were never followed by complaints and finally I concluded that what I had heard of your Englishman's unsubtle wooing must be true, and my own efforts by comparison were but gentlemanly essays!

Curiously enough it was my weakness that first brought me into contact with Robin Essex. A wench who served me wine in a Westminster tavern sparked the attack. She was plain, just past first youth. Already the peach-blossom of her skin was turning to a vinous flush, doubtless derived from the consumption of too many heeltaps. But the aesthetic principle never played a large part in my bouts. I downed my wine, ordered a fresh bottle, followed her into the cellar and met with little resistance over a barrel of Rhenish. I then gave her some coin and would also have given her some moral advice, for I feared from her demeanour she might be a woman of too easy virtue. But a footfall on the cellar steps prevented my sermon. My new respectability had not yet dulled my old cautiousness and I had no desire to get into a fracas with the landlord who, for ought I knew, was the woman's husband or lover. So putting a hand over her mouth, I pressed her into the shadows between the racks and waited.

There were two men and they did not descend the steps but stopped by the cellar door, conversing in whispers. I could not make out much of what they said, but I caught the name Pym and I heard a sound which I would have recognized in a thunderstorm, the decelerating click of the ratchet of a wheel-lock pistol being spanned. My heart sank. These men were up to no good. Whether hired professionals or dedicated amateurs I did not know, but if they knew enough not to wind up their pistols till shortly before use (else the wheel-spring may grow stiff and fail to work) there was bloodshed soon to be done.

The name Pym I recognized. He was a leading man in this English parliament which through some deficiency of law is allowed to defy its King and go unpunished. This was before their war started, of course, and it seemed to me quite natural that, in this unseemly state of things, gentlemen of honour and loyalty should make shift to teach the rogues a lesson by shooting their leader. For all I knew, the King himself was privy to this plot. It would be foolish then to interfere.

On the other hand I could scarcely step forward now and say, 'Gentlemen, whatever your purpose, I approve it. Commend me to His Majesty. Good day.' Men surprised in ambush shoot first and listen later.

I could, of course, remain quiet and let them get on with it. But I had no idea how expert they were. A botched-up job could have this cellar full of angry men in minutes, none of them keen to listen to protestations of innocence from a sinister foreigner.

I suddenly recalled how many years ago, I had set up the phoney attempt on Wallenstein's life to ingratiate myself with him. Here I was now with no desire at all to ingratiate myself with Pym or his party, yet saving his life seemed the best way I could find of preserving my own.

Yet this too was fraught with danger. I carried no pistol (thus far my new respectability and sense of security had taken me), only my sword. The men were forty feet away, at the head of a narrow flight of steps. To rush them would be fatal. If saving Pym's life were the means of saving my own, I would do it, but I had no intention of sacrificing myself on his behalf.

Suddenly one of the men hissed the other to silence. The door into the tavern was open a crack, letting an axe-edge of light fall through. Obviously their prey had arrived, perhaps manoeuvred here by some complotter. The time had come to act.

I decided quickly. One man firing in alarm into the dark was a takeable risk; two men weren't. I needed to draw their fire. Against me I felt the body of the serving-wench still heaving either from fear or the aftermath of our recent exertions. She was a fine sturdy girl, well able to take a ball or two with no ill effect. Women should wage war, I have often thought, not men. They are better fleshed for it. Slowly I released her. She had sense enough to make no noise. I edged round her till I was behind her and she faced the door.

Then I swiftly drew my sword and plunged about an inch of steel into her right buttock.

She screamed like a trapped boar and ran towards the steps.

'God's cods!' roared one of the men as he span round and discharged his pistol. Whether by luck or skill, his aim was true. The ball struck I knew not where, but the woman went down at the foot of the steps and lay there moaning.

I came after her at the run. As long as the man who had fired remained where he was, his companion could not shoot at me. I trod on the recumbent wench and she grasped at my ankle nearly bringing me down. It was a fortunate stumble, for the man, with a speed which denoted an expert, had hurled his useless pistol at me and drawn his sword. Upright, I would have been struck by the first and spitted by the second. As it was the pistol passed over my head and I came up under his guard, running my blade beneath his rib cage into his left lung. I withdrew it quickly and pressed against the wall to let the poor fellow tumble past me. The woman shrieked as for the second time in ten minutes she was covered by a hot-blooded hard-breathing man.

But I had no time for ironic reflection. The second man was still to deal with; I could see his face clearly. His eyes were round with terror and the sweat hung on his youthful beard like dew on the maidenhair fern. He must have been absolutely wrought up to the business in hand and had no nerves left to deal with this interruption. I slashed at his wrist so that he shrieked and dropped the pistol which hung loosely in his hand. It proved more dangerous out of than in his grasp for as it hit the stone step, the wheel was released and it went off. The ball ricocheted off the step and I heard it whizz past my head. Angrily I punched him in the belly, knocking him to the floor. Then, recollecting myself, I stood over him with my sword poised till the cellar was flung open and crowded with chattering figures.

'Die, traitor!' I cried, thrusting my sword into him. But I took care to insert the blade just beneath the shoulder. I wanted to establish my credentials with the onlookers, but I also wanted at least one of these two would-be killers to be fit to answer questions.

As it was, some fool did not pause to work things out but fired a pistol down the steps at almost point-blank range. The ball caught me glancingly on my right shoulder blade, flinging me against the wall. Next moment I was seized roughly, my sword was wrenched from my grasp and my arms were forced behind my back by a pair of eager bully-boys. No one seemed capable of taking charge and I could not even identify Pym, the cause of all this trouble, in the mob. I was mightily relieved at the arrival of a troop of part-time soldiers from the London Trained Bands who were at this time reponsible for guarding the approaches to the Houses of Parliament. Part-time they might be, but at least they were disciplined, and the situation was further improved a little later by the arrival of the Bands' overall commander, the Earl of Essex, who had been in the vicinity.

Pym was now identified to me, an undistinguished enough fellow though with a kind of knowing cunning in his face which made him a man to look out for. I was now able to tell my story which, apart from my reason for being in the cellar (suspicion that the wench was watering my wine), the wench's part in the fray (she had run to the door in hysterics) and my own motives (desire to preserve such a noble bulwark of democracy as Pym), was the truth. This was confirmed by the few words the badly shocked but lightly wounded girl could say and by the almost incoherently complete confession of the second ambusher. The first was meanwhile uttering nothing but frothy blood.

Essex ordered me released and grasped my hand.

'Sir, we are much in your debt,' he said warmly. Immediately those who had so recently been manhandling me crowded round to shake my hand and clap my back. It was almost as painful as my former treatment. When I winced, it was recalled that I had been hit by a ball. But when my tunic was removed, nothing but a light bruise was found.

'God must have you in His special care,' observed Pym who had been the least forward in expressing his thanks.

'Aye, sir,' I answered. 'While *your* health He has merely consigned to mine.'

He grinned as though genuinely amused.

There was no way of preventing news of my part in this affair from being carried rapidly throughout the city, therefore as is my way I made the best I could of the business. While the King's followers could scarcely do less than express relief at the failure of the plot (variously laid at the door of the Court, the Papists, and, most subtly, the Puritans who it was alleged wished thus to rouse the ire of the people), privately they must deplore my albeit accidental intervention.

It would be long before I could look for royal favour. But every man needs a friend in a position of power. I had little choice. It had to be Robin Essex.

Mind you for all his tobacco stench and Puritan cant, he wasn't a bad fellow. He was no man to hand out idle favours though; he had to feel they were deserved. We talked often of warfare and he listened with keen interest to my views on the armament and disposition of cavalry in the modern army. The ideal, I suggested, would be for all cavalry men to be trained in all the cavalry modes – as cuirassiers, as harquebusiers, as lancers. Also a good cavalryman ought in a fix to be able to dismount and fight as a dragoon, though I have the true cavalryman's contempt for these second-raters with their spavined beasts.

Realistically I knew no paymaster in Europe could afford the outlay necessary to train and equip such a force, but the point I was making was that there is no such thing as 'the best cavalry'. The winning side will be that which is best equipped to deal with the *kind* of cavalry opposed to it. It's rather like that children's game in which scissors cut paper, paper wraps stone, stone blunts scissors. A force of cuirassiers will smash through an equal force of lighter cavalry who try to meet them head on. But well-trained harquebusiers who avoid the head-on clash and concentrate on bringing down the horses, may then leave the floundering cuirassiers to their infantry.

Likewise, bullets are obviously stronger than spears, yet once fired a pistol or carbine cannot quickly be reloaded and men with lances can often spit a harquebusier before he has time to take a good aim. The infantry also are most vulnerable to a charge of lance-men. As heavy armour for both horse and foot has grown rarer, so vulnerability to the lance has increased. In many situations, a front rank of lancers followed by two or three of harquebusiers is a devastating formation. But not, of course, against cuirassiers. That is why it is so important to know exactly what your enemy's strength is.

I held Robin's attention whenever I spoke on these matters, particularly in my defence of the light lance or 'staff' which was rapidly following its heavier medieval counterpart into disuse. Of course, at this time I did not know enough of English politics to believe that internal war was possible. To me our talk was all theoretic, an area of common ground useful to graze over while I worked out what advantage could accrue to me from his patronage. That I needed patronage, I was becoming aware. While I still had every confidence in Mr Thomas Bushell's schemes it would be some small time yet, as that gentleman had explained to me in his charming, reassuring way, before the vast returns which were promised us began to appear. Till then I had need of employment and I had even begun to think of a foray to the mainland in search of a small war for five to six months to restore my fortunes. England I had begun to regard as men I had served with regarded those of their own estates they felt most secure. I had always mocked this need to have somewhere to return to and angered many by suggesting that when they went back they would find their houses burnt, their goods stolen, their women ravished by just such an army as ours.

So it was with real horror that I became aware that this quarrel between King and Parliament could go further than noisy protests and a few broken heads. Essex was much moved by my reaction, for he loved his country dearly. When I asked him how he could bear to fight against his own monarch, he smiled sadly at me and said, 'Carlo, you mistake us. 'Tis not against His Majesty we fight, 'tis against his evil councillors. We fight to *rescue* the King from those who would lead him into danger.'

I let the matter rest then. What motives these good men and politicians produce for killing people! I have dreamt sometimes of a totally professional army whose loyalty extends only as far as the last clause on the contract their leader signs. We came close to it in Germany but always the purity of such an organization was sullied by a general's ambitions on the one hand or the soldiers' indiscipline on the other. God's bones! If I had enough money to keep five thousand men for a year while I drilled and trained them, I would have an invincible force which would put the mastery of Europe where it belongs – in the hands of the highest bidder! Riches and power were created to go together. It is only the foolishness of man that contrives sometimes to keep them apart.

So, to keep the matter short, this was how it came about that I was sulking by my fire on this cold October night. I could not remain neutral. My association with Essex forbade that. And I could not claim unsuitability. My displays of theoretic expertise forbade that. Nevertheless, despite both these causes, I would have sought a comfortable retirement in the country had not my current impecuniosity forbidden that also!

'Tomorrow we fight, Carlo,' said Essex poking destructively at my little fire with a willow rod. 'How say you? May we win?'

'Any man *may* win,' I answered. 'So may we. I wish it so for I have no wish to fight at Christmas.'

'Yes, I think we may, with God's help,' he went on. The old sod didn't want a discussion I realized, just someone to answer his own uncertainties. I would have preferred to do without God and have another regiment of horse, but I did not say so. The first of Essex's Articles of War promised to reward blasphemy by having the blasphemer's tongue bored with a red hot iron.

'Our cause is just,' said Essex. 'Our men are ready. Our hearts are strong.'

He gave an emphatic thrust with his stick and extinguished the last flame.

'Come back to my tent, Carlo,' he said. 'I have invited all my senior officers to gather there.'

I agreed readily. I could do with a bone to chew on, and a glass of wine. But as we crackled our way through the frosty undergrowth, he disenchanted me by saying, 'Aye, 'tis good for God's soldiers to pray together before a battle,' and my heart sank even further when, pushing me ahead of him into his tent, he announced cheerily to those assembled there, 'Fantom says it will all be over by Christmas.'

I will say little of the battle. I was with Sir James Ramsay who commanded the cavalry on the left wing to such effect that later he was tried for dereliction of duty by a council of war. He was found not guilty, and so he was not, if a commander be not responsible for the way his men comport themselves. I fought as long as I saw cause, but when our line broke under the Royalist charge and our men turned and fled, I too rode away. The chase I saw ranged far over the countryside (which was to our advantage also, for the pursuers were as far removed from the battle as the pursued) but I was able to escape this ignominy by courtesy of Petrarch whom I was riding that day.

As with all my horses, I had early trained him to jump which was something omitted from the schooling of most cavalry mounts of the time. All horses will jump in a pinch, but some 'experts' felt that a trained jumper would tend to try to leap over infantry lines, thus exposing the belly, rather than crashing through, which is much more forceful and devastating. Myself, I feel that any horse which runs or jumps of its own will cannot be described as 'trained'. I am not satisfied till my own mounts will take a six foot gate and a seven foot hedge without a qualm. Usually I find that such a barrier is enough to deter nearly all pursuers so I never have to run far. On this occasion, one fool came crashing through the hedge behind me but, as is my custom, I brought Petrarch to a stop and turned him as soon as we had landed, so I blew the young fool's brains out and caught his reins as he fell. The beast was a fine black stallion which would have done credit to a royal stable. Indeed I wondered if I had completed what I had nearly done four years earlier at Vlotho on the Weser when I had fired at Prince Rupert. He it was, so our intelligences reported, who led the King's cavalry that day. But when I returned to take another look at the stallion's rider, I decided that neither five years nor even a shattered temple could change a man that much.

But this was no time for reflections on mutability. I was in a small area of peace and tranquillity but all around me the battle was joined and my pay was still to earn. I picketed the stallion in a small copse, doubting much that he would remain undiscovered till the end of the day, and set about reorganizing some kind of formation on the left flank which Rupert's charge had left totally exposed.

Many men have written that it is impossible to know more of how a battle goes than what befalls in the circle of your own eyes. Such men perhaps cannot tell if a storm approaches till they feel the rain or whether a building is a church or a bawdy-house till they enter the door. A battle is movement and noise; I watched and listened and felt. Above all, the trick is to be able to recognize that sense of emptiness at the centre which means your leaders have been overrun, or withdrawn. Then the professional's wages have all been earned and he is free to retire.

Well, we were in dire straits on the left, but there was still strength in reserve. The greatest danger was panic and the assumption of defeat. A trooper on a badly wounded horse came blundering through the smoke crying, 'Flee! Flee! We are lost! The General is taken!'

I shot his horse from under him and caught him by his shoulder as he fell. He was only a boy, pale as a Polack's paps with fear.

'Boy,' I said sternly. 'Dost believe in God?'

'Aye, most truly,' he gasped.

'That is sad, boy,' I said. 'For your feet dangle in a bottomless vat full of devil shit which, if I once let you go, will suck you out of God's grace for ever.'

He shrieked as I urged Petrarch forward and his legs dragged and bubbled through the hot entrails of a gutted horse.

'You have one chance,' I said. 'See, through yon hedge, there, in that wood you will find a horse. Mount him and return to me within the quarter-hour, else Satan's teeth will sink most excrutiatingly into your scrotum. Go!'

He ran like a peppered ferret and I laughed to see it. Sir James Ramsay happening near at that moment cried, 'For God, Fantom, what is there here for any but the devil's spawn to laugh at?'

'Keep your faith, Sir James,' I reproached him sternly. 'And God will keep his faithful.'

I had been around Essex long enough to pick up a good line in this Puritan cant. As I spoke, there came a change in the din which arose from the battlefield. Ramsay noticed it too but could not isolate it.

'It's the King's guns,' I explained to him. 'They have stopped firing.'

It was Balfour, I later discovered, who had led the attack which silenced the guns and so gave our infantry heart to continue the struggle. Thank God for professionals!

Naturally many of our side were made as certain of victory by this as Rupert's charge had made them of defeat. The young trooper returned on the black stallion (he rode well I was pleased to see) and was as flushed with ardour to fight as before he had been pale with terror. I held his reins to prevent him galloping off towards the enemy lines.

'Boy,' I said, 'that horse is mine. Any wound it receives I will redouble on your own hide. Now, keep close to me and protect my back.'

Well, that is all that needs to be told. When darkness fell, no one had won. Both sides camped in the field, claiming possession thereof. It was bitterly cold, that I do remember. I made the boy trooper, whose name was Christopher Allen, lie with me in my cloak. I think he feared my lust at first, but all I wanted was his heat and with a fire at one side and Christopher at the other, I kept tolerably warm. The following day we withdrew towards Warwick, being harassed all the way by Rupert's cavalry. I suppose on balance the King's men had the better of it, but what cared I? I had earned my pay and I was alive to spend it. As we moved along the road, I started to sing a song recalled from my youth. It tells a singularly obscene tale of a princess who is held in a castle by a giant with four cocks. But the tune has a stately catchiness, like one of the livelier Protestant hymns, and soon all around me the men were la-la-ing the chorus or even imitating the strange words.

Essex, as he rode along the line, smiled approvingly and I sang the louder. Suddenly I felt optimistic. It had struck me that all the smart operators would be with the King, which meant that in a sense I had a cash monopoly with the Parliamentarians. For the first time in my life, I resolved to come out of the war stinking rich.

1642–3
London – Winchester

I WAS in London in November. Essex may not have managed the army with complete success at Edgehill, but his strategy in reporting the battle in London could not be faulted and he was received as a hero. Parliament voted him £5000 in recognition of his services. What in God's name would he find to spend it on? I wondered.

All I got out of the battle were my wages and the black stallion, in whose saddle-pouch I found matters of interest but little value. First a roll of two or three love letters which addressed him as 'my most sweetest Daffyd' and were signed 'your ever-loving, ever-longing wife, Annette', and what lay in between promised such a wealth of carnal delight on his return that I was shocked a lady should know such terms. I thought of the poor bastard having his eyes picked out by hungry crows, hoped his wife would find someone worthy to console her, and put those hot letters into the scarcely hotter fire. But I kept the other object which 'most sweetest Daffyd' had seen fit to bear with him into battle, a lady's ring with an amethyst set in tin. My researches into Wallenstein's idiotic belief's recalled to me that this was a talisman to attract the influence of Jupiter which was especially valuable in gaining wealth, health, position or friendship.

'You are a fake, ring,' I said rhetorically, but later I remembered that Jupiter could also be useful in helping a man become invisible, so perhaps the ring had worked after all! It is by such ambiguities that these soothsayers and magicians control the minds of the gullible!

In London I had found comfortable lodgings close by Drury Lane. With me was Christopher Allen whose services as orderly I had begged from his company commander when I saw how skilfully he cared for horses. He was a pleasant lad of a well-to-do seed merchant's family in Norwich. He had run away from home, intending to enlist with the King's army, but having in error made contact first with the Parliamentarians he was wise enough not to admit his mistake, but to accept the pushings of fate, for the time being at least. It was this lack of soul-searing commitment which appealed to me most. His motivation was a lively curiosity and a kind of contrariness which made him seek that which was most denied him. For instance, having recognized that I had no desire to sodomize with him, he began to try to rouse my lust and when I called him he would come as if from his bed naked or but lightly clothed. I smiled to myself at his pride in his fair unblemished skin and would throw open a window so that he stood and shivered in a wintry blast while he listened to my slow instructions. Eventually he started coming to me in shirt and breeches.

But the sight of his body though it did not rouse me made me think of my own and it came to me oddly that though I was twice his age and more, my flesh was as unblemished as his. For a priest or a soft-living courtier this may seem no oddity, but for one in my profession it was near miraculous. I had been struck with steel and bullets enough, yet none had left their mark. And into my mind again came those old stories from my native land of hard-men, recalled to me in the Saxon forests by that villain, Josip. His store of dried leaves had by now run out but since my arrival in England I had noted a common enough plant (of the family *saxifraga* so one of my acquaintances told me) whose leaves, appearing similarly shaped though rather smaller, I had first dried and then infused, finding to my pleasure the taste very like that of my Croatian brew to which I confess I had become as addicted as Essex to his pipe. Could there perhaps be some truth in the old stories? I took my pistol in my hand and stood before a mirror. There was only one way to test the tale and the proof could be more painful than the uncertainty. What an absurd old fool I was getting, I thought with a grin.

This is a true mark of age, to start dreaming of immortality.

Suddenly I was seized from behind and my arms pinned by my side in a strong embrace.

'Captain! Captain! Be strong and take heed of your soul, I beg thee!'

It was Christopher, I realized, fervid to save me from self destruction!'

I was half amused, half angry, the amusement growing less as I wrestled in vain to break his grip. Finally I relaxed.

'It is well,' I gasped. 'The devil has left me.'

He slackened his hold, I spun round, kneed him gently in the groin and as he groaned in pain, I flung him face down on the bed which silenced him and buggered him most roughly till he cried out loud again.

'That is how it is, lad,' I said grimly as I dressed. 'Perhaps now you will be industrious to watch over my stable and let my body and my soul fend for themselves.'

I left the house angrily, but my anger was with myself. Women I had decided were put in my way by divine will with which no man should quarrel, but what I had just done I had chosen to do and I was sorry for it.

I sat down in the Horseshoe Tavern and ordered a flagon of wine. When that was done, I ordered another and after that I felt it best to seek my bed.

As I stood outside the door, breathing deep of what passes for fresh air in a large city, a sound penetrated my reeling head, a melodious tinkling noise putting me in mind of the goats I once herded as an innocent boy. For a moment I was back in that childhood scene. Then the noise grew louder. I turned. Approaching me wearing the uniform of a Lieutenant of Horse, his boots weighed down by great jingling spurs, was another vision from the past.

'D'Amblève!' I shrieked and drew my sword.

I would have thrust through him before he had time to draw, but the drink made me stumble and next thing his steel was in his hand and running at my chest. I felt my tunic part and I stepped back before the force of the blow. But he might as well have blunted his sword on the tavern wall. I parried, passed at his head, checked, withdrew, and gave him the point through his heart.

He sighed like a girl in love and tumbled over into the frozen kennel. I peered down at him, eager to make certain of his death. The moon glinted back off his spurs, off the ice which his fall had splintered into temporary diamonds, and off his pale, surprised face.

It wasn't D'Amblève. It was a young man I had never seen before in my life.

Sobered suddenly and completely, I sheathed my weapon and fled. There were no witnesses, or none that would do more than rob the corpse when I was gone. What a day's work was here! I had bestialized one young man and murdered another. And yet there were days in my past more soaked with blood than this, days when the dead were past counting and the ravished far more innocent than young Christopher. Was I growing a conscience in my age? I wondered uneasily. Perhaps I was too much in the company of these sodding Puritans! Their cant must be contagious. I awoke next morning, resolved to seek a cure even if it meant the moral equivalent of standing in a steam-barrel in the spital.

Essex sent for me that day. The King's army was to the west of the capital, threatening Brentford, and Essex's army reinforced by the London Trained Bands was preparing to march towards them. It was goodbye to the hope of peace which had followed the near stalemate of Edgehill, though with Pym totally committed to the overthrow by arms of the Royalists, the fabric of hope had always been so threadbare that it would have burst under a nun's fart.

I was not to go with the army, Essex instructed, but to go to the south country, ostensibly with missives for various vacillating townships; but when I protested that as a foreigner it was not to be expected that I should find my way around with ease or be listened to with enthusiasm, it became clear that my real function was to oversee the activities of Sir William Waller, whose rivalry with Essex, though not yet of the mature proportions it came to achieve, was already a hearty infant. At first I demurred. Though astute and observant enough in my own self-interest, and willing to practise deception where this will best serve it, I have little taste for spying, that is, passing what I know of one master to another for reward. But Essex, blunt honest Essex, had been so oblique in his suggestions that he was able to be offended at what he called my implications though we both knew well enough what he meant.

So I joined Waller, a short stout man and, like many of that build, of considerable fieriness as though to compensate for his lack of inches. He had fought in the German wars some twenty years earlier and though we had never met, some warped rumour of my career had reached him, and perhaps because of this or my present association with Essex, I was greeted with much coolness.

I, for my part, bore Sir William no ill feeling, but I could not look with favour on the force under his command, which consisted in the main of dragoons. A true cavalry man would almost as lief be a pioneer as a dragoon, or at least such as dragoons were wont to be before the army was reformed. These had mounts which bore the name of horses as alders are called trees; skinny stunted things, scarce able to take a man's weight. My heart sank the more when I saw they were armed with match-locks. These were often as dangerous to one's allies as to the enemy. A stray spark could set off a musket beforetimes and wound a comrade placed ahead; or set fire to a charge in a man's bandolier, tearing him to pieces as his other charges ignited; or worse still (and this I had seen as recently as Edgehill) ignite the powder in the budge-barrel, blowing up all those who stood around it. Dragoons were merely mounted infantry, it is true, but with match-locks the option of firing from horseback was entirely removed.

Let it not be thought that I am simply prejudiced against all arms of the military service save the cavalry. Without foot soldiers there could be no army, and to use horses to move foot soldiers quickly from one area to another makes excellent sense. Wallenstein used to send dragoons ahead with shovels and matlocks to level the way and make good the passes – in a sense, as mounted pioneers. But possession of a horse can give an infantryman ideas above his station. Even these broken 'nags', as they are called, will bear a man further and faster in his search for pillage, and then allow him to carry away a great deal more. So, much energy was wasted, much indiscipline engendered (and, incidentally, much booty, properly the perquisite of cavalrymen, stolen) by these so-called dragoons. Because of this, in France dragoons as a corps of their armies almost disappeared altogether. Now, the circumstances of war in England were very different from those on the Continent, the quarrel more clear-cut, the area less diffuse. Yet these dragoons still had to me something of the look of those wild men I had served with in the past. And their horses . . . ! Well, you could buy any two of them for what you'd get from selling an ordinary cavalry horse – and half a dozen for what one of my own family would bring.

I left Athene in London and took Petrarch with me and also Luke, now matured into a fine beast, rather short in the neck, but deep-chested, strong, nimble and above all eager-to-please. I always felt of Luke that he had observed enviously the gentle imperturbability of Orfeo and the controlled power of Petrarch and somehow determined to try even harder in order to win my love which I gave him most unstintingly.

Also with me was Christopher, riding the black stallion I had won at Edgehill and which I had named Digby after Lord George whose lively vigour was so well known. Christopher's manner to me had changed in some subtle way since I had fucked him, but whether he felt debased or elevated by the experience (I mean socially) I did not know. Either was dangerous, for him I mean. I wanted neither a resentful nor a presumptuous servant and if I detected signs which confirmed either diagnosis, then I would rid myself of him quickly enough. But perhaps I was wrong. Perhaps, like Luke, Christopher was simply eager to please.

'What gift shall I give you at Christmas?' I asked him one

night in December as we lay about a dozen miles from Winchester.

'Nothing,' he answered. 'There is nothing I know that you can give me.'

Well, that was ambiguous enough to tickle a Jesuit. I pondered it all night. Next day, a Tuesday as I recall, we attacked the city. Those dragoons must have scented rich pickings and small resistance for they drove into the town with the power of a troop of Tilly's veterans and the small force of Royalist cavalry which held it was overrun in only an hour. Waller most civilly permitted the surviving Cavaliers to withdraw to Oxford where the King was, but the good people of the town held such courtesy was for baronets and took revenge for remembered wrongs by hurling stones after the marching line. Meanwhile those ungodly dragoons were tearing the inside of the cathedral to pieces. I watched with distaste as they ripped tapestries, danced on books, and smashed the organ, then after selecting a couple of pieces of silver plate (which I quickly beat into an unrecognizable mass for these English tend to be squeamish about such booty) I went with Christopher in search of lodging, first for our horses, then for ourselves.

We found a decent clean house owned by a once handsome woman of middle age who had a daughter dressed to look about ten years old but whom I suspected to be some years older and accoutred thus in order to foil the lecherous Cavaliers. I was too tired to have been interested in her had she been dressed like a Turkish dancer and as my second boot hit the floor at the foot of the bed, I fell asleep.

In the middle of the night, I was awoken by a terrible commotion. A woman's voice was screaming most violently, though whether in fear or pain I could not detect. Seizing my sword, I ran out of my room and followed the noise to the floor below.

I had been wrong in both cases. It was neither fear nor pain, but outraged anger that was making the older woman set up this din. And the cause was not far to seek. Naked on a bed and rolling over and over to avoid the mother's blows were the daughter and Christopher. I had been right about the girl, I noted as I seized the woman from behind. She had bubs like a pair of fool's baubles.

'God's knees, woman!' I roared. 'Will you not be quiet?'

But she struggled still and turned her wrath and her assault against me. Suddenly, whether it was the sight of her daughter crouched naked and heaving before me with Christopher's hands, despite his fear, still roaming compulsively over her flesh, or whether it was just the appointed time, my trumpets sounded and I tipped the woman onto the bed, pushed her nightgown up to her waist and set on.

Now the girl too started screaming and Christopher had to drag her away from me else she would have pulled my hair out by the roots. She turned against him and they began to fight.

So it was that the Watch found us a few moments later when, summoned by fearful neighbours, they broke into the house.

Waller was hardly sympathetic but nor, fortunately, was he summary.

'This is a grave offence, Captain Fantom,' he said coldly.

'Grave *charges*, sir,' I said. 'But I hope you will believe, no offence.'

'How do you defend yourself?' he demanded.

'Is this all the trial I shall have, sir?' I asked politely. 'Or shall perhaps I have the pleasure of seeing you on a judicial bench on a later occasion?'

This reminded him of his duties and also, of course, made him angrier still. How strange it is that reminders of duty, which we should all be grateful to have before us everyday, can make a man so angry.

'You shall have a trial if that is your wish, sir,' he pronounced.

Of course it wasn't my wish. Nothing was further from it. But since being arrested I had bribed three different people to take a message to Essex for me, informing him (with glosses) of the sad state of things and appealing for his intervention to prevent a miscarriage of justice. Being expert in human nature, I had promised each of the messengers another large sum on the day I was released. Without incentive, nobody feels obliged to work very hard for a man who is to be hanged in a day or two.

I pleaded provocation, of course. It is always the best thing in these circumstances, but I discovered too late that the woman was famous (infamous, I would say) in the town for her strict morality, that she was a pillar of the Church, that after the birth of her daughter she announced that she had gone as far in matters sexual as the wedding service required her to go, and that according to local tradition it was this resolve, unswervingly adhered to, which had caused her late husband to waste away and finally expire five years later.

Five years! I thought. Why, it would have done for me in a six-month!

But the thought was merely an ego-boosting boast, I acknowledged instantly. I was not a man of frequent sexual needs. Why, in the field I had known myself to go for a month or more with no desire whatsoever. It was just that when it did come it was irresistible. Perhaps, I wondered, perhaps there was some link between all those carnal occasions. Perhaps something I had not yet identified triggered them off, some common denominator. . . .

It was an interesting line of speculation. When I came back from it to the world of so-called actuality it was to hear myself being sentenced to death by hanging.

It came as a shock though I had expected no less. I could not blame those who sat in judgement on me. Only the previous month, Parliament in an effort to repress the wide-scale plundering and general indiscipline rife among the military had issued a declaration more or less ordering that the laws and ordinances of the Army should be strictly applied. Rapes, ravishments and unnatural abuses got you death.

It was the week before Christmas and I settled down to wait for word from Essex. They could not hang me without first having the sentence confirmed by the Lord General and I complimented myself on having (I hope) ensured that he had received a version of events other than the totally condemnatory abstract of the trial. But it is well not to put one's trust singly in man, so I turned to God, begging most civilly that I might be visited and instructed by one of the chaplains who so swelled the ranks of every Parliamentary force. At Edgehill a man could hardly swing his sword for these pious frantics who galloped up and down the lines, singing psalms and shouting encouragement. The one I picked was the famous Master Obadiah Jones, a fiery Welshman, who came gladly to lead me into the ways of truth. If a man's time on this earth is short and he is in need of good counsel, then Master Jones is his best hope, for he could utter more words in one minute than your ordinary pulpit preacher could manage in five, thus keeping a constant stream of holiness playing over the hot and sweaty soul.

And if that were not enough, he had another great attraction. He was not one of your canting words-are-mightier-than-the-sword men. No, he rode into battle with a stout blade swinging at his side, and a snaphance pistol thrust into his breeches.

More importantly, he wore these when he came to the room in which I was confined and should Essex fail me, I had a plan to beat him over his red shaven neck with a chair-leg as we knelt together in our final prayers and make my escape with the aid of his weapons.

But thank God (as Obadiah did most fervently) it never came to that. On Christmas Eve, Waller's adjutant came with the news that a pardon had just been received from Essex. With it he brought me a private missive from the General which contained a great deal of nonsense about his knowledge of my character and a man not being condemned for a single untypical error. I laughed aloud as I read it and went out into the town to breathe the icy air and add my portion to the season's merriment. I was more relieved than I would have thought possible – the idea of death must have entered deep into my being despite all my contingency plans for escape. And when I turned a corner and saw in the square before the city gaol a pair of gibbets looming high, my relief was so intense that I could almost in sincerity have knelt with Obadiah and given thanks.

Poor devils, I mused as I walked beneath the dangling corpses, which the hard frost had tinselled till they shone like Christmas angels, you had no friend to send you pardon.

A harsh wind rose of a sudden, spinning the silver figure I gazed up at, so that one stiff bare foot (for his boots had been stolen) brushed against my shoulder. I shrank back, still looking up. That face! He had died hard; no quick breaking of a neck here, but the slow agony of strangulation which leaves a man unrecognizable . . . almost unrecognizable . . . I cried out in fear and alarm; the Watch was passing so I begged him to shine his lanthorn in the face of the dead man. He looked at me oddly, but complied. I peered close as I could. Through the frost, through the contortions, the features emerged at last. I had no doubt. It was Christopher Allen.

Poor Christopher. In my concern with my own plight, I had forgotten his. My excuse is that I had not thought he would be taken up for any offence graver than fornication which the ordinance states 'shall be punished with discretion, according to the quality of the offence'. (Did this mean, I wondered, that a good screw would get you more punishment than a mediocre one?)

I resolved to look further into his death, but first went to check on the health of my horses which Christopher's taking off must have put in jeopardy. My fears proved true to some extent. Petrarch and Luke were in excellent condition, but Digby was gone – stolen so the shifty-eyed ostler claimed, but I doubted him much. The villain, I swear, knowing Christopher to be hanged and anticipating that I would soon follow, had got rid of my trooper's horse and was fattening the other two with thought of selling them also. I beat him till he cried for mercy, but he would not confess. Which was wise as then I would surely have killed him.

After that I made inquiry into Christopher's fate and discovered that the girl of the house in fear both of her mother and for her reputation had claimed that she too had been ravished. The trial had been much speedier than mine. The sergeant who had been his custodian told me that, realizing that the daughter would stick to her story and the mother was adamant in confirming it, Christopher had appealed to have me fetched as a witness on his behalf, but this had been refused on the grounds of my incompetence as a prisoner under the same charge.

That night with my cloak wrapped round my head I went in search of a pair of those thorough-going villains who are to be found in any town. They thought I was crazy when I told them what I wanted, but the sight of gold in my one hand and a pistol in the other persuaded them to comply.

Next morning early risers discovered, bound tight to the two corpses hanging from the gibbets, the mother and daughter, naked and half frozen to death.

Waller glared at me angrily when we met later in the day, but I greeted him courteously and there was nothing he could say. Nor did any countermand my orders when I commanded that Christopher's body be taken down. I had it pulled behind me on a cart as I rode out of Winchester and started back for London. In a village some miles beyond the town, I bribed and threatened the sexton and his grave-diggers from their squalid hearths and stood over them while they hacked a hole in the frozen churchyard. When the parson came out to see what the activity was, I kept him there also to speed Christopher's soul on its journey to wherever the innocent dead may go. And when I reached London, I wrote a letter to his family in Norwich telling them how their son had died bravely in the taking of Winchester (which, I discovered, Pym and his gang had inflated into a great steeple-ringing victory).

Such are the sentimentalities which age can bring a man to if he does not take care.

1643

Bedford – Lincolnshire – Nottinghamshire

A MAN who has been very close to death suddenly realizes how futile and vain are those things so valued by the commonalty of man, as friendship, honour and the so-called comforts of religion. My resolve to grow rich was confirmed by my experience in Winchester. A wealthy man could die as easily as a poor one. So I set about surrounding myself with a troop of like-thinking fellows, who were not far to find. The constitution of regiments was not yet so clearly regulated as it was to become in the New Model Army after 1645 and my troop of some fifty men though small was nonetheless acceptable. I had as my lieutenant a crop-shaven shabby boy of twenty-two or -three who had the look and language of one of those bible-waving preachers who were the only entertainment permitted in this miserable army. His name was James Croft and I would have avoided him like the plague had I not caught him ransacking my quarters one night when I returned unexpectedly. When I challenged him he showed no alarm but answered, 'In the name of Our Saviour, Captain, this is well met, for I have been instructed by the provost-marshal to search your belongings, upon traitorous and malicious information that you carried missives between the King and certain disaffected gentlemen of our party. But, praised be the name of the Lord, I have found nothing and was presently hastening to you with the news – you are innocent!'

He made it sound like a genuine discovery worthy of celebration and I found myself on the point of taking his outstretched hand. Instead I hit him in the stomach and as he doubled up, I went behind him, seized his ankles and shook him in the air till most of what he had stolen fell to the floor.

After that, I gave him a glass of brandy which, for a fervent denouncer of the evils of strong liquor, he downed with great skill. When he had drunk another and regained his composure, we talked. An hour later he was my lieutenant.

My cornet was Thomas Turner, a fresh-faced lad who reminded me of Christopher. I found him sleeping drunkenly beneath a bush one night with a poinard in his hand, its steel dulled by dried blood. He was a thorough-going villain despite his looks, yet because of his resemblance to the dead trooper I always kept him at a distance.

There only remained one more commissioned place to fill, that of quartermaster, and this I left vacant till the right man should present himeslf. The combination of talents needed in a good quartermaster is most rare – he must have the accountant's gift of reckoning, the lawyer's gift of concealing, the merchant's gift of trading, the carrier's gift of transporting, the priest's gift of deceiving, and the soldier's gift of not caring. Such men are hard to find and they are usually politicians or prelates – or sometimes kings. To be a quartermaster a man needs something extra – a disability which keeps him out of great place.

My three corporals were three brothers called Parkin from a place called Yorkshire which, though I had not visited it, I had heard reputed as a breeding ground for a hard and vicious race of men. If this were accurate, then the brothers Parkin were true sons of their soil.

As for my men, they recuited themselves. No one who was not the kind of soldier I wanted lasted long in my troop.

We were attached to Sir Robert Pye's regiment and between Sir Robert and myself existed a kind of armed truce for though he did not approve of me or my followers, yet he knew that in battle we would bring him nothing but honour and high reputation. Also my position as a favourite of Essex was still taken into account by those who held commands under him. I had seen little of Essex since the start of the year which perhaps was well, for I had felt but small inclination to comply with his Puritanical admonitions. I had thanked him civilly for my pardon though I made it clear that I regarded it not as an act of mercy but merely as the correction of a manifest injustice.

Now it was high summer and we lay at the town of Bedford on our way north to Lincolnshire where fortune had fickled between the two sides all year. Presently Gainsborough was held by Lord Willoughby but a Royalist force under the great horseman, Cavendish, was threatening and various Parliamentary groups had been summoned in support. Whether we would arrive in time to help I did not know, nor much care. I had grown even more disenchanted with this war than when I entered it. The two sides swayed back and forth across the country like drunkards wrestling on a frozen pond. The only hope of a conclusion seemed to lie in the earth cracking and swallowing all the armies! Like the German wars I had wasted my youth in, there seemed no reason why this should not continue for a whole generation. The thought frightened me. Death in battle had always been a possibility, with death by hanging now a good second. But to grow old in arms and die of age, still a soldier, that had a ring of futility about it. Not for me the willing acceptance of such a fate which I had once found almost admirable in old Lauder. No; I suddenly had ambitions to be a rich old civilian.

Lauder. I had not thought of him for half a decade. It was nine years since I last saw him, his sword dripping with blood at the massacre of Eger. He had been ancient then. Surely the old bastard had had his quietus by now.

I smiled at the thought of him. Our friendship had been the kind professionals ought to have. It was based on mutual awareness of the limits of our contract. Risks we would take for each other, but well within the bournes of reason. Lauder had warned me and saved my life, but had I been sitting at that table at Eger, he would have slit my throat with a steady edge.

I smiled at the thought, then roused myself and left my

tent. Mine was the only troop in the Army (so far as I knew) to have tents. I had used them in Germany for years – men on a long campaign must not be left to the vagaries of night and weather – but here in England, when no buildings presented themselves, the common soldiery slept in ditches and under hedges. I had no desire to be faced each morning with cold, damp, sullen men, coughing and wheezing like broken-winded nags. No, what I wanted to hear was what I heard now, coming to me through the morning mist, lusty voices raised in the 144th Psalm – 'Blessed be the Lord my strength; who teacheth my hands to war and my fingers to fight.' Jem Croft was a stickler for religious observances and to outward appearance we were the most devout gang of slit throats who ever robbed a poorhouse. I joined them in the Amen, then went to the picket-line to say good morning to my family. They neighed in delight at my approach, Luke almost pulling himself free in his joy, a display of emotion which Athene regarded with cool disdain. I had discovered the beginnings of sweet itch on Petrarch's mane and after giving them each an apple, I examined this carefully while my groom looked anxiously on, knowing what would follow if I were not satisfied. But the fellow had followed my instructions to the letter and I congratulated him, at which the great fool simpered like a dairymaid being chucked under her chin.

There had been some new arrivals late the previous night and I strolled along the line, examining their mounts. Nothing of interest, I thought, till I heard a loud neighing which had in it something familiar.

I looked round. There picketed some distance from the main line as was often the custom with uncut stallions was Digby.

I greeted him with pleasure and he obviously recalled me though our acquaintance had been but brief. 'God is just,' I said, sending my thanks winging heavenwards with all the other hymns of praise which were now rising all over the camp (the Fantom troop were always earliest at their devotions). When I looked close at Digby I saw evidence of hard use – a saddle cloth had been laid on with a fold in it, raising a tender area on his back, and his mouth was also sore, probably from too much pulling on the over-strong bit some fool had needed to control him.

'You like my horse, Captain Fantom?' spoke a voice behind me. I turned. A long gangling fellow with a fair wispy beard smiled complacently at me.

'You have the advantage of me, sir,' I replied.

'Captain Hector, at your service,' he said, bowing. His accent and this parody of courtly manners placed him instantly as some trademan's son whom dyspeptic chance had belched up to a commission in this democratic army.

He continued, 'Captain Fantom's name is, of course, famous wherever soldier's deeds are talked of.'

The long streak of pigeon shit was trying to mock me. My only notable feat in this war had been to escape hanging at Winchester. But I would still have answered him politely (for the penalty for quarrelling in the quarter was cashiering) had not the fool persisted, adding lest I should miss the subtlety of his wit. 'I bought my horse in Winchester where I believed you too were well mounted; and nearly well mounted for it.'

He laughed most heartily and one or two troopers attending their mounts near by grinned openly.

I regarded him coldly, wondering if he were a thief as well as a fool. But I decided he could not be such a fool to talk thus if he knew whence the horse had come.

'What did he cost you, Captain?' I asked.

For a moment he demurred, but some men cannot resist boasting of a bargain.

'Faith, I beat down the rogue who was selling him and I had him for five pounds.'

Five pounds! That was scarce more than the price of a dragooner's nag!

I reached for my purse, which in the field I wore always tied to my body, and took out a sovereign.

'Five pounds,' I said. 'Well, I shall take two off for the hire of the horse, and another two for the treatment he will need to recover him, so here is your compensation.'

'I do not take your meaning,' he said.

'The horse is mine,' I said kindly. 'Stolen of me while I lay under false arrest in Winchester. You have been cozened, Captain Hector. Take your money.'

'Nay!' he replied, striking my hand aside so that the coin flew through the air, fetching up in a mound of newly dropped horse shit. 'Go your ways, sir. These may be your lecherous foreign ploys for taking a man's horse, but they shall not hold here, sir.'

I grew tired of the fellow and boxed his ears soundly. His mouth dropped wide in amazement and his hand went to his sword, so I kicked him hard just below the knee and as he capered around on one leg, I took his left arm and forced it up behind his back.

'Now, Captain Hector, take your money and go in peace,' I said and pushed him down over the pile of droppings in which the sovereign gleamed. He tried to resist, so I pushed harder and with a high scream he thrust in his hand and plucked out the coin.

I let him go and returned to Digby whom I now untied.

'The Colonel shall know of this!' screamed Hector after me.

Half an hour later when the general muster was called, I was ordered to the Colonel where he stood before his own troop in the centre.

Dismounting from Luke, I saluted him. In the background I could see Hector, his face rendered almost mature by hate.

'Captain Fantom,' said Sir Robert. 'This gentleman says you have assaulted him and stolen his horse.'

'Not I, sir,' I replied. 'I helped him seek some money of his which he had let fall. Nothing more.'

'And his horse, sir? What say you of his horse?'

'There was a horse,' I answered. 'One which I lost in Winchester. Captain Hector had bought it in error. I gave him compensation and took back what was mine.'

Sir Robert glared angrily at me.

'Sir, any man can say these things. What if I should say to you that yon nag you ride is *my* horse, taken from my stable in time past? What then?'

'Why then,' I said clicking my fingers so Luke came up to

my shoulder, 'I should say, take your horse again, Sir Robert. I am most heartily glad to have recovered such a fine beast for you.'

Those who stood around smiled to see the Colonel so baffled and he, seeing them smile, grew angrier.

'This will not serve your turn, sir,' he said. 'We are concerned here with law, not a man's word. What evidence can you produce?'

'Ask Captain Hector how much he paid for the beast,' I said, adding when I saw that he was reluctant to speak, 'Surely he has boasted to some of these gentlemen present of his bargain?'

'Aye,' said the other field officer of the regiment, Major Colloboy. 'He told me he had the animal for five pounds.'

They all looked significantly at one another. Such a price for a good mount smelt strongly of some illegality.

I pressed home my advantage.

'When occasion arises, I shall produce some comrades who were by me at Edgehill to identify the beast. Now, sirs, is it not time to ride, else our friends in Gainsborough may fare the worse for our tardiness?'

This was a mistake I realized instantly. As I've said before, reminding people of their duty is often worse than sneering at their ancestry.

As I walked away, leading Luke, for I would not mount in my colonel's presence, Sir Robert bawled after me, 'You are insolent, Fantom! You are known for a brawling, lecherous Papist, and I will not tolerate you, no, not though your friends were thrice as powerful. Return Captain Hector's horse within this quarter hour or I shall . . . I shall. . . .'

He choked on his threat, unable to find one vicious enough within his power. I looked around at him and said, 'I would obey your order, Colonel, as is my duty, but I have no horse of Captain Hector's, so I cannot. Good day.'

'Fantom!' he screamed as I continued walking away. 'Fantom! I will not tolerate . . . halt, or I . . . Fantom!'

There was a loud explosion, something struck me on the back making me stagger against Luke. I turned. Sir Robert stood with a smoking pistol in his hand, his face already aghast at what he had done. At my feet I saw the ball which had hit me. I bent and picked it up. It was still hot so that I felt it even through my gauntlets and I had to juggle it from one hand to another as I made my way back to the Colonel.

'Sir Robert,' I said, 'take your bullet again. Our cause is just, but we still have need of all our shot.'

This time as I returned to my troop, no one spoke.

Jem Croft examined my back later and told me there was only a faint bruising of the skin though the leather of my buff coat was crushed and burnt where the bullet had struck. He was greatly impressed and eager to know wherein the trick lay, believing there was some spell or conjuration which gave immunity. In the end, I muttered a few words in my native language over him and told him that now he too was shot-free if only he had faith in the efficacy of the charm. But when I pointed my pistol at him, he turned pale and refused the test, which is perhaps why miracles are now so rarely known.

I myself twisted uneasily between explanations. One was physical – that indeed there was something in the herb brew I still drank which rendered my skin immune to bullets; one was coincidental – that each time I had been hit, the force of the ball had been nearly spent, either through distance or a weak charge; and the third was metaphysical – that my life was being spared for some great purpose.

Well, be that as it may, until the great purpose was revealed to me I saw no reason to divert from my chosen course, and a reputation for invulnerability was no impediment here. It was a nice irony in this most holy and unctuously self-righteous of armies to be known as a man in league with the devil! It certainly gave me that extra degree of control over my own troops which was necessary if our excesses were not too quickly to be known in the wrong quarters.

Our technique was carefully worked out. We looted in bands of five, two of whom were always posted as look-outs, for there were still plenty of authorities civil and military who exercised themselves in preventing – or punishing – this time-honoured campaigning activity. All valuables were held in common; in a sense we were the most democratic community existing in the country at that time, every man in the troop had a voice and one vote, including myself though it is true to say that mine was a casting vote – whatever the division. Anyone caught trying to appropriate plunder for himself was summarily dealt with – on the first occasion by a fine equal to ten times the value of whatever he had tried to steal, on a second occasion by death. Beatings, mutilations, and such bestialities were pointless. They merely produced dissatisfied vengeful men who might vent their spleen by betraying us all.

Share-outs were based on seniority of rank and service. I took twenty-five per cent of the total, Jem Croft got ten per cent, Tom Turner seven and a half per cent, Nob, Coll, and Perce Parkin got two and a half each, and the men shared the remaining fifty per cent between them.

Coin was easily divided; plate I nearly always had melted down which though it meant some loss in value gave us a good safe untraceable lump of metal to carve up. Other goods such as bales of cloth, glassware, china, clothing, carpets etc. were more difficult. They had to be sold for what they were and to find a market and get a reasonable price posed considerable difficulties. It was at these times that I felt most in need of an experienced quartermaster and I was close to issuing a directive forbidding the collection of such booty.

You must not imagine that we neglected our more obvious soldierly duties in the pursuit of riches. Just as we were the first to rise and praise the Lord each morning, so were we distinguished by our application to the martial arts. I drilled my men and their horses to the point of mutiny, following my precept that a true cavalryman must be expert in all branches of the horse-soldier's art. When noise of complaint from my men reached me I told the Parkin brothers to offer any who wished to depart a fair discharge, and to my critics amongst my fellow officers I replied by leading the troop with more distinction and fewer casualties than any other in our engagements in the north that summer.

It was a curious thing to see how my men were at the same

time motivated by the lust for wealth and also by a burning pride at being a kind of elite. Once they realized what all their drilling had made them, they became infected with an absurd *esprit de corps*. Each cavalry troop had its own distinguishing banner and to start with mine was a white cross on a black ground with the motto, 'Veritas Vincit'. But the simple tastes of my men made them eager to have something more illustrative and dramatic, such as the picture of an armed soldier waving his sword over a kneeling bishop which one troop had as their emblem. I gave way to this harmless if naïve wish and we had the more symbolc device of a rearing white horse trampling underfoot a serpent with the head of a cavalier, and the motto 'Latet Anguis In Herba'. But I drew the line when they wished to have the same device painted on their buff coats. One gang of soliders looting a house looks much the same as any other gang. I had no desire to make identification easy.

In every group there are weak links, of course, men who cannot subordinate their selfish desires to the general good. Nob Parkin, having led a small party to plunder a grange just outside Nottingham, delayed the group's departure so that he could ravish a wench who had taken his fancy. The others, deprived of leadership, started to drink or pursue the older women who, apart from a couple of elderly servants, were the sole occupants of the house. They were surprised by the return of the master of the grange with a group of his farmhands who set about my troopers with such wrathful energy that they were constrained to flee, leaving behind one of their number and all of their booty. As soon as I heard the news, I led a larger party back to the grange, thinking it imperative to rescue our man, but when we approached our destination it was to discover that we were forestalled by a troop from the regiment of that canting bastard, Cromwell, who was then making such a sound in the north. Any other lot would have accepted my lad as their prisoner till out of sight of the house, then let him go. But these were fanatics and would certainly take him back to face trial. So I laid an ambush along the road, put balls into a couple of Cromwell's men and blew our lad's brains out. It was for his own good. They would certainly have hanged him and this way he was saved the tedium of their endless sermons.

I imposed a swingeing fine on Nob Parkin, but I realized that this was just one of a line of near-misses which all stemmed from the same problem. Just as indiscriminate looting by individuals would almost certainly result in the end in capture and punishment, so with indiscriminate ravishing. Jem and I sat down and worked out a strategy which would minimize risk. The first principle was never to mix the two activities. Parties would go out with a single well-defined objective – loot or sex. Sexual parties who returned with booty would have no share in it; looters who indulged in rape would be heavily fined. We devised a roster so that those with the strongest needs went out most often. This meant that at first Nob Parkin went on every rape detail but in the end we had to stop him as he could hardly sit on his horse.

Choice of targets was the big problem. In large towns there were willing dames enough, or at least enough so close to the edge of willingness that they raised little complaint, especially as the man in charge of the detail had a bag of coin which he shared out among the ravished women. Small towns and the countryside posed other problems. Best were hamlets under some threat of attack, for the women tended to group together for safety while the menfolk were out in the fields.

I led one such raid myself in a small midlands village. Posting look-outs at all approaches to the place, I went on foot up to the church door and rapped gently thereon.

There was a ripple of noise within then silence. I knocked again.

'Who is there?' asked an uncertain voice.

'A servant of the Lord's,' I answered, 'come to seek shelter from the ravagements of these most violent soldiers. Pray let me enter or I shall sleep on these steps till it please my Master to rouse me unto Him.'

Silence again. Then slowly the door was unlocked and creaked open; and my men, crouched in silent anticipation behind the stones in the graveyard, rushed in.

I took no part in these exercises myself. As I have pointed out, my needs were no regular craving for animal pleasure, but something much more erratic and compulsive. I strode around amidst the spasmodic bodies, urging haste and applying the flat of my sword where I felt brute energy was decelerating into art. Not that much urging was needed. A competitive element had arisen among the men, and the whole business had become something of a race.

But this time the runners were not fast enough. One of the look-outs came panting into the church to say that a troop of cavalry was approaching.

'Whose?' I demanded. But the question was academic. Even if they were our own regiment, I had too many enemies there for the chance to be missed of getting one over on me. But more likely it would be a troop of Cromwell's psalm-singing East Anglians led by some bullet-headed Puritan with his balls packed in ice.

Our horses were hid in a barn at the edge of the village. We could not make a run for them without being noticed. It seemed best to stay still and hope the newcomers would ride through.

I gave commands.

'Everybody, get down among the pews. And keep these women quiet.'

The clatter of hooves was clearly audible now. They got nearer and nearer. I held my breath waiting for them to pass. Then, 'Whoa!' I heard right outside the church door.

'Lieutenant,' I heard a deep voice say, 'let the men rest here a while. I shall go alone into the House of the Lord and seek spiritual guidance for our further work this day.'

Christ, I should have locked the door! I thought. It was too late now. It creaked open once more. Someone entered, silhouetted in the light for a moment, then the door closed and the shadows took over again.

The troop captain (or so I surmised) moved forward. Oh these pious fools! I thought. Could he not worship as well from the back of the church as up by the altar? A glance to left or right and we were discovered.

But he had stopped again. Crouched at the end of a pew, unable to retreat any further because a half-naked woman blocked my path, I contemplated rising to my feet and bluffing things out. But it might not be necessary. This fool's silent meditation must soon come to an end. He seemed to be in the grip of some strong emotion. I heard his throat working as if the right words were not to be found. Then came a long sigh that smacked more of relief than regret. Surely he would go now.

His feet sounded on the stone floor once more, this time moving away. He was going. Praise be to God! I thought fervently.

Then one of the women screamed. Or squeaked rather. Just a semi-breve of noise squeezed through the gagging fingers of her assailant. But it was enough.

The footsteps halted. Resumed. Returned. The figure came abreast of me and peered into the pew opposite. Slowly, realizing the futility of concealment, the three men hiding there rose, their breeches round their ankles, still holding tight to the women, their skirts round their waists.

All over the church my men rose up in the same condition. Slowly, silently, the captain turned to observe this strange phenomenon.

I rose too, wondering whether I should try to conciliate or intimidate him. With five times our number outside, all properly dressed, the case seemed hopeless. He turned now almost full circle. He was holding something in his hand – a pistol, I thought at first. Then a shaft of sunlight pierced a window and I saw it clearly.

It was a bottle of brandy.

I felt a pang of hope. He had retired to the church for a drink, not to pray! Now he spoke.

'I might have known,' he said. 'Soon as I smelt the flesh, I might have known it was you, Fantom, you cock-worshipping Goth.'

And now I saw his face.

'Oh Jesus!' I said, weak with relief and amazement. 'Why the hell aren't you dead, Lauder?'

1643-5

St Albans – Donnington – London – Oxford

A WEEK later Lauder was my quartermaster. It was a demotion he accepted gladly. In all armies there are ordinances against drunkenness on duty, but the general disapproval of strong liquor he encountered in his present company made life almost intolerable.

'My stomach is mutinous against it,' he told me.

'What?' said I, misunderstanding. 'The drink?'

'No, you turd-brain,' he answered. 'The onions.'

I discovered that he had taken to carrying onions with him so that whenever he had a private nip, he followed it with a bit of onion to mask his breath.

Working out terms proved rather difficult. Demotion he was happy to accept, but he wanted his share of the goodies. I offered him five per cent to come out of my own share, for to attempt to redistribute any of the man's dividends would have caused great protest. Lauder laughed and demanded at least an equal share with Jem Croft. I refused indignantly. That would have reduced my cut to a mere fifteen per cent. Finally after I had taken him to the ruined mill, where we kept our hidden store of material booty (which I began to fear we would have to abandon when our force moved on) he settled for seven and a half per cent, spotting, as I knew he would, that QM's perks out of the sale of this lot would probably double his cut. Well, that's the way army stores have always been run and always will be, I suppose.

Naturally we sat late into the night at first opportunity, drinking and exchanging news and reminiscences.

When I mentioned D'Amblève to him and told of the man's many attempts on my life and my fears that he would track me even to England, he looked at me closely through the monk's spectacles he now wore all the time in private, then roared with laughter.

'What's so funny?' I asked, irritated as a man must be whose fears are not taken seriously.

'Nothing at all,' he said. 'Save that yon bairn had his head blown off at Breisach in '38!'

'What! Then who . . .? all these attempts . . .?' I stuttered.

'In your mind, laddie,' he asserted laughing still. 'It's the Laird's way of giving ye a taste of fear, for He created ye sairly deficient in conscience!'

'Well,' I said. 'Well!'

For it was true in a way. Nothing had I really feared these past twenty years and more except for D'Amblève. I refilled my glass and drank deep. I felt empty, cheated, like a man who, having turned religious on being told he has a terminal illness, discovers that for years he has been cured without knowing it. Suddenly I felt a deeper hatred of D'Amblève than I had ever known. Without him who knows what my life would have been? Drunkenly I said as much to Lauder who regarded me curiously.

'You've changed, Fantom,' he said.

'Yes, yes,' I babbled eagerly. 'I've changed. It's not too late. Now without D'Amblève, there's nothing to worry about. After this war, I shall be rich, you'll see. Twenty-five per cent, sorry, seventeen and a half per cent of what we take, it'll set me up. And I have investments, good old Tommy Bushell, yes, I'll be a gentleman, live in a mansion, raise a family. Oh yes, I've changed.'

'No, all I meant was you didn'a used to be a fool,' said Lauder.

I threw my brandy in his face and lunged across the table at him. He it was after all who had taken D'Amblève from me. But my hands grasped empty air and when I looked up, Lauder's pistol was an inch from my breast bone. By his own account he was over eighty; by any reckoning he must be ancient, and he had just downed a flask of brandy; but the pistol barrel was as steady as a cossack lance.

'Shoot!' I sneered. 'But take care when your ball rebounds.'

'So,' he mused. 'Now he believes his ain fantasy! Oh Carlo, Carlo! If I were a younger man, I'd abandon you in fear of my life. But I'm old enough and curious enough to stay with you even if it takes me over the edge. So sit up like a soldier and take your drink!'

He pulled me upright, replenished my glass and raised his own. His pistol had disappeared but I had the feeling it was held under the table ready for use if need be. Suddenly my skin felt as soft as a cherub's cheeks.

'A toast!' he said. 'To God who bears with fools, and to fools who bear with God!'

'Amen,' said I. 'A-fucking-men.'

With Lauder aboard, we now had a complete crew and for a time the pickings were good. My men were kept fat, but I never let them forget they were soldiers, for among thieves success breeds enmity while among soldiers it breeds unity. They could take their discharge when they wished (save if a battle were imminent) which a few did as their wealth grew, but most stayed on, though still talking round the campfire of the businesses they would found and the girls they would impress with their new riches. I smiled to hear them. I had heard such talk in a dozen different languages across the face of Europe these thirty years.

The only complaint came from Nob Parkin who assevered that he no longer found it possible to achieve his orgasm unless one of his brothers stood by, beating his buttocks with a sword and crying, 'Make haste! Make haste!'

I talked with many of the men about their experiences – it is ever a common topic among soldiers – but none seemed to undergo a sensation like mine. While my trumpets sounded less frequently now, their call was still as strong and the discretion with which I ensured the men satisfied their needs could not apply to me. I was taken up once more with a country squire's wife near St Albans who, though her husband was a nobody, herself had powerful if distant connections, and once more it was only Essex's intercession that saved me from the rope.

I saw him near Basingstoke soon after – for the last time though I did not realize it then. I expected sermons and reproaches, instead I found him abstracted and inward-looking.

'Carlo, Carlo,' he said, shaking his head, but this was all the reproach I had of him. He went on to talk most gloomily about the progress of the war. His concern seemed to be as much with the strength of his fellow leaders in the Parliamentary armies as with the enemy.

'There are mines beneath my feet,' he said. 'Who is there to trust?'

'Nay, sir,' I protested. 'The men love you and fight for you as much as for a cause.'

Normally any suggestion that the soldiers in his army were not inspired solely by a sense of God's purpose would fill him with anger. Now he merely smiled sadly and said, 'Aye, Carlo, had I a thousand Fantom Troops, what might I not do for my country?'

My mind boggled at the thought. What indeed!

'You have one, sir,' I answered promptly, 'whose loyalty shall serve for a thousand.'

He took my hand then and I saw there were tears in his eyes. I was filled with alarm. When a sober Puritan like Essex started putting his trust in the likes of me, the time perhaps had come to leave.

I returned to my troop, but did not speak of my misgivings yet. Things were in a balance – against the heady victory at Marston Moor in July had to be set the ignominy of Essex's defeat and flight out of Cornwall in August. The present engagement on Speen Heath between Newbury and Donnington seemed to me to be decisive. It was not just a matter of who won. Essex, Waller, Manchester and Cromwell were all taking part and I knew that in any victory there is only room for one victor in the public eye. Naturally I was all for Essex – I could see no protection coming from any of the others.

But I suspected from my interview with him that his star was declining.

Well, as it turned out the problem for the Parliamentary leaders was not who to honour for victory but who to blame for its absence. It was a confused and misdirected business and though the Fantom troop fought with the customary skill and courage, my nose and ears told me that nothing good was coming out of this diffuse and disorganized battle. In the end we were left hanging around Donnington Castle (I will not call it a siege!) while the King's army relaxed and fêted themselves in Oxford. Prince Rupert, we heard, had been proclaimed Lieutenant-General, which, with the young Prince of Wales as so-called Commander-in-Chief, meant that control was effectively in Rupert's hands.

Early in November they returned to Donnington, recovered the artillery which they had left in the Castle, and marched away again, almost unopposed.

In the weeks following the most serious fighting that was done took place in the Council of War, the Committee of Both Kingdoms, and ultimately Parliament itself. There comes a time in the life of every soldier when he realizes that, fight he ne'er so bravely, it is politicians who in the end will rule the world. I followed the arguments with keen attention and when in December at Cromwell's prompting the Self-Denying Ordinance was laid before the House, I summoned my own council.

Some of the others were slow to see the significance of this proposal which would make it impossible for any member of the Lords or Commons to hold military command while the war lasted.

'It seems to me a good measure, inspired by the Lord,' said Jem Croft. 'It will put command of the army where it belongs, in the hands of a soldier, under God.'

'Ay, ay,' growled Nob Parkin who spoke as usual for his two equally brutal but more inarticulate brothers. 'Let Parliament parley, while true soldiers get on with the bloodshed.'

It was a not ineloquently stated point of view. Tom Turner,

my cornet, who notched the staff which bore our colours each time he slayed a man (it felt now like an Ethiop's backbone, and many mornings after we had lain peaceful all night in our own quarters I noticed new notches) offered a different view of things.

'It may mean the Presbyterians and the Independents will fight each other which will give an opportunity for more killing. And more booty,' he added as a concession to our base material lusts.

'What say you, Quartermaster?' I said to Lauder.

He took a long pull of brandy and said reflectively, 'Peers may not resign from being peers.'

The others looked at him in puzzlement, not taking his point for a moment.

Nob Parkin, sharp witted for three, saw it first.

'Then Lord Essex and Manchester must give up their commands,' he said slowly.

'But Cromwell need not,' said Tom Turner. 'There is blood in this.'

'I think Cromwell would find a way to stay both a member and a general,' I said. 'But *certes*, the Ordinance has no teeth for him.'

'But the House of Lords will not pass it!' declared Jem.

'Who knows?' I said. 'There are many who might be happy not to fight by law.'

I saw Lauder observing me quizzically. He saw which way my thoughts were tending and knew why. With Essex gone, my shield was gone and where should I seek another? Not in Cromwell, certainly; nor in Waller. Who then? The only person of distinction on whom I could make any call was the man whose star was now reaching its zenith – Prince Rupert.

But my own personal feelings would not be sufficient to carry with me the whole of my troop into the King's camp. There needed to be better reasons.

Lauder came to my rescue.

'Methinks we have served this army well,' he said musingly. Everyone nodded except Jem who was beginning to catch the drift.

'And our wages are grossly in arrears,' continued Lauder.

'Ay, ay!' agreed the Parkin brothers with nods to emphasize their sense of being badly done to, though if each did not average in a day what your ordinary trooper earned in a week, he believed himself cozened.

'For my part, I have no interest in their quarrels. I do my duty as a professional and when my work is ended, then I seek a new contract – or a new master.'

There, it was spoken.

'Go to the King?' said Nob Parkin incredulously.

'To the King?' echoed his brothers.

'Go to the King?' repeated Nob, but this time with the note of incredulity modulating into one of reflection.

'Nay!' protested Jem. 'This cannot be! How shall it be answered before the Throne of the Most High?'

I looked at him sympathetically. I could see his point. None had worked harder than he at establishing our religious credentials and in his dress, manner and physical appearance he was their epitome.

But once the idea had been broached, support for it flowed thick and strong.

'The King's party looks set fair to win,' I declared. 'The wise soldier fights for the winning side.'

'Our stores are low,' said Lauder. 'A change of master gives us new crops to reap.'

'Ay!' laughed Nob. 'And we know where the richest grain lies.'

'And there are those of our own side at present I should dearly love to kill,' murmured Tom.

'Stay!' said Jem. 'The Ordinance is not yet passed. I say the Lords will reject it.'

'They might indeed. Once, perhaps even twice. But I see Cromwell as the coming man,' I answered grimly. 'He has the gift of victory which Essex has lost if he ever had it. And I know for a fact that Cromwell has plans to reorganize the army on lines which would make life intolerable for the Fantom troop.'

I was guessing, of course, but it was not time for vagueness.

Jem made one last try.

'If Cromwell has this gift, what do we then if he should finally prevail against the King?'

'Why then, Jem,' I answered gaily. 'We change back again!'

The Parkin brothers undertook to sound out the men as they lay in quarters that night, offering honourable discharge to any who were prevented by conscience from joining us and dishonourable death to any who might be pricked by conscience to betray us. These may seem strange precautions, but conscience is a vegetable which can oft best grow on a dungheap.

Yet it should not be thought that what we proposed was unique. In wars civil the shift of loyalties, creeds, interests – call them what you will – is common and inevitable. Earlier that same year Sir Richard Grenvile, a man of spirit and intellect, had abandoned William Waller and offered his services to the King along with thirty troopers and more than five hundred pounds of Parliamentary cash. He now prospered in his new position and though he would do well not to be captured by the enemy, he looked to have made a wise choice, for his disorders would not long have been tolerated by the Parliamentarians.

Nob Parkin came to me to say that all the men were firm; where I led them, they would follow. I was moved despite myself by this declaration though I knew it was based on self-interest and nothing more. I trusted my family of horses more, and of those it was only Luke's love that I was absolutely certain of. But at least none of them would ever betray me for wealth or advancement.

We made no move yet for it was the dead of winter and the various campaigns proceeded only fitfully. The King feasted at Oxford and the Parliamentarians tried and executed a string of 'traitors' to entertain the mob and menace the vacillating. The sight merely confirmed me in my desire to be away. These were an uncivilized race.

Even the rejection of the Self-Denying Ordinance by the Lords was no incentive to stay, though Jem Croft took it as such. The pressures on the much depleted Upper House were powerful and increasing. Essex would be out by the spring, and I felt that one or two of my superiors who did not love me (I know not why) were regarding me speculatively as though thinking, *were it not a good idea to take up Fantom now and let his trial move slowly so that by the time of sentence Essex might be out?* Perhaps I imagined this but it gave spurs to my intent and when early in March troop movements began to accelerate in preparation for the inevitable spring offensive, I rode out of London at the head of my men with such a variety of forged orders in my cloak that, had I been challenged, I doubt if I could have easily produced the forgery to support the chosen lie! But no one stood in our way, and we made such a brave show that many passers-by in the London streets stopped and cheered us. We made our way carefully west, taking our time, and avoiding contact with other units of either side. When at last we came within sight of Oxford, I ordered a halt and from our baggage horses we unpacked several large bales which contained short cloaks of gold lined with green silk and plumes of green and gold for the men to fit on to their helmets. The officers too put on new gear of the same colour and by the time we were finished, even Jem Croft looked gay enough for a cavalier, though the shortness of his hair (by this time a rare sight, for practically all officers of the Parliamentary side wore their locks down to their shoulders) was a deficiency which only a wig would correct, and this he refused most scornfully. But I was pleased to see he joined in the laughter when our banner was unfurled, unchanged except that the figure under the horse's hooves was now completely bald and in profile looked not unlike Jem.

So we made an even braver show as we rode into Oxford than we had as we left London. But I was glad when we were arrested at the first ring of defence posts, for had *we* been able to penetrate the city on no better authority than our finery, then others less honest in their intentions might have done the same.

I introduced myself to the officer of the guard who appeared to be a good professional man, so I saved the flowery speeches I had prepared about *seeing the light* and *divine motivation*, and said merely that I and my troop wished to transfer our allegiance to the King. He recognized my name and talked of one or two common acquaintance for a while, then suggested that my men should disarm and wait here while he awaited instructions. I demurred politely, acknowledging his intentions to be honourable but pointing out that at this stage in the transfer my men were extremely sensitive to any slur on their own honour. I suggested instead that my men should picket their horses and prepare their meal – which was the equivalent of a fierce dog rolling on its back in an attitude of friendliness, but without any muzzle being placed round his savage jaws. Meanwhile, perhaps, word of my arrival could be taken to the Lieutenant-General, Prince Rupert, with whom I had some previous acquaintance?

An hour later I was summoned to the King's presence in the Tom quadrangle of Christ Church College. I do not flatter myself it was my reputation that won me this honour of a public reception, it was simply that any defection has a good propaganda value particularly if it is accompanied by apparently informed assertions of the enemy's weakness and confusion. These I gave most readily – and in a good loud voice – as I knelt before His Majesty and pledged my allegiance.

He was well satisfied and gave me his hand to kiss which I did in a manner somewhat perfunctory for my eyes had fallen on a lady of the court, a woman of some twenty-nine or thirty years, whose beauty struck me most strangely. For a desperate moment I thought one of my visitations was upon me and I might be driven to try to board her here and now, in full view of all the court. But with relief I realized that it was not those particular trumpets which were sounding but other less strident and more bewitching instruments.

'You are acquainted with my nephew, I believe, Captain Fantom,' said the King, recalling me to myself.

I stood up.

'We met, sire, in Germany where he so early displayed that fiery courage for which he is justly renowned wherever heroic deeds are sung.'

I caught the girl's eye as I spoke and she raised her eyebrows and smiled slightly as though mocking my hyperbole.

'Yes, Captain, I remember you.'

Rupert himself, whom I had not observed when I arrived, stepped forward from a group of noblemen shaded in one of the arcades to my left. He spoke flatly and for a second I I wondered uneasily whether anyone had been so foolish as to whisper to him the scandal which associated his mother's name with mine. Well, he was hardly going to bring that up here and now.

'When last we met at Vlotho, sir,' I said, 'you said that you owed me a life and I owed you a horse. I come to pay my debt.'

I clapped my hands and Nob Parkin, looking splendid in his new uniform, led Digby in. Groomed till his black coat shone and with his head held high as he took in this unusual scene with great interest but no nervousness, he looked a splendid beast. The lady spectators whinnied appreciatively while the gentlemen neighed and reared. Only Rupert remained unmoved.

'And do you ask me to pay my debt now, Captain Fantom?' he enquired coolly.

I drew myself up and looked slightly affronted. It was important to get this right. I couldn't very well say, *no you stupid bastard. I just want you in reserve next time some sod gets nasty ideas about stringing me up!*

Instead: 'What debt is that, sir?' I cried. 'When first you led the King's armies to glorious victory, you cancelled all debts. How can any man be owed a life by one who has so nobly preserved all our reason for living?'

I gestured dramatically at the King who looked well-pleased at these histrionics and a ripple of applause ran round the quad though I dared not catch the young beauty's eye again.

Rupert meanwhile moved forward to examine his gift, running an expert hand along his withers.

' 'Tis a fine beast,' he said appreciatively. 'How do you call him, Corporal?'

Had he asked me, I would have invented some flowery and complimentary name, as Bucephalus, the steed of Alexander. But Nob saw no reason to hide the truth.

'We calls him Digby, sir,' he answered. 'On account of he jumps over anything.'

There was a second's silence, then the whole quadrangle was filled with laughter. Even the King smiled and Rupert grinned from ear to ear.

'Captain Fantom,' he cried. 'Give me your hand. I accept your service and your gift. We have need of brave men and can never have enough Digbys.'

'To ride,' he added in a low voice audible only to me as he turned away.

I discovered later that relations between the Prince and Lord Digby were not of the best. Digby, the King's favourite, was not a military man and when his boundless optimism and Rupert's tactical advice coincided, all was well between them. But more and more they differed, particularly as Digby was very jealous of his position in the King's favour and resented Rupert's advances in that quarter. Well, Rupert had another backer now, I thought, one long experienced in supporting the great. This fellow Digby when I spotted him was laughing as much as the rest, but I did not doubt his enmity. I could have done without it, but if it were the price of Rupert's friendship, then it was worth paying.

But the troubles brought on me by Digby (the horse) were not yet ended.

As I left the court to return to my troop with Rupert's commission in my pocket, a red-faced fellow with a patchy ginger moustache and ragged beard, grasped my arm.

'Sir,' he said aggressively. 'Olwyn Matthias, Baronet, at your service, sir. That horse you gave to the Prince, without offence, sir, may I ask where you had it?'

'You may ask, sir,' I answered. 'But without offence, sir, I see no reason to answer.'

'I'll give you reason, sir,' he said excitedly. 'That horse looks much like one owned by my brother Daffyd Matthias, of most blessed memory, who was butchered at Edgehill.'

'Indeed, sir? And you look much like a jackanapes I once saw at the court of Emperor Ferdinand. But I shall not chain you, sir, I shall not chain you. Good day.'

It was foolish perhaps. I could easily have invented some story of purchase at a London horse-market which may have satisfied him. But after receiving courtesy at the hands of a King, who could tolerate unmannerliness from a Welshman?

Anyway, I had other things to think of. I discovered that the face of the woman who had caught my attention at court would not leave me. I have generally been reckoned a better judge of equine than female beauty; when the trumpets sound, the object of my charge has always seemed the apex of desirability, but once the notes have died away I have often discovered that what I imagined a thoroughbred is after all a nag. But this one was different, or so I had convinced myself by the time I returned to my troop.

I made haste to settle the men in quarters. Lauder had already made some enquiries and though we were the latest arrivals in what was already an overcrowded town, yet a combination of his expertise and our comparative wealth soon saw us comfortably settled in St John's College, to the surprise and chagrin of some of our new allies. I always tried to keep my men as close as possible, for an early quelling of their riots before any of our secrets could be revealed. For though many among the common soldiery of both armies, and some among the officers also, undertook to plunder and ravish whenever opportunity arose, yet they did it but intermittently and *extempore*. Only my troop of all I ever heard of was properly organized and trained in these most basic of the soldier's arts. Lauder kept a record of each man's share which was given to him week by week except for one shilling in ten which was set aside till a man received an honourable discharge from me. This system the men approved for it meant that even if they squandered all their wealth in riotous living, still something would remain – and if a man should commit a misdemeanour meriting a fine, the money could come out of this store without being felt immediately in his pocket. Looking after their money was each man's own problem, though if it were proved that any of my men had robbed or cozened one of his fellows, then he was straightaway punished with death – which was simply to apply the common law of the army, though in the Fantom troop we proceeded without the publicity of open trial.

My own wealth which was now considerable I had concealed in small parcels at various points across the country. Thus if some were discovered by accident, yet would enough remain to make me comfortable, while to keep it all in a lump sum would invite theft or even, were I disgraced (as indeed I was by now in the eyes of Parliament), confiscation. My excellent memory which enabled me to be so skilled in tongues found it no hardship to keep precise details of each hiding spot so that nothing appeared on paper for the curious eye to read.

But I was not concerned with material matters at the moment. Once my men and my horses were settled, I returned to Christ Church with hasty gait at first, but gradually slowing as I was suddenly beset by doubts, fast burgeoning into certainties, that on closer examination the woman would have a face scarred by small pox, black teeth, one leg shorter than the other, a squint, and certainly stink to high heaven. I had early discovered that the English gentry though elegant and gay in their dress, were less nice about their persons and their manners than almost any other nation in Europe. In Oxford I have observed ladies of the court rise from their meat, go into a neighbour room, or perhaps into an alcove, shit on the floor, and return to their table. Soldiers who live often in close and uncomfortable conditions are less beastly than this, nor would the most of them even in their cups offer such offence to tavern wenches as I have seen gentlemen of the court offer to their ladies. No, it is certain that manners were not known in England except as they were brought, like silks and wine, from abroad.

For myself, I had all my clothes steamed in an oven after each campaign and I bathed myself all over in fresh water twice or even three times during a summer. And to a lady I would offer only the courtesy I had learned of the Spaniards and Italians, except in those few cases I have told you of, where politeness bowed to necessity. So when on passing through the great portico which leads into Tom quad the first thing I saw was the lady of my thoughts suffering the horse-play of a pair of gilded poltroons, I forgot my concern about her possible defects and straightway grew angry.

She was trying to walk across the quad which, having been so recently used as a cattle market, was spotted with heaps of cow-dung into which these two gallants were attempting to steer her, the whiles making comments on her person and attempting to thrust their hands into her bodice. She seemed unmoved by their foolishness but I could not be so philosophical. I boxed the ears of the nearer fellow so violently that his eyeballs rolled and he tumbled to the ground. The other looked at me in such amazement and terror that I did not strike him but instead approached him slowly, then with great suddenness snapped my fingers in his face and cried, 'Boo!'

Startled, he cried out loud and sat in a cow-pat. The lady seemed far more amused by this than impressed by the chivalry of my intervention. But at least her laughter gave me the chance to check that her teeth were sound, nor were any of my suspected deficiencies manifest to a close inspection. She was truly beautiful and with a beauty which for some reason twined itself around my sensual being.

'Your servant, madam,' I said, essaying a bow.

'No servant of mine,' she answered in a melodious, soft voice with something of Spain or France in it. 'This work is none of my instructing. I had heard you were a sudden man, Captain Fantom, but did not appreciate what this meant.'

'They are not hurt,' I said defensively.

'You only score blood, do you?' she mocked. I fell into step beside her as she continued her progress, leaving the uninjured man to tend his fellow.

'You have heard of me, madam?' I enquired, feeling flattered and perturbed.

'I saw you presented to the King earlier,' she said. 'Afterwards I heard people talking of you, as they do of all turncoats.'

It is to the professional soldier the commonest of gibes, but today it hurt me.

'I turned no coat,' I said angrily. 'Any man who says so is a liar.'

'And woman too? Forgive me, Captain Fantom. Was it on the road to Damascus that you were converted to the King's cause?'

Said I, 'I care not for your cause. 'Tis the King's money I fight for; and perhaps some of his lovely ladies.'

This piece of gallantry seemed only to amuse her the more and I continued angrily, 'Those are fools who fight for their politics or religion. My father was a Roman Catholic, and his father too, but I have fought for the Turks against the Christians as well as the Christians against the Turks. It is not seemly to mock a man for practising of his profession.'

'Strange,' she said. 'I see you are an honest man. Yet a fellow much like you within these two past hours swore allegiance to the King, whom he called his "reason for living", and said nothing of his wages.'

We had now it appeared reached her destination, a tall overhanging building near St Aldate's Church. All the advantages of my usual method of wooing had been made manifest to me in the time we had walked together. Abuse and outrage after the event I could understand (and in any case it was always fading away behind me) but this unprovoked mockery before any advance had been made was barely tolerable. I wondered what she would do if I now pushed her against the door of the house and ravished her on the threshold. But such a project required more than annoyance to make it feasible and I was in no wise properly inclined at the moment.

She smiled as though recognizing my thoughts.

'Good-day, Captain Fantom,' she said. 'If your wages keep you in Oxford long enough, we may meet again.'

'Madam,' I said, preventing her from closing the door, 'I do not know your name. Nor yet if you are wedded wife or free maid.'

She looked at me thoughtfully.

'Neither sir,' she answered. 'I am a poor widow, made so by this awful war in which you earn your salary. I exist here by the charity of my dead husband's brother, who loved my spouse enough to want to keep his memory warm at whatever cost. So I have neither wealth nor youth nor virginity to recommend me.'

'You are wrong,' I said. 'And your name?'

'Mistress Annette Matthias,' she said.

But I had somehow guessed it before she spoke.

1645

Oxford

LIFE in Oxford proved much to my taste, except insofar as Mistress Annette Matthias seemed unwilling (or, I hoped, simply unready) to rub flesh with me. Yet strangely I found this complicated dance which they call wooing began to commend itself to my liking. Just as in matters military I have ever felt it behoved a soldier to make himself expert in all the proper arts, so now I began to realize that there may be more to taking a woman's citadel than a simple charge. And the element of danger was not lacking for Sir Olwyn Matthias, offended by my personal affront to him and suspicious still that I had slain his brother, put himself in the way of my courtship at all turns.

Annette, seeing this, most mischievously swore that she would never lie with a man who had hurt her brother-in-law. It was not that she had any great fondness for the man – indeed she disliked him heartily – but it amused her to see me sitting beneath his insults unable to reply. Sir Olwyn had naturally slandered me to her in terms general and particular, but she took little heed of this save to repeat the slanders to me in mockery.

'Sir,' she said. 'I have it on authority that you are brutal, vicious, grasping, licentious, and a very great ravisher.'

'Madam,' I said, 'what do you need of authority when you may test these qualities for yourself?'

Of her husband she spoke but once.

'Did you kill my husband?' she asked.

I resolved on honesty, having already sold the ring.

'Who knows? I slew many good men at Edgehill. As for

the horse, as I have since told Sir Olwyn, I had it of a gentleman of Sir Robert Pye's regiment at Bedford.'

Nothing but the truth there. She seemed satisfied and spoke no more of the matter. When we talked of matters military, Edgehill was never mentioned. Indeed she showed much more interest in my European campaigns than in the English wars, but this was understandable when I discovered her family were French.

Militarily speaking, my troop took its turn at all the duties of a garrison town. We stood guard, manned outposts, rode on vedette patrols, foraged, even appeared in court on ceremonial duty which honour was accorded us by Rupert in the face of much opposition by Lord Digby. As Rupert's enemy, he was my enemy also, but I could not dislike the man. To hear him talk, victory was always just round the corner; the Irish were coming, the French were coming, even the Dutch were coming (though God knows why anyone should believe that; I had lived in The Hague long enough to understand that cautious, mercenary, Protestant race). But Digby cheered even *my* spirits when he talked, though I knew that he spoke very stupidly.

News of the reformation of the Parliamentary armies was greeted with amused interest and regarded as a sign of weakness. But I felt uneasily that all of what I had foreseen was coming true. Essex had resigned the day before the House of Lords finally passed the Self-Denying Ordinance early in April, so my decision to withdraw my labour had been well timed. But Cromwell somehow survived the Ordinance as General of Horse under Sir Thomas Fairfax, the Commander-in-Chief. And with leaders like these, not even the story that at nearby Abingdon, Colonel Pickering had provoked a mutiny among his troops by preaching to them, could make me agree with the Cavaliers' contemptuous dismissal of this 'new, raw army' as one of them called it. To me it sounded like an efficient and well-ordered machine of war.

Still, I had great respect for Rupert and, were the direction of the King's tactics left in his hands, there was still a good chance of a Royalist victory. But I doubted much if he had the political strength to win his way. And another factor was the sheer wanton stupidity of so many of these Cavalier commanders. Even when courage and tactical sense were not wanting, often these qualities were negated by purely personal considerations, quarrels over precedence, a readiness to feel slighted, a desire to behave in the 'right' way. It is no wonder that democracy flourished first in England!

An example – or rather two examples – of this inconsistency of behaviour occurred at the end of April. Annette was going with some other ladies to visit a friend, Mistress Windebank whose husband commanded the garrison at Bletchingdon House, one of the outlying posts which guarded the northern approach to the city. On a hint from Annette, I volunteered my services as escort, pleased at the thought of having her company away from the constant threat of interruption by Sir Olwyn. As it turned out, opportunities for seeing Annette alone were even fewer than in Sir Olwyn's house, for the ladies kept in a gaggle all night, talking and laughing, while I sat with Frank Windebank drowning my sorrows and his reminiscences of youthful debaucheries in a bottle of brandy. He was still but a stripling which of course is when evidence of dissoluteness is most highly valued. I liked him well enough but tonight I had hoped for pleasures less verbal and vicarious than his conversation offered me.

Bed time came and still I had not spoken to Annette except in company, but as the ladies retired I took the candelabrum from Mistress Windebank and lit them up the stairs. My act of courtesy in no way deceived Annette who took great delight in revealing that she and one of the other ladies were sharing a bed – 'for a timorous maid needs company in a strange house, do you not think so, Captain Fantom?'

I retired myself some hours later, full of brandy, anger and lust. Sleep would not come and after a while I rose from my bed and asked myself the question – if Annette had put herself out of my reach, who would be the best substitute; that is, which among the ladies would be most like to make me welcome (for I wanted no scandal?) Finally I settled on the Lady Henrietta Furnell whose husband was at present campaigning in the west country. A woman of a certain age and no great beauty, yet she was decaying in splendour like autumn and all men were invited to the harvest-home. My only fear was that I would be prevented there, but Windebank would hardly dare neglect his wife and the junior officers of his guard were either on duty or drunk – or, I feared, both. But the efficiency of the guard was not my responsibility.

I entered her room with stealth till I was certain that she was alone, then I pulled back the covers and shook her bony shoulder for I felt it wise to wake her first.

'In God's name!' she cried. 'What is the matter?'

'No matter, lady,' I said. 'Just a simple soldier come to make his devoirs.'

She sat up and stared at me till her eyes penetrated sleep and darkness and made out my identity.

'Why, 'tis the hard-man!' she said. 'Nay and how hard are you, Captain Fantom?'

'Hard enough,' I said, falling on top of her.

'God's guts! take care!' she cried, now fully awake. '*I* am not shot-proof!'

As though cued by her words, a rattle of musketry sounded about a hundred yards from the house. To Lady Furnell's ear, if she heard it at all, it must have been nothing more than a nightjar's grating and she was understandably puzzled when as nimbly as I had leaped on, I leapt off.

'By Our Lady's womb!' she said. 'They did not tell me you worked so speedily!'

But now there came a fresh outbreak of firing, much closer and followed by the shattering of glass as a window was struck.

'Ahh!' shrieked Lady Furnell displaying great agility in her turn as she scrambled out of bed and through the door.

'We are attacked! Attacked! And shall all be ravished. Oh help!'

In the circumstances I found her fears rather unflattering. As I followed her into the corridor I ran into Annette who, in company with all the other ladies had been roused by the shooting or the shrieking.

'So, Captain,' she said. 'This is how your devotion overflows.'

Had it not been for another burst of firing without, I would have thrust her back into her room and settled things between us once and for all, but the defence of the house was going to need every man so I pushed by her unspeaking and made haste to my room.

Had I been in command, I would have gone to my duties naked, for rapid action is of the essence in cases like this. A surprise attack gains or loses momentum within the first ten minutes. If the defenders can make some kind of show of strength and readiness, the enemy will often hesitate and lose an advantage, for it is hard then to press home a surprise attack when you believe the surprise has failed.

Windebank was a gay young spark, not yet able to hold his drink too well, but I knew him by reputation as a soldier of courage and dash, so I did not doubt he would be making all preparations for a stout defence. But I reckoned without that fatal 'gentlemanliness' which, despite the general foulness of their court manners, still managed to rear its stupid head on ill occasion. (The story they tell of their great hero, Philip Sydney, passing his water-bottle to a common soldier at Zutphen is a case in point, though some bawdy verses I have read on his death show the other side of the English character.)

When I descended into the drawing room, instead of a garrison-commander instructing his troops I found a knight-errant surrounded by terrified damsels pleading for his protection. Dishevelled, his tunic unbuttoned, his sword in his hand he looked the perfect picture of careless youth roused to action by a threat to his ladies' honour, but such allegorical groupings have always made my heart sink.

I approached and saluted him. Frankly, whatever he decided to do was none of my concern. If I could make him behave like a professional soldier, well and good. If not, then at least I would establish to those present (I mean the corporal and wounded sergeant who stood by the door as if awaiting commands, for I did not count the ladies) that I was ready to do my duty.

'Sir,' I said. 'What are your orders?'

'Orders?' he said as though the word were Sanskrit.

'Yes, sir. What part shall I take in the defence?'

'Defence!' shrieked Mistress Windebank, half swooning round her husband's neck. 'Nay, but my ladies! We must treat!'

'Ravished! We shall all be ravished!' cried Lady Furnell.

'Then we must prepare ourselves as best we can,' said Annette demurely. 'Are you not prepared, my Lady?'

Lady Furnell glared angrily at her, but Annette took the wind out of her sails by sinking on her knees, closing her eyes and clasping her hands. After a moment the others began to follow suit. Later I would be amused by memory of the sight, but this was no time for tomfoolery.

'Sergeant,' I said to the wounded man. 'What is the state of the outer defences?'

'I know not, sir,' he said. 'My post was quickly overrun and I fear the others may have gone too. Those of us who lived have fallen back to the house and await command.'

'What is the enemy's strength?'

' 'Tis a large force, sir,' he said, adding when he saw doubt on my face, 'Nay, 'tis not my fear that speaks, sir. There is horse out there, and I fear me a battery of minions or drakes, for I heard their wheels on the road as I withdrew.'

This was ill news. A small raiding party was one thing, but a large force with artillery at their back would be irresistible.

'With permission, sir, I shall look to the disposition of our troops within the walls and send one to tell the King of our situation. Have courage, ladies. We will be reinforced by morning. And if one of you will add bandage and dressing to your prayers, perhaps God will spare this brave sergeant's life.'

As I turned to leave, Annette rose and went to the sergeant who by now was standing in a pool of blood. Windebank still had not spoken, but now he at least shook himself free of his wife and began to button his tunic.

When I reached the front door of the house which I saw

with a shudder stood ajar with only one soldier to guard it, I heard a voice call from without.

'Flag of truce! Flag of truce!'

Peering into the darkness I saw approaching two figures, one with a lantern.

To the soldier on guard I said, 'Take these men to your commander,' and myself stepped back into the shadows for I had no wish to appear as a principal in any parley that took place.

I was very glad of my discretion for behind the drummer who led the way with his white flag and lantern came a long, gangling awkward figure whom I recognized instantly as Captain Hector, the man who I had quarrelled with at Bedford.

I followed them to the drawing room and listened at the door. What I heard filled me with fear. It was certainly no mere raiding party out there but the advance guard of Cromwell's army. Hector, like a second-rate actor, was painting a crude but effective picture of the carnage that would ensue if the Parliamentarians breached the walls with their artillery, then took the house by storm. The ladies reacted with 'oohs' of horror and some subdued weeping. I didn't blame them. If they knew as I did what the opposing forces could do to us, they would have been terrified out of their minds.

Now Hector changed his tune and offered terms of surrender; all arms, supplies, monies and furniture to be left in the house while the inmates would be left unharmed and given safe conduct to return to the city in the morning.

Of course to a civilian, particularly a female, this must have sounded an offer too good to refuse. They cannot know how essential it is in war that every part of any army from a corps to a private soldier resists to the utmost extent possible. As a professional, I have never considered myself being paid to die, but certainly I am paid to risk death. And these men who fight for a cause, well, one would think their motivation would take them even further.

But now came a silence and as I counted the seconds, I began to realize what Windebank's answer would be. It would sound chivalrous and correct in that room full of frightened women, but it would not be frightened women who listened at his court martial. I shrugged philosophically. That is what philosophy's for, to make other people's misfortunes bearable.

But I had problems of my own which required action, not philosophy. Windebank's decision meant that I wasn't going to be killed by a culverin ball which even a hard-man would find it most difficult to resist. But I had other fears. Both armies had plenty of turncoats in them and theoretically I would have the same status under the surrender terms as any other officer. Yet I felt uneasily that Hector would be reluctant to miss an opportunity to pay me back for the affront I had given him and Cromwell himself would not be averse to using me as a dreadful warning to other waverers.

It was not a risk I wanted to take. In the drawing room, Windebank in a faltering tone which showed that deep down he knew the enormity of his deed was accepting the terms. But officially I knew nothing of them. Swiftly I went round the house issuing instructions for constant vigilance. I found a lieutenant who seemed to know what he was doing and I described to him the situation without of course mentioning the truce offer.

'Someone must to Oxford instantly to warn the King,' I said. 'I will go myself, for I am better mounted than any man here. But it is a dangerous business and I doubt me if one man alone can hope to succeed. Pick me another two, Lieutenant, bold fellows who can ride and who do not fear to risk themselves in His Majesty's service.'

The lieutenant tried to dissuade me from risking my own life in this venture, but I insisted that the speed of my horse (Petrarch on this occasion) made it essential. He was an emotional boy and wrung my hand as I was preparing to leave.

'Never fear,' I said. 'But defend the house bravely. The enemy are strong but our cause is righteous.'

I led Petrarch into the night closely followed by the two soldiers who were pleased to be accompanying me. Had they known of the agreement their commander was just making, nothing in heaven or hell would have made them stir, of course, but in their minds they were abandoning a position which would certainly be overrun within the hour.

About fifty yards from the house in the cover of a box hedge I judged it safe to mount. Ahead I could hear the noise of an armed force – clinking, jangling, muttering – but nothing was to be seen except that in the orchard which lay to our left front match-ends gleamed like fireflies showing that a troop of musketeers lay in readiness there.

'Quietly, boys,' I said nudging Petrarch forward. 'Then when I give the word, dig in your spurs and there's a purse of gold for which of your first reaches the city.'

Slowly we advanced. Suddenly a figure rose before us, round metal helmet dull-gleaming in what light fell from the spectating stars.

'Halt!' he cried. 'Quickly, the watch-word?'

I levelled my *donderbuss* at the shadowy figure.

'Fellow,' I said edging nearer to be sure of him, 'General Cromwell has ordered a new watch-word to match his great deserts.'

'I know not of that,' he said, puzzled. 'What be it?'

'The devil's arsehole,' I said squeezing my trigger.

'Ride, brave lads!' I cried above his shrieks. 'For God and the King!'

'For God and the King!' the poor fools answered as they spurred their horses into a gallop.

I turned Petrarch quietly to my right and back into the cover of the hedge where I dismounted. The orchard exploded in a volley of musketry, the horses screamed, one went down instantly but the other still held on and it took a volley from the second rank to give him his quietus.

Meanwhile I was now back on Petrarch wearing the round helmet I had removed from the dying guard and with my own plumed bonnet tucked beneath my cloak. Slowly I advanced along the line of the hedge. A party of musketeers came running towards me.

'Good work, my lads,' I cried. 'But there is more to do. 'Tis said some of those decadents within may try to leave the front of the house in the guise of our officers. Hie you round there and put a ball into any who so appears.'

They were well drilled, thank God, and went trotting off into the dark where with a bit of luck they might blow Hector's brains out. I meanwhile by dint of moving at a slow but purposeful gait rode right through the attacking formation and, once safe, increased my speed slightly, though saving the gallop till I reached the outskirts of the city where I was intercepted, wild-eyed, and with Petrarch in a fine lather.

The King was roused and listened gravely to my news. I spoke most modestly of my actions and most urgently of the desperate plight of those in the beleaguered house, volunteering to be in the van of the relieving expedition. A council of war was called. Cromwell's army, I learned, had already that day – or as it was now, the day before – beaten the Queen's regiment as he moved north from Watlington. I began to see that Windebank had been sadly negligent with the enemy so close, but uttered not a word against him and preserved a most manful silence when questioned about the state of readiness at Bletchingdon.

In the end shortly after dawn two regiments of cavalry set out on the fifteen miles north, but they had not gone half way when they met with one of Windebank's men sent ahead with the most chivalrous intention of reassuring those concerned at court that their ladies were safe. Such chivalry deserved recognition, and those concerned showed their gratitude by avoiding duty on Windebank's court-martial which took place that afternoon. I was called as witness and gave him what help I could, but the result was inevitable. Courtesy is no excuse for surrender.

I watched him die that same afternoon, shot by a file of musketeers against the wall of the Divinity School. His wife and her friends shrieked and wailed most touchingly. Had they kept their peace the night before, then the poor fellow they lamented might yet have lived or at least died with honour. Instead he forgot what it is to be a soldier and all his past brave service was wiped out in a moment.

I saw Mistress Annette after the execution and she berated

me most foully, for not taking responsibility with Windebank for his decision, for riding away from the house, for saying too little in his defence at the trial.

Finally my patience ended so I struck her across the mouth, cutting her lip against her sharp little fore-teeth.

'Understand this, madam,' I said. 'I am not such a brave man as that poor fellow we have just seen killed, but had the decision been mine last night, then you and all your ladies might have been slaughtered before I surrendered. But it was not mine and a soldier must abide his own decisions. Madam, you have blood on your mouth. I think it becomes you.'

I left her and went to the stables to see that Petrarch had suffered no harm from his night's exercise.

1645

Oxford – Leicester – Naseby

My star was now in its ascendant and I was offered various forms of advancement all of which I modestly refused, for though they would have given me rich opportunity to line my pockets with bribes or profit from the redisposition of supplies, yet I had no ambition to shine as courtier or accountant. The cobbler should stick to his last and my trade was in the field of battle where a man earned his right to dishonesty by blood, sweat and the looseness of fear.

One thing I did accept was a Forlorn Hope medal from His Majesty. This was cast in silver, embossed with a picture of the King himself, and given for great valour. Its purpose here was to underline what poor Windebank's death had made clear enough, that the King expected his soldiers to fight, not treat. In the affair at Bletchingdon I was the only one to have engaged the enemy and so, in the best tradition, I was dubbed hero. I discovered to my amusement that the idea of the medal itself had derived from my old acquaintance, Mr Thomas Bushell, who, I also learned, had provided more than two dozen cannon for the King and in addition clothed four regiments, including the Life Guard, out of his own pocket. I say 'to my amusement', for I had also learned in Oxford that 'out of his own pocket' usually meant out of *my* pocket, or *anyone's* pocket who could be persuaded to part with money! Nothing that I had heard before of Bushell's engineering skill was untrue. The trouble was that his projects often proved vaster than even all the pockets of his investors could support and he lived constantly in debt. But so persuasive was his oratory, so amiable his personality, that even in the confines of prison he inspired trust and was rapidly released. Were he never so amiable, I fear I would have cut his throat had I discovered his misuse of my money in time of peace. But in war commerce changes its face and I was on my way to becoming rich by other routes, so I could afford to be entertained by a fellow rogue.

My men by now were eager for more action, partly because they had been too long with little real work to do, and partly because Oxford offered too many opportunities for the rapid spending of money. Rupert was on the Welsh border but early in May he returned to Oxford, just in the nick of time. Since my quarrel with Annette I had found my old trouble returned in an exacerbated form. I commanded the Parkin brothers to attend on me constantly for I feared what my lust might bring me to, and on several occasions they dragged me struggling from the presence of women of good repute who unknown to themselves had sounded my trumpets.

Lauder laughed loud and long when he chanced to witness one of these scenes. I had been strolling down Broad Street when the wife of the Master of Trinity College happened to come walking by me. I leapt forward, one hand outstretched, the other plucking at my breeches. Dextrously Nob Parkin tapped my heel and I ploughed into the ground at her feet. Leaving his two brothers to drag me away, he doffed his cap to the puzzled woman and said, 'Forgive my master, mistress, for he has suffered most grievously in these wars. Sometimes in a lovely face he fancies he sees the General Cromwell and the lovelier the face, the stronger the fancy.'

Flattered, the woman offered her condolences and went her ways, while Lauder who had been standing near almost laughed himself into the grave and gave Nob Parkin a small silver coin which the great oaf put in his mouth and swallowed, this being a common test of such coins, for true metal after being passed and washed shines bright and even, while base and mixed metals are patchy and dull.

When the women were of no importance, however, and the places dark or ill-frequented, the Parkins offered no restraint, and indeed if there were wenches enough to go round they joined me in my toil, despite my warning that ultimately they would suffer the pangs of hell, for while I did it for necessity, they did it for pleasure. Finally their vigilance failed. I had been in a brawl, or rather more than a brawl for some ruffians lay in wait for me as I walked down the narrow passage they call Turl Street. One fired a ball at my chest, the force of which knocked the breath from me though it did not pierce the skin. Instantly the other two ran at me with clubs and began beating me around the head and even as I fell to the ground the thought came to me that these fellows – or he who sent them – knew their herb-lore.

At that moment Nob and his brothers came running up, whereupon my attackers broke off and fled, save one who stumbled and on rising received Nob's fist on the back of his skull so that he fell to the ground once more. When they came to take him up, they found he was dead.

I myself was badly bruised and somewhat dazed. Quickly they took me to a chirurgeon's house, then thinking no harm left me to go tell Lauder and Jem what had befallen. When they returned it was to find me arrested. The chirurgeon's wife had come to me to bathe my head, and with her husband only a few feet away in his dispensary mixing a posset for my aching brains, I had attempted to ravish her.

My defence that I had been disturbed in my wits by the beating I had received might have been acceptable had not Digby taken an interest in the case and put forward witnesses to my previous offences. These I dismissed as purveyors of malicious gossip, admitting only (what was not easily denied) that I had twice been convicted of the offence during my service under Essex.

'But then also I was the victim of false testament,' I averred. 'These Roundheads like not foreigners and especially not those of the Catholic faith. Nonetheless, that godly though misguided peer, Lord Essex, who is a great hater of lechery, gave me my pardon, acknowledging my innocence.'

This citing of that old Puritan, who still was known for his honesty if not his intellect, might well have brought me out of my scrape scot-free, had not Digby pursued his malevolence towards me. These gay, pleasant fellows can bear any amount of other people's misfortunes but cannot abide a joke against themselves.

Fortunately Rupert arrived as the court were considering their verdict and as 'twas one of those times when his breath was blowing stronger than Digby's in the King's sails, I was given my release. Two days later I rode with my troop behind Rupert's banner as the King's forces marched out of Oxford in search of the battle that would end the war.

The night before, I had visited Annette and met with her brother-in-law, the fiery Olwyn Matthias. He drew his sword on me and lunged at my gut but his rage made him unsteady and I parried the blow with my gauntlet, drew my own weapon and would have slit his throat had not Annette appeared at that moment and cried, 'Stay!'

I obeyed and with much pleasure heard her scold the stupid Welshman till he left the house in a rage.

'Forgive me,' I lied. 'I would not have hurt him.'

She smiled but said nothing and led me into her chamber where she offered me wine and a fresh ham bone.

I accepted the refreshment with a smile and some puzzlement at her kindness, but soon it came out that her conscience had been much moved by the consequences of the attack on me which she was almost certain had been arranged by Sir Olwyn. Naturally I did not dissuade her that my assault on the chirurgeon's wife had been consequent on the addling of my brains by those villains' cudgels, but I did say (to tickle her conscience the more) that I would certainly have swung if Rupert had not returned when he did.

' 'Tis a good friend,' she agreed. 'With a friend like that, who would need another?'

'Nay, I have need of many friends,' I answered. 'The Prince may not serve every turn.'

'What lies there in another's power which the Prince cannot perform?' she asked.

'What no man can perform,' I answered, dropping on one knee before her and taking her hand.

'I do not take your meaning,' she said coyly.

'Take it now, and with it, everything!' I replied slipping

my hand into her bodice and squeezing first her right and then her left breast. She moved away, I pursued; she protested, I insisted; she softened, I hardened; she subsided, I ascended; she shuddered, I exploded; we swore eternal faith and I departed, thinking that in her letters to her husband, she had made no empty promise. Why she should have decided to yield at this particular moment I did not know.

Strange are the ways of women. Though as soldier knows the eve of war has ever been the special time for treats.

Now followed a good campaign, culminating in the sack of Leicester. Our artillery spent the afternoon blasting a hole in the south city wall. Then at midnight, the infantry (mostly Welsh recruits) attacked while we sat on our mounts and waited for the gates to be opened so that we might ride in and scour the town.

'God's leeks!' said Nob Parkin impatiently after half an hour. 'Those Welsh locusts will strip the town bare!'

'There are plenty yet to kill,' said Tom Turner confidently. I hoped so. I often felt my cornet would start on his own side if he felt his thirst for blood unslaked! Lauder went round the men, making sure they knew where our plunder waggons were stationed and that each group was equipped for its particular task. We had developed certain specialist skills so that nothing of value would be overlooked. Our gold and silversmiths' party, for instance, carried with them powder barrels and long fuses to break their way through the heavy locks these distrusting tradesmen protected their wares with. And our china, glass and porcelain experts bore padded boxes for the safe transport of their fragile plunder.

At one o'clock, the city gates opened. The victory was ours. We moved quietly forward, heedless of the raging gallop of the rest of the cavalry and went about our business with the dignity of professionals.

Two hours later Jem came to me with word that our waggons were full and the men requested permission now to frolic a little. After work, play is the soldiers' maxim, so I gladly gave command.

'Wilt not join us, Captain?' called Nob.

'I will come to see you have not forgotten how to comport yourselves,' I answered gayly and leaving the perforce continent Lauder to ensure the security of our waggons, I set off through the streets at a canter.

Everywhere I saw death and destruction. Doors smashed, windows shattered, smoke belching skywards from fires no one surviving dared appear to quench. Only the dead of that city remained in the streets; men, women; children even. All living things are enemy to the conquerors of an intransigent city. The citizens had been invited to surrender and refused. The garrison had no choice, of course (as poor Frank Windebank had discovered), but the citizens themselves were free to make their own decisions and put their trust where they thought it most like to be rewarded. Well, they had backed the wrong horse.

My sword was still undrawn and unblooded. It did not bother me. I met Tom Turner and saw his right arm red to the elbow and beyond. He had taken my share and more.

Nob and his mates had found a tavern in whose cellars sheltered a dozen or more women, most of them no better than they should be. I went among the men offering encouragement with the flat of my sword and making the usual jokes but my heart was not in it. In the end I left them to their sweaty joys and rode through the devastated streets, thinking of Annette. A strange adventure befell me on that ride. As I passed an old stone church I heard the bells jangle in most devilish discord and on curiosity I turned Luke's unquestioning head and rode in through the great open doors.

The source of the noise was easily seen. Some drunken soldiers had broken in to loot the church and the parson and some of his officers had attempted to prevent them. For their pains they had been bound around the gut with bell-ropes and the soldiers were amusing themselves by sending the struggling parson and his friends soaring into the bell-tower, vying with each other who could achieve the greatest height.

The noise of their laughter and the clang of the bells masked the rattle of Luke's hooves on the stone floor and I was upon them before they were aware. The apparition of a man on a horse in a darkened church is a fearful thing or so I judged by their reaction. Their noise ceased, they desisted from their sport and pressed back against the wall with faces aghast.

'Unbind these men!' I commanded in sepulchral tones, more to test my newfound power than out of any particular sympathy with the hanging men. The soldiers hastened to obey me but as they finished their task, Luke raised his tail and dropped a mound of smoking shit. This homely act emboldened one of the soldiers to decide that if my horse were capable of such a deed, perhaps I also was just as far from being a spirit, and with a vile oath (which in that place must surely have marked him down for hell) he plucked a pistol from his waist and fired at me. The ball struck my shoulder, fell to the floor and bounced back towards him. With a scream of terror he fled and his fellows who on his example had drawn their weapons also flung them to the ground and followed him.

The released men lay half stunned on the flag-stones, regarding me as if they would have preferred the more comprehensible inhumanity of their tormentors to this strange revelation.

'Be comforted, Master Parson,' I said. 'God has abandoned you, but you have friends in the underworld who love you.'

I laughed hollowly to underline the joke and backed Luke away. But the stupid vicar leapt suddenly to his feet and crying, 'An thou be the devil himself, thou shalt not mock God in my church,' he picked up one of the discarded pistols and fired it at me.

The ball took Luke in the neck and because of his brave heart he stood there solid as ever for a moment and I scarce knew he was hit. Then his forelegs buckled and I slid out of the saddle, sick with fear. Now he went over on his side and his legs threshed for a moment as he tried to rise again. His breath came and went in ugly gasps but his eyes held calmly to my face as though waiting for my command to stop this pain. There was nothing else to do but draw my pistol and put an end to it. After the explosion I closed my eyes. All was quiet now. When I opened them again I was standing among the swinging bell-ropes my sword in my hand, and all around me lay the mangled bodies of the parson and his friends.

Among them Luke lay quiet and still and comparatively unbloodied. Even in death they have more dignity than us. I wept now, remembering his love for me. He had been perhaps the least *bien dressé* of all my mounts and many a time his waywardness had almost put me in danger, yet his courage and affection had always got me safe away. This was a great loss.

Yet as I walked away with his saddle on my shoulder I felt a sense of loss greater even than that I had just sustained. It was as if a wheel had turned a full revolution. My life as a mercenary had begun thirty years ago with the slaying of a priest; suddenly I felt that the killing of this last one had brought it to an end.

'Lauder,' I said as we made breakfast of a cold capon and small beer, 'do you think I am fit for marriage?'

He spat a bit of gristle into the fire and laughed, showing the ragged row of stumps which did him service as teeth.

'If you may find the right lass, well then, aye,' he said.

'And where should I look for her?' I asked.

'In a booth at a Bart's Fair,' he said promptly. 'Where else will you find a woman able to be on her back in bed, on her knees in prayer, and on her last legs in desperation, all of which things are necessary in any fool who'd marry Carlo Fantom.'

I grinned at his insults and drank some beer. It was sharp and cold, a good taste to go with the smell of smouldering wood and the pleasant sharpness of a late spring dawn. We had not looked for quarters in the city but remained without, guarding our plunder and watching for the return of the men. I had not slept, nor Lauder either who had found with age he needed scarce more than one hour's real sleep in twenty-four, though he could doze on an ambling horse for mile after mile.

'What think you of Mistress Annette Matthias?' I asked next.

He picked the chicken carcase clean and cracked the rib-cage between his palms.

'I have not met the lady,' he said. 'But from report, she is of good repute and fairly fleshed. But poor.'

I smiled at his warning and gestured towards our waggons.

'I have enough,' I said.

'Perhaps. She is not reported to be a fool, though?' he continued.

'I hope not.'

'Then she can scarcely be the lass you're thinking to wed,' he mocked.

'Lauder!' I said warningly, unamused this time.

'Well, man, look at yourself! What can you offer a respectable widow? She is a widow, you're sure of it? There's nae chance her man will prove to be but lying low till these troubles pass?'

'Oh yes, I'm sure. I blew his brains out at Edgehill,' I answered.

'Oh, Fantom, Fantom,' he sighed. 'You're a strange and bloody man.'

'I did not know him,' I protested. 'Nor her till we met at Oxford. Something about her face has charmed my mind, Lauder.'

'If it's just the face, then all's not lost,' he answered caustically. 'The smallpox may pit it, or powder scar it, or wind and sun rough it, and age will surely wrinkle it. Man, you will not condemn the girlie for something so accidental as a face?'

'Lauder, you stupid old sod, will you not understand what I'm saying? I want to change my life, marry, settle in peace somewhere, rear horses, children even. I'm sick of soldiering!'

But he just laughed the more, as if a blackamoor should put flour on his face and call himself Queen of the May.

'Though this I will say, Fantom,' he added finally. 'I will see this *face* for it must be a rare *face*. Eh, man, *faces* are not things ye've ever paid much mind to in the past.'

I rose and left him, my breakfast quite spoilt. He shouted

after me, 'Fantom, regard yourself, man! You're like me. Ye'll live forever before you'll die a good man!'

Later we divided up our plunder. A trooper was discovered attempting to conceal a piece of gold plate in one of his boots. He had offended in this before (hence his fellows watched him closely) and had suffered the tenfold fine which was our first punishment. Our rules laid down only one penalty for a repeat of the offence – death. This had been necessary only once in our short history and I had carried out the sentence instantly in plain view of the others, who had been much chastened by what they saw, proving the insight of mother church and father law in these matters.

This time I passed the task to Jem Croft who without a hesitation went to where the poor fellow lay bound beneath a waggon and slit his throat. If Jem had had a conscience he would have been a mighty man for God, for he brought to everything he did the fervour of religious fanaticism.

Lauder was sitting on the waggon which was taking our goods to the impromptu market which always springs up after a big looting and at which local people attend to snap up bargains of their neighbours' treasures, or even buy back their own. He looked down at me strangely, then gave commands and the waggon moved forward leaving the dead man at my feet.

'Bury him,' I said. 'His portion goes to the general fund.'

I left them digging a shallow grave with Jem giving directions, eager to get to his funeral oration which was one of our best entertainments.

We did not stay long in Leicester itself, but dithered in what seemed to me a state of uncertainty all over the midlands. My men took the opportunity of picking the area clean and I began to wish that they should have the chance to spend as well as get money, for too much possession makes a soldier begin to take his future seriously. Perhaps this was my trouble. As usual I had lodged the greater part of my share in a safe place in Leicester, beneath a very old flat tombstone in the yard of the same church wherein I had killed the parson. Making allowances for accidental discovery or destruction of as many as three or four or my caches, I still had a goodly store of riches to be collected after the troubles were over. Or perhaps before. Annette was French by birth and would surely be happy to live over the sea with me till England came to its senses. Then we might return, for I had grown fond of this landscape and liked the feel of a great salt moat all around me.

But still there was fighting to be done. Fairfax's army had raised the siege at Oxford and marched north which was cause for joy. Cromwell too was on his way, also cause for our pleasure if Prince Rupert's counsel held, which was to continue our own march north, reviving support for the King there, and eventually joining up with, or at least sending reinforcements to, Montrose in Scotland. The Covenanters once defeated, the King would have a solid base stretching from the Highlands to Yorkshire out of which to face Parliament. The West Country, hitherto so important in all Royalist strategies, was now too unstable to make a division of the King's powers worthwhile. Our generals there, Berkeley, Grenvile and Goring, spent more time fighting each other than the enemy. I speak metaphorically, though a report had reached us of the two halves of Goring's force in the west each mistaking the other for Fairfax's army and fighting together for two hours before realizing their error. Now Goring with his cavalry should, according to his orders, be riding north to join us. But there was no sign of his approach or even of its intention, only news of the growing Parliamentary strength.

So Rupert wanted to keep going, as far as Newark at least, but there were others, notably Lord Digby, who were hot for a fight. The battle to end all is a concept much favoured of civilians. As if a cause can be snuffed out in the space of half a day! You can't even really manage to destroy an army in a single battle. Kill a few, capture a few, there'll still be those with the wit, stamina, agility to head for the hills. No, this war had a lot of mileage in it yet, whatever might happen this windy June.

But as so often happens the civilian with his catchy slogan got his way while the military commander, able to advise nothing but caution and the biding of time, was not listened to. When our intelligencers told us that Cromwell's troops had joined Fairfax's, making a force of some fourteen thousand to our seven or eight, I waited the command to turn and withdraw. No one in his right mind would accept such odds unless time and circumstance forced them on him, will he, nill he. But the command did not come. Instead we all went forth on a gusty summer morning and arranged ourselves for what might pass for a battle near a village called Naseby. It was about eleven o'clock when all was ready – if such a term can properly be used of so outnumbered a force as ours.

The Fantom troop was on the right with Rupert, facing Henry Ireton. Petrarch was standing quiet beneath me, his head turned to lick at the sugar in my gauntlet palm, a treat he only received on days when I wished him to know there was fighting to do. We stood on a ridge with the northerly wind almost at our backs and I watched the long summer grass ripple wildly away from us down a shallow dip then up another slope till it broke against the waiting lines of Ireton's horse.

A thick hedgerow ran towards us from the left marker of Ireton's line and I thought that, were I in his shoes, knowing Rupert's proclivity for charging first, I should interlard those hedges with sharp-shooters to take us on the flank as we galloped forward. Indeed as I looked I glimpsed movement thereabouts and further back I could see groups of unmounted horses. Dragoons, I thought, and turned to send one of my men to the General lest he had not been made aware of this danger, but before I could speak Rupert had doffed his scarlet monterey cap, waved it in the air, the whiles shouting our day's slogan, 'Queen Mary!' and we were off. The order came so quickly that I had some difficulty in falling back into line with my troop, but I would have been angry if it had proved easy. We were drawn up in the Swedish formation, in column of three, and we charged at the close order, that is with the right knee close locked up against the thigh of the next rider to the right. This produced a line not exactly straight, but which, properly constructed, was as taut and strong as a steel-link chain. The Fantom troop, I prided myself, rode tighter and closer than any in either army. We had once broken through a line of cuirassiers in Yorkshire and found ourselves on the other side with five of our lads shot dead, yet still held on their saddles by the pressure of the formation.

There are some who have felt that an officer's place is ahead of his troop, but they are mostly dead or civilians. In broken or in wooded country where there is a free charge, why, the sight of the captain ahead with his cornet by his side may indeed be a spur to those behind and I would venture myself so when the occasion demanded it. But any officer I saw riding in advance of his line at the close order across even terrain, him I would cashier – or rather turn with contempt from his funeral for the poor fool must certainly die. Well, a man's life is his own, but an officer's life is his men's and to put himself where he will certainly be shot in full view of his troop is wrong; and to put himself where he cannot fall back into line without causing the line to break is wrong; and to put himself where his corpse and his horse's corpse may cause the line to break is wrong; and to put himself where those men immediately behind him cannot fire forward lest they strike his back is wrong. Have I said enough? These heroes who ride out in front, I would let my horse shit on their graves.

But we on the right that day had a straight tight line and our General's scarlet hat bobbed in the middle of it. I myself as all my officers wore a harquebusier's 'pot', that is a helmet open before with plates to protect the cheeks, and, of course, a light cuirass or 'back and breast' armour. There was a tendency amongst officers of both sides to neglect the use of protective armour on the grounds partly of comfort and also, implied rather than spoken, of courage. More targets for my stable droppings! My troop, officers and men alike, were trained to respect their bodies and when they saw that their captain, the famous hard-man, did not scorn to wear 'back and breast', they never complained of the extra weight.

Back to our charge. The time – eleven of the clock. Down the slope we went, gathering speed till we reached the full trot (no gallop is possible – or necessary – in this formation). As we began the slight ascent out of the dip, I heard the dragoons concealed along the hedge open fire. Let them, I thought. You do not stop a cavalry charge with a few musket balls from the flank. As yet none of the enemy ahead had fired and neither had our men. They each had three shots, the first from the carbine held at the ready across the horse's neck, the other two from the pair of pistols primed and spanned in their saddle holsters. I permitted my men only two shots in their first charge, keeping one of their pistols in reserve so that they might rapidly reform and be ready armed for a second charge. But I had spoken to them so seriously about the need to kill a man with each shot that it was now part of their most sacred credo and they felt the shame greatly if they had not made sure of their men in the first charge.

Now the enemy's line was close; some of them had started firing, I picked my man, a big red-faced country lad wearing only a buff coat and no cuirass, and as we struck I put a musket ball in his chest. Their front line broke like rotting cloth on a week-drowned man. I drew a pistol and sent a young corporal to his Maker. He looked scarcely old enough to have sampled sin, in which case I had done him a favour.

Now we were in the midst of them and I began to swing about with my pole-axe, the little battle-axe many of the King's cavalry wore tied to their right wrist, with a sharp blade on the one side and a hammer head on the other. It was a weapon I had found mighty useful in space too constricted for the sword, and all around me my lads were putting them to good effect. I saw Nob Parkin take a man's head off with his, a fine blow, though a shameful waste of energy when compared with the economic slaughter perpetrated by Tommy Turner despite the labour of having to bear our standard.

Suddenly we were clear; the enemy had broken. One, perhaps two of their regiments were galloping wildly off the field. A cheer went up from the King's troopers but I did not join in. What booted these small advantages when Fairfax had so many thousands to spare? But small advantages should be pressed home and I rallied my men round, hoping for a second charge against those of Ireton's troops we had still to deal with. I could see them where they stood, obviously dismayed by the ease with which we had shattered their fellows. A charge now might carry them away.

But it was not to be. My own men apart, these Royalist troopers had no discipline for a rapid re-formation and a second onslaught hard on the heels of the first. They were broken up now into parties, some attacking the infantry, others pursuing the flying regiments and yet others doing nothing as though all were now done and the victory ours.

This was the high point of that day. It was now close on a half after the hour of eleven. By twelve the battle was lost. By one, all resistance had ended and the King's army was in ignominious flight. Little care was taken to bring any order to that retreat and into the enemy's hands fell our artillery, supply waggons, the King's entire correspondence, most of the army's baggage train and dozens of coaches full of women, legitimate and loose, and of wealth the same.

The Fantom troop suffered least of all. As soon as I had seen the odds against us, I had ordered Lauder to make a discreet withdrawal with our personal waggons and when we rendezvoused with him near Leicester and counted our losses they amounted to no more than six horses and a handful of men. My reputation reached a new height among my followers. Any fool can triumph in a victory. It takes real talent to come comfortably through a defeat. So the men laughed and chattered happily as they made a late dinner.

Fools.

Why do I call them fools?

Because they had fought with courage, come off with honour and reputation intact, and earned their pay. Any who asked me for it would have been given an honourable discharge from the army which, though not strictly legal for I would have had to lie about the reason for discharge (such as, wounding, illness etc.), would certainly have satisfied most who read it and permitted the men safe return to their homes with their booty.

Yet none asked, which meant that none foresaw what I did, that though there were many battles yet to fight, each would be more desperate than before, and all for nothing. In a way Digby had been right. Naseby *had* been a battle to end all, for I was sure now that without the intervention, long promised by Digby, from Ireland or the Continent, the King had lost his war.

1645

Hereford – Bristol

My life now was like a weary horse which starts galloping downhill towards a cliff and has not strength enough to pull up short of the edge.

I had written to Annette telling her of my fortunes and asking for her hand in marriage. Having had little ground in romantic composition, I fear my letters must have swung between military chronicles, full of blood and tactics, and a schoolboy's *billets-doux*. Our last encounter had given me hope of a kind answer, but never a word came back though those new come from Oxford reported her in good health, if somewhat subdued from her former lively self. This I optimistically laid to my absence and wrote again, but still there came no reply. I asked the Prince's favour to be posted to Oxford, but he told me as plain fact without hint of flattery that his best troop could not be spared. I could have by now been a colonel at least had I so wished, but I refused the promotion. So short were we now of men that many of our officers (of whom there was ever a superfluity since the King's habit had been to squirt out commissions like a boar pissing) formed themselves into companies of *reformados*, and to be the captain of a loyal troop was, to my mind, better than to be a colonel without a regiment.

So I followed the Prince, first to Hereford then down into the West Country. It was a busy summer with enough of good news from the Scots under Montrose to give colour to jolly George Digby's continued optimism and this coupled with minor successes at Stilton, Huntingdon and Hereford revived the hopes of the King's side. But my spirits remained low, partly because of Annette's silence and partly because of my certainty that the war was lost. Do not think I had become a devotee of the King's cause. If monarchs are appointed by God then God has it in his power to give them enough sense to retain their thrones. As a bad Catholic, I might deplore the rabid Protestantism of the Parliamentarians, but the episcopalian system they opposed (among other things) was equally schismatic, perhaps more so because it flaunted many of the trappings of the True Church. No, my concern was simply that these hypocritical Englishmen showed scant respect for the professional soldier and his right, service done, to take new employment. I began to dream at nights of hanging and to wake in a cold sweat, reaching for the brandy flask by my pillow.

God's arse! I told myself angrily. You have been nearer hanging than this, Fantom, and never felt a pang.

But thought alone cannot soothe the troubled spirit and when I saw Fairfax's army preparing to lay siege to Bristol where Rupert and his force now had their quarters, I took steps.

I went wandering around the sailors' taverns on the waterfront, sitting quiet and curbing my natural exuberance of spirits (save once when, blinded by drink and the flaring of my trumpets, I took this strapping wench against a bollard on the dock and found when I had excavated a vast confusion of petticoats that I had a man. Pah! such are the filthinesses of these sailors! I tipped him in the water where perchance he drowned, I know nor care not.) Finally I found my man, the captain of the *Albatross*, an old lugger fit to run small cargoes along the coast, or sometimes, if wind and weather promised fair, over the sea to Ireland. His name was Hugh Trengold, a silent brooding kind of man with all the yearnings of mighty villainy, but nerve enough only for small.

At our second meeting I offered him a hundred guineas for passage on his ship with another hundred to be paid on safe arrival at my chosen destination. His eyes glinted.

'Where would you go, master?' he said. I could see he was thinking what other rewards there might be in this.

'Where, and when, is my business,' I answered. 'This payment will bind you to take me off at slightest notice any time in the next twelvemonth. Agreed?'

'Aye, master,' he said reaching for the purse of gold.

'Wait a while longer,' I said. 'There is yet another condition. That fellow offends me. What is he?'

The fellow I pointed out was a great ox of a man, strong, certain of himself, the kind in whose company all men laughed or kept silent as he laughed or kept silent, out of fear of his correction. Tonight he was in a laughing mood and the raucous noise filled the smoky air.

'Meddle not with him, master," said Trengold, suddenly fearful for his money. 'He is a brute who maims men for sport.'

I rose and approached the merry group.

'Sir,' I said addressing the big man.

He took no notice so I seized a mug of wine from one of his fellows and poured it over his head. That won his attention.

'Sir,' I repeated. ''Tis a matter of the noise you make. My ears are sensitive and I would appreciate a *diminuendo*. My nose too is sensitive, but I am not so sanguine as to look for a quick improvement in your scent. But the noise, sir, let there be an end to the noise.'

Prepared as I was, he almost got me, lunging with great speed for a man of such bulk. Fortunately the table lay in his way and I was able to step back from his grasp. A fellow to my right reached for his sea-cutlass so I smashed the pot mug I held over his head and with the shard that remained I leaned forward and scored a bloody gulf across the big man's brow.

Blinded with rage and blood he came running at me. I stepped aside nimbly, having no desire to wrestle with this ape, seized his left hand as it clawed for my face, broke his little finger deftly, saw with some relief the broad-bladed knife appear in his other hand, drew my own dirk and slit him up the belly and breast, neat as a filleted fish.

'Take him to a doctor,' I ordered. 'He may yet live.'

And to Hugh Trengold I said as we walked along the darkened seafront, 'Captain, the other condition of which I spoke is that should you fail in any part of your bargain, you die.'

I left him then, feeling happier now that I had an escape route at my back.

It was not a route open to large numbers, however, for there was a squadron of Parliamentary ships blockading the sea roads. Rupert had had foresight to stock the town with plentiful supplies in anticipation of the siege and for a while things went well. We had a jolly time, sallying once or twice a day to hack a few of Fairfax's men to pieces, then returning to a good dinner. But gradually the grip of the besiegers tightened and there was no sign of relief coming from the King. Early in September Fairfax summoned the garrison to surrender. Rupert played for time, exchanged messengers, entered into protracted negotiations. Two years earlier, the position had been reversed. Rupert then had been outside the city and the Parliamentarians within, so now he knew the strengths and weaknesses of both sides. He must also have remembered the tremendous losses his army sustained when they stormed the city, and also perhaps that the enemy's garrison commander, Colonel Fiennes, had been court-martialled for surrendering and sentenced to death. Robin Essex had pardoned him (good old Robin – he was a great pardoner) but it was an unsettling precedent.

Finally Fairfax grew impatient. Guessing that the assault was soon intended, Rupert had made preparations accordingly. I and my troop were given the task of manning one of the forts on the outer wall, not a job normally performed by the cavalry, but there would be little chance of performing our usual role and I realized our general was putting his stoutest men at the most important positions.

Early in the morning of the tenth day of September, I sat with Lauder playing cribbage. We talked low, not to disturb Jem Croft and Tom Turner, who slept in a close antechamber till it should be their turn to mount the watch. Lauder too might have been taking his rest but as I have said, age seemed to have freed him from the snares of sleep which trap a man from so much of his life. Three times in succession as I cut the cards, the Queen of Spades was turned up and Lauder's face grew long.

'What, are you growing superstitious, you old fool?' I asked.

'Always believe a warning,' he said sternly, 'no matter how foolish.'

'Why then, I believe it. But what shall I do?'

'Take care,' he admonished.

I laughed long and loud so that Jem stirred restlessly in his sleep.

'So, I shall take care. But does it mean flee, or stay? Fight, or not fight? Eat, or starve? Piss, or hold my water? Tell me, thou Pictish wizard, tell!'

'I know not. But this I know. Were I you, which heaven forfend, I should ride off now with whatever I could carry and take my boat to anywhere.'

I put my cards down and said quietly, 'And what do you know of a boat, wise man?'

'I? Nothing.'

I turned the pack over and spread the cards face-up before him.

'Look well at these, Lauder,' I said. 'Each one commands *thee* to take care. Now, what's this of a boat?'

'A guess,' he said. 'I heard you visited the waterfront.'

'Did you? From whom?'

He jerked his head towards the sleeping chamber.

'Jem?' I said.

'Aye. He is with you more than you know, I think,' he answered.

'And he spoke of a boat?'

'Nay; only of the waterfront. I guessed at the boat. I thought as I would have thought myself, forty years since. A man should take care, especially a man whose profession and character puts him in the way of dangers.'

'And what would you do now, Lauder, old friend?' I enquired.

'Who knows?' he said. He put out his hand and sorted out the cards till the Queen reappeared.

'Ordinarily, I think I'd do my work and take my pay,' he continued. 'But with this one staring up at me, why, I might be tempted to mount my horse and ride for the sea.'

'And is this your advice?'

'Advice, laddie? I give no advice. Ask yourself the question, then listen close and wait for your answer.'

'Right, my grandfather. I have asked. Now I listen.'

For perhaps ten seconds we sat in silence. It was complete. Even the sleepy breathing in the other room seemed still.

'Alas,' I began mocking, but got no further. The air was shattered by a succession of thunderclaps whose echoes rolled and rolled till they were consumed by other closer explosions.

'Fairfax's siege-guns,' said Lauder rising slowly. 'And our batteries reply. There's your answer.'

I went into the other room. Tommy Turner was sitting upright on his bed, a slow joyous smile spreading across his fresh young face, as though awoken by church bells and a woman's hair tickling his cheeks. Jem still slept. I kicked the bed sharply and he awoke starting with fear as he saw me looming over him.

'Nay, Jem, it's not the devil,' I laughed. 'Rouse yourself now. There's work to do.'

I have had little experience of sieges from the inside, for Wallenstein's tactic of settling in comfort behind a strongly fortified position and letting the enemy waste his strength without could hardly be called a state of siege. And while I can read a pitched battle pretty thoroughly from the confused pattern of noise and movement which shows itself to the tutored sense, this kind of warfare left me baffled and frustrated. I had no idea what was going on anywhere except in the immediate vicinity of my own wall-fort. And, worse, I was static. To a cavalryman whose whole fighting life consists of movement – advance, charge, regroup, charge again, withdraw, run like hell! – this sitting and waiting was unbearable.

Mind you, I felt safe, oh yes. I walked round and round the battlements and saw no way in which anyone *down there* could persuade Nob Parkin and his lads to allow them *up here*. Yet fortresses had fallen, and castles had fallen, and citadels twice the height with walls twice the thickness of these had fallen, I kept on reminding myself; but I still felt invincible.

'They won't shift us from here in a hurry, Lauder,' I said as we peered out into the darkness, lit from time to time by the flash of powder and rent by the boom of cannon and the cries of fighting men.

'Not in a hurry,' agreed Lauder. 'But if there're enough of them, and I trow there are, they'll shift us right enough. Two of those siege pieces will knock these walls down, stone on stone, if they've time enough.'

I was angry and afraid to hear this hardened veteran accept so matter-of-factly that we could be dislodged.

The attack on our position direct did not start till half an hour later, during which time we irritated whatever enemy came into our range with fire from our muskets, while a detachment of gunners under my command covered a wide area with their sakers and minions. The noise of battle had never bothered me before, but now I found that to stand still with the monotonous rattle of explosions sounding constantly in my ear began to wear me down (I mean our own for at least the enemy fire that was directed at us made me duck and fear for my life). Fortunately they seemed to have little more than a single demi-culverin bearing on our fort and though it chipped away at our battlements as regularly as a mason's hammer (though somewhat slower, only one shot every five minutes) it would be broad daylight before they could hope for a breach. Nevertheless I was almost relieved when a great cry came up to us from the darkness and I saw their troops rush forward to attempt the assault proper.

Out of the darkness they lumbered. I say lumbered because all those who were not carrying ladders (of which there were perhaps a dozen with two men to each of them), bore huge faggots of fresh chopped branches wherewith to fill the ditch running beneath our walls. This burden made their progress slow and gave our shooters easy targets, but these were brave fellows, and still they came in spite of all, and in the end our shooting did but speed their task, for the ditch was soon level with bodies.

Now came the ladders. At first we reached over and simply pushed them off whenever they came to rest on our walls but soon groups of their musketeers were positioned to send a hail of fire at the head of each ladder as soon as it came to rest, and after losing several men we let the ladders lie. In addition a small mortar had been brought into play and the gunner with more craft than those of his art usually show (for gunners are frequently stupid men, as like to blow up their own side as the enemy) had found a good range and was dropping his shot onto the platform of our fort with deadly effect. Of course, I had men stationed at the fort's narrow windows, but these were so deep for purposes of defence that unless the ladders ran straight outside one of them, my men could get no aim at the climbers.

For the climbing had now begun. The first I saw to rise above our battlements was a whey-faced lad whose spirit must have been great to overcome such fear. I saw from his accoutrements that he was a cavalryman, for it is a barbarous custom in some of the Parliamentary armies to let a horseman lead the assault in a siege, for the infantry claim that their riders do not share an equal peril with them. God's piece! let some of these footmen ride at the close order into a regiment of cuirassiers flanked by culverin and they will understand the meaning of peril!

Taking pity on his plight, I said, 'Go find thy horse, boy,' and struck him with the hilt of my sword. In gratitude for my mercy, the young bastard attempted to hurl a hand grenade among us even as he fell, but it bounced from the wall and fell with him, blowing him to pieces and the ladder from the wall with all those who were climbing it.

I laughed, thinking this easy sport. And so it would have been with men of self-respect and wisdom, who would soon have withdrawn to lick their wounds and plan for the morrow. But these fools, they knew nothing of the morrow save what their canting preachers told them and still they came, some mouthing psalms, some mouthing oaths, some speechless with teror; but still they came!

I heard at one point a voice something familiar promising

all the glories of heaven to those who fell in capturing the city (which seemed to be a combination of Babylon, Nineveh and Sodom) and all the pangs of hell to those who defended it. Quickly glancing over the walls I saw below the moon-face of Obadiah Jones who had laboured so long to save my soul in Winchester gaol. From the colour of the sword he waved over his head, he was not averse to acting as a recruiting agent for the devil.

Turning, I looked for my lieutenant.

'Jem!' I cried. 'Give us a tune to raise our hearts. Yon doggerel of Martin Luther's will do!'

For I recalled the fear we had felt before Lützen when the German apostate's music had risen out of the mist which hid the Swedish forces.

Jem started singing, his eyes lit up with a fervour that made Obadiah Jones look like a puling hypocrite. Soon the other lads joined in, some from mockery, some from belief, most from a mixture of both (for though a soldier may rob and murder and ravish in quieter times, yet religion is oft woken up by the assault trumpet). If the hymn lifted our spirits, it amazed the enemy. Perhaps they thought the fort had been taken, or that we had been moved by God to join them, for all round the battlements they paused and in a trice, my lads drove forward, swords swinging and suddenly the walls were clear.

But the respite was only of a moment.

'Blasphemers! Blasphemers!' screamed Obadiah below and the Parliamentarians came back with renewed vigour. More and more ladders were brought up till the walls looked like the rigging of a galleon under full sail and I thought suddenly of my dirty little lugger rocking quietly in the mouth of the Avon.

It was now after five and the eastern sky was lightening, though the sun would not appear for another hour. But the light seemed to cheer my men more than the attackers for though sorely pressed we still held the fort and men press less eagerly to the peril they can see than to that which stands hid in darkness.

But then came a great outcry which seemed to run all round the outer walls of the city and this was followed by a mighty cheer from the enemy.

'Oh, Captain, Captain, we are beaten!' cried one of my men. Looking over our battlements I saw what he meant. Breached in several places and put under terrible pressures everywhere, the outer walls were being abandoned by the defenders. Rupert had ordered a general withdrawal to the castle where his sadly depleted and outnumbered force could better stand the next wave of attack. This was the time for us to go also, but even as I watched, I saw troop after troop of enemy cavalry gallop through the nearest breach in hot pursuit of the retreating defenders. There was no way out for us, or any others who remained in the outer forts. We were trapped.

Now it was the Parliamentarians who had new heart. With psalms and hymns and Obadiah's Welsh wail proclaiming the coming of God's kingdom in Devon, they pressed forward again.

My men fought well. We were professionals with a pride in our skills. But as a leader of professionals, I watched and waited till my mind was clear; we had earned our pay, let those who fought for faith and belief give up their lives, the Fantom troop could now treat with honour.

As though catching my thought, the enemy slackened off the assault and a trumpet sounded below followed by a loud voice summoning us to surrender on peril of a further and final assault without quarter. With a sense of relief, I realized the time had come.

I turned to Lauder, who had been doing the work of a twenty-year-old for five hours now, and told him my decision. I expected instant agreement but he shrugged and said nothing. Well, that was his privilege. I was in command and the decision was mine.

I summoned my trumpeter and ordered him forward to play a parley while one stood alongside him with a piece of white cloth tied to his musket. But as the pair went to take up their positions, Nob Parkin stayed them and tore the cloth from the musket end.

'What, Nob!' I cried in a rage. 'Do you know me?'

'Aye, master,' he answered. 'But I know not why you shame us.'

'Shame!' I echoed. 'Dost say I bring shame on myself?'

'No, Captain. Not on yourself. 'Tis well known thou wouldst fight with the devil, aye, and fuck him afterwards if he wore skirts. None will think shame of thee. But us, for whom you do this thing, we may be shamed. You do it for our sakes, loving us, but I know these men and it shall not be!'

God's lights! I thought. He thinks I set my own life at nought, yet love these stinking, illiterate, lecherous grotesques! He is surely mad, and they will tell him.

But to my amazement and horror a murmur of assent ran round those close enough to hear.

'What, lads?' I cried. 'Will you not take honourable terms and go forth to fight another day, if you will, or else back to the bosoms of your families, rich with coin and reputation?'

There was a silence while they thought of this, then an amiable rogue from Lincolnshire piped up.

'Well, sir. I'd as lief be here as in the bosom of *my* family.'

They all roared with laughter as though at the best joke they had ever heard and I knew we were lost. These stupid dolts were going to fight to the death – not for their King, not for their religion, not for their honour (their *honour!*), not for reward, not for *anything* I could think of. For fellowship perhaps? For me? God forbid! No. For *fun*. That was about the nearest I could get to it.

I recognized their insanity but suddenly felt a strange lightening of the spirit.

'Corporal Parkin.' I said. 'You are insubordinate and must be punished.'

I approached him gravely, my sword aloft. He held his ground. Then I skipped behind him and struck him with the flat blade across his buttocks, as I was wont to do when he was labouring on top of some favoured wench, crying, 'Go to, Nob! Show them thou art a man!'

The silly fools all around laughed and cheered and threw up their hats in glee.

'A song!' I cried. 'Like swans, let's die in singing.'

Jem Croft began to intone a hymn, but I stopped him impatiently.

'Enough of that cant! Let those who fight for God sing of God. The Fantom troop has fought for other things and will die singing of them.'

And I struck up my catch of the four-cocked giant which I had translated and taught to these child-like men.

There needed no more answer to the enemy's summons. Below I heard Obadiah Jones's cry of outrage as he caught the words of our song and next moment the assault was resumed.

I have fought with the Turks and I have fought with the Swedes and I have fought with the Germans, but I have never seen men fight as my troopers fought that morning. And these were cavalrymen fighting on foot, far removed from all hope of escape or succour. As the attackers scaled the walls, coming from all sides now that they were inside the city, we gave them volley after volley with pistol and musket till our powder ran out. Then we drove them back with cold steel. Three times they came over the battlements at us and three times we charged them and sent them tumbling back to the ditch. But each time we regrouped there were fewer of us. No one was singing now, for none had breath or cause. Nob Parkin saw his two brothers slain at his side and fought the harder as though he would do work for all three. Only Tommy Turner remained cheerful, standing beneath our banner of the prancing white horse with a sword in either hand and a pleasant grin on his face which spread and spread as the number he had killed mounted.

Now we no longer charged but with our back to the small central tower we received the enemy's charge and again and again repulsed it.

The top of the fortress was now swarming with the Parliamentarians, so many that they got in each other's way and dared not use their muskets at us for fear of slaying their own. We were down to some twenty or less, scarce a fifth on the numbers I had started with. Not one of us but was wounded. I had a gash an inch wide in my thigh and as I put weight on it to thrust at one of the foe, my leg buckled and I fell to the ground.

'Now perish, thou spawn of Satan!' cried a near-hysterical voice and a great pair of knees descended on my chest and a bloody sword was raised above my head.

'Nay, Obadiah,' I gasped. 'Thou broughtest me to the brink of salvation at Winchester. Wilt not say a prayer for me now?'

The mad eyes cleared, looked puzzled, then, 'Fantom!' he said. 'Thou traitor!'

The sword started to descend again but the respite had given me time to clasp my dagger beneath the tangle of my cloak and now I struck up from behind, driving the narrow steel deep into his anus. He shrieked horribly and sprang upright, straight into the inexorable sword of Nob.

'Thanks,' I gasped as Nob pulled me back to the relative safety of the wall.

He grinned at me, but did not speak and the grin turned to the tautened rictus of death. I saw there was a hole in his chest through which the lives of a dozen lesser men might easily have issued.

'Oh, Nob, Nob!' I cried. But a hand plucked at my shoulder and turning, I saw Lauder on the outer flight of stairs which led to the top of the small tower.

'Come, man,' he said. 'No time for elegies.'

He was right. As the last half dozen of our force protected our backs, I half crawled, was half dragged up those steps. At the top, I lay on my belly and observed the scene below. I saw Tommy Turner steadfast beneath his banner still. He was cut almost to ribbons, his left arm dangled limp almost severed above the elbow, his scalp was shredded like a mothy old wig and his face was a mask of blood, though the shine of his teeth showed he was still smiling. His right arm still thrust and parried, but as I watched he took three or four more savage blows on the head and chest and sank slowly to the ground. The men who were attacking him now paused and looked at each other in wild amaze at the slaughter this one man had wrought. Then suddenly he leapt to his feet once more, swinging his weapon like a stripling youth at exercise, and dispatched five or six more before they drove him down again, this time not desisting till his head rolled separate from his body. He smiled still.

Below at the foot of the stairs, my remaining troopers fell one by one. Jem Croft alone survived and as his last companion fell, blocking the stair, he took advantage of this respite to turn and run. But on that open stair he was a fair target and as he reached almost to the top, a pistol cracked and he staggered and fell. He was not yet dead and his hands clawed at the topmost stair. I reached forward and grasped them.

'Come, Jem; come, Jem,' I called as I pulled. But it was a dead weight, though he was not yet dead.

He looked up towards me, his face grey.

'Carlo,' he said. 'I have wronged . . . forgive me. . . .' Then he died.

I rolled back from the edge, sat up and looked at Lauder.

'Well, Lauder,' I said.

'Well, Fantom,' he said.

'What hope of quarter?' I asked.

'Man, we've made carrion of a couple of their regiments!' he exaggerated. 'If we had a hundred lives apiece, they'd torture us out of each of them in turn.'

'What's o'clock?' I asked.

'What the devil have you to do any more with clocks?' he asked.

I looked at the sky. It was now broad daylight and had been for an hour or more. It must be soon after eight.

'I could eat a breakfast,' I said.

'Man, your appetites will kill ye,' he said.

We both laughed.

They came rushing up the stair.

The first to appear wore a major's insignia. Lauder struck his sword from his hand and I thrust forward on my knees but as I did so I heard trumpets sound, from all quarters of the town it seemed, and the din of distant cheering, so I stayed my sword with its point at the man's throat.

'Major,' I said. 'The Prince has come to terms. We are your prisoners.'

I pushed myself upright and sheathed my sword.

'I would be honoured, sir, if you would join me in my quarters for breakfast,' I said, hoping to God my interpretation of the din was right.

'For Christ's sake, keep down!' urged Lauder anxiously. 'They'll kill you anyway.'

He was right. These men had fought too long and seen too many of their comrades slain to be thwarted by a few seconds.

There was a rattle of musketry. Several balls whistled past my head, one glanced off my shoulder. I staggered but remained standing.

'Are these the terms General Fairfax will have offered?' I asked. I bent and picked up the Major's sword and returned it to him, reminding him without words how close to death he too had been for he flushed and turned, shouting angrily, 'Hold your fire there! The battle is over.'

One spurred up on a horse at that moment and excitedly shouted confirmation of the news and in a trice the mood of our conquerors changed. They cheered wildly, slapping each other on the back; some sank on their knees in thanksgiving but the most, I was glad to see, began to hurry away in search of plunder before their fellows in the city had taken it all. Well, go to, I thought. They had fought bravely and deserved it.

'Gentlemen, will you come below till we hear the terms of your surrender?' said the Major courteously.

Slowly I limped down the stairs, past Jem Croft, his glazed eyes still pleading for forgiveness (for what, in Christ's name?); past Nob Parkin, huger than ever in death; past Tom Turner, shrouded deep in blood; past all my brave lads who had died in honour with their wounds on the front. For a moment I was moved, then I saw Obadiah Jones who had crumpled on his knees in death, like a Mussulman at his prayers. My dagger still protruded from his arsehole like a stiff tail. The sight did me good.

I looked back once more at my lads and wondered where they had all cached their money.

1645
Oxford

WE came off from Bristol quite well, I believe, being permitted by the terms of surrender safe convoy to Oxford with our horses and baggage. Though they took our firearms, we kept our swords and to one who had but a few hours earlier composed himself (in a manner of speaking) to death, this trek from the city felt like a wedding procession.

'So much for your cards!' I mocked Lauder.

'There were *three* Queens,' he muttered darkly. 'Best still that you board your lugger.'

I laughed. Even the pain from the gash in my thigh could not flaw my joy at being alive and on my way to Oxford and Annette.

Rupert and those nearest to him were less joyful, however. Well, I suppose it mattered to them that the war in the west was now virtually lost, and in addition there is always a doubt gnaws in the mind of a man who surrenders a garrison at whatever stage. Colonel Fiennes had come close to death for surrendering this same town but two years earlier; Frank Windebank had paid the full penalty for giving over Bletchingdon House and one of Prince Maurice's lieutenants who gave up Taunton Castle to my old commander, Robert Pye, had faced a firing squad too. Not that any such risk faced Rupert even were he at fault, which not a man who came alive out of that battle would dare accuse! Indeed I wished he had surrendered an hour or more earlier, whereby I might still have men under my command instead of being like so many others a trooper-less reformado. Still, I had my life and I had recovered Petrarch and Athene before they were stolen, and that was the main thing.

At Oxford we were received well though without much ceremony. Those who survive a pitched battle on the field may claim an honourable glow or even, as time passes, a degree of victory, but there's no way the loss of a large and important port with all its arsenal and provisions, can be turned into a triumph.

My intention was to seek out Annette instantly and discover the reason for her long silence but when I dismounted from my horse outside my lodging, my wounded leg pained me so much that I fainted with it. When they got me into the house and removed the dressing placed there in haste at our departure from Bristol and not touched since, the wound was discovered to be deeply infected. The chirurgeon said it was gangrenous and recommended amputation but I drew the sword I kept always ready by my bed and assured him that any man who would cut off my leg must needs suffer the same operation himself first. After that I lay in a tertian fever, awaking from each bout with the fear strong in me that my leg had been sawn off as I lay unconscious. Lauder assured me, however, that as I tossed and turned in my burning, my sword never left my hand and none save himself dared approach me. He fed me the medicines the chirurgeon had prescribed, plus his own catholicon of brandy and hot water, but the potion which did me most good I believe was a double infusion of my old herb, used both as a draught and to bathe my hurt. So efficacious was this that the doctor, greedy for profit as all his profession, offered me a hundred crowns for the name of the herb (which was not identifiable in its dried up form) but I only laughed and told him to go cut off more legs.

Still, the cure was a drawn out business and it was some time before I was well enough to make my way to Olwyn Matthias's house. My reception was extreme, even for that household. The servant who opened the door looked at me aghast, then ran from me, calling for her master. Matthias when he appeared was so flushed with rage that I would have laid odds that apoplexy would carry him off before he reached the threshold. Perhaps he felt the same for, while still some yards distance down the long corridor which ran from the entrance hall, he drew a pistol and took a pot at me. The ball struck the ground between my feet and without thinking I pulled out my own pistol which was primed but not spanned.

As I spanned it, I collected my wits sufficiently to speak to him.

'Sir Olwyn,' I said. 'It is not willingly that I approach your doors but I have urgent business with Mistress Annette which if it be brought to a satisfactory conclusion will mean that you see me no more.'

This seemed a very reasonable offer to me, but it only served to enrage him the more and now he came running at me with his sword raised, so I shot him in the foot.

A man in pain on one foot is fairly easy to push aside and I made my way rapidly to Annette's quarters. It was no time to observe the courtesies and I pushed open the door without knocking. Annette stood before me, pale but composed.

'Then you have returned, Captain Fantom,' she said.

'Did you ever doubt it?' I demanded. I rushed forward to embrace her. She neither flinched nor responded, but it was not this coolness that made me draw back, it was the realization that something stood between us. I looked down.

'God's womb, madam!' I said. 'You are in foal!'

She smiled then, without much humour.

'Look not so surprised, sir,' she said. 'You are the only begetter.'

I was amazed. It was a possibility which had not entered my mind, perhaps because my relations with women have generally been of such a nature that I have rarely stayed to discover the outcome.

'The child is mine?' I said, calculating quickly in my mind.

'Aye, sir,' she replied. 'It is your doing.'

'Well then,' I said. 'Well then. Let it be mine!'

For the prospect suddenly began to please. I saw the new Fantom in my mind's eye, rich, respected, his loving wife waving from the door of his mansion as he rode out to the hunt on his fine horse with a convoy of children behind.

'Is it for this that you did not answer my letters?' I asked. 'You goose!'

I laughed but her answer stopped my laughter.

'Letters?' she said. 'I neither had nor wanted letters from you.'

'What?' I said, beginning to feel angry at this coyness. 'Will you play with me, madam?'

Behind me I heard the noise of men approaching. I turned meaning to shut the door and bar it, but before I could act, two troopers of the King's guard with weapons drawn entered followed by a lieutenant.

'Captain Fantom?' he enquired.

'Yes.'

'Good-day, to you, Captain. I must require you to disarm and come with me, sir.'

'What?'

'You are arrested, sir.'

'No!' I protested. ' 'Tis monstrous. I did but shoot him in the foot and he had tried to kill me.'

Now he looked puzzled.

'There is nothing in the charge of shooting,' he said. 'Come sir. Can you not see you offend the lady?'

Annette indeed looked most offended.

'I'm glad you are come,' she said to the Lieutenant.

'Has he menaced your person, madam?' he asked pompously.

For answer she gestured eloquently at the smoking pistol I still held in my hand. The Lieutenant looked at me angrily and nodded at his men who moved forward and seized my arms.

'Do you treat a gentleman thus?' I demanded, struggling.

'Gentleman!' he retorted. 'No gentleman would have acted as you have. And this is strange impudence for a gentleman to come here again.'

'What mean you? What is the charge against me?'

'Will you make me speak it before the lady, sir? Why then, you are charged that in May of this year you did most unlawfully ravish this lady here present and the evidence of your misdemeanour is most plain to be seen. Fetch him away!'

Lauder came to see me that night. They had taken my parole so I had avoided the indignity of a cell, but I was close confined to quarters with a large well-armed trooper hanging around outside my door. What small value they place upon an officer's word, I thought gloomily as I considered whether it was worthwhile slitting the oaf's throat and making my escape. Yet what had I to fear?

'Lauder,' I said. 'This business, I understand nothing of it. What have you found out? Tell me, for God's sake.'

'It seems the lady concealed her condition until some weeks ago, about the time of our return from Bristol.'

'What? Is that significant?' I asked.

'Who knows? But she steadfastly refused to name her seducer until this very morning when she had Sir Olwyn lay a complaint against you, alleging that you ravished her in May and shame and fear for reputation kept her quiet till she was certain of her pregnancy.'

I was bewildered stilll.

'But why? And why this morning? They could not know I would go to her this very day.'

'Nay, they knew not that. They came to your quarters first to arrest you and, learning you had gone a-visiting, followed you to Matthias's house. But I think the reason for waiting till now to name you has little to do with your health.'

'What then?'

He looked at me doubtfully as though gauging my strength.

'Have you not heard?' he asked. 'Your protector, the Prince Rupert, was himself arrested last night.'

This was such heavy news that for a moment I was rendered speechless.

'What!' I said incredulously. 'Rupert arrested? And who do they say *he* has ravished?'

' 'Tis not the only crime, Fantom,' said Lauder. 'He is suspected of collusion with the enemy in this business of surrendering Bristol. The King has revoked his commission and commanded him from the country. He and Colonel Legge, the Governor, are placed under arrest.'

'Oh shit!' I said.

'Indeed,' said Lauder. 'You're a hanged man, Fantom. You have enemies enough to stretch your neck a dozen times now your patron has become a thing of straw.'

'Nay, but Rupert will have power still,' I said, alarmed.

'Not to pardon a guilty man. That is the General's prerogative.'

'And who will be general now?'

Lauder shrugged.

'God knows. The King himself must direct for want of a better. He has a close adviser.'

'Digby! But he is not a malicious man, Lauder. He would not advise against the pardoning of an innocent just to settle a private score!'

'Innocent!' echoed Lauder. 'Innocent! If they put you through a mincer there would not be found one particle of you to call *innocent!* If the lady's testimony stands firm, you must tread air, Carlo.'

He enjoyed his image so much that I heard him chuckling in the distance as he made his way from me. Despite all, I could not believe that Annette would bear false witness against me. What motive could she have? She had given herself willingly. I searched my memory, there was no mistake. I had not been carried away by an excess of zeal to force her against her will. Then she had had my letters in which my honourable intent was clearly stated. How could she say she had had no word from me? They could not all be lost – unless Matthias had found a means to intercept them. That must be it! I decided. He was behind it. Perhaps he had convinced her that I had slain his brother, her husband. Or perhaps after the taking of Bletchingdon House, that long turd Hector had spoken of me, telling the tale of the black stallion which I had taken from the dead cavalier. But that would mean she knew of my connection with her husband *before* we had lain together.

My head was spinning. I was still weak from my time in bed and these coils of thought were too much for me. I drank half a bottle of brandy and fell asleep.

By the time of my trial, I had convinced myself that some simple misunderstanding lay at the base of Annette's accusation and all would yet be well. But as I listened to her statement to the court martial, I realized that things were far more complicated. She wasn't just mistaken, she was lying. With downcast eyes and faltering voice, she described how I had brutally assaulted her and at pistol point forced her to submit to me. I was furious with indignation at this calumny. Never in any of my tangles with women had I resorted to such barbaric methods. A man who cannot ravish without resort to physical threat is no man at all.

Suddenly everything began to ring most sinisterly. She denied my letters. I had no acknowledgement of them and the messenger who had carried mail between the army and Oxford had been slain in the late siege at Bristol. Witnesses were produced all of whom denied ever having heard Annette treat me, or even talk of me, in terms other than of indifference or dislike, while at the same time testifying that I had pestered her to her great discomfort. Only Lauder could I produce to counter these allegations but he made a very poor impression staring fixedly at Annette all the time and sounding like some senile drunkard bribed to report mythical conversations. He left the court immediately, in shame, I hoped. Other testimony was brought which portrayed me as an evil, licentious man and even the fact that I had come to the King's party from the other side was educed as a blight on my character. Hypocrites!

Eventually the officers of the court withdrew to meditate their verdict but I had no doubts what it would be. After a while Lauder appeared in the antechamber where I was placed till the court should re-assemble.

'Thanks for your help,' I said sarcastically. 'You did not even stay in the court after you had spoken, as a friend would, but left most suddenly like a man in need of drink!'

'I was,' he said. 'This woman of yours, do you know yet why she is lying?'

'No. Can you tell me?' I asked eagerly.

'Today I saw her for the first time,' he answered. 'You find her beautiful?'

'Surpassing all,' I answered indignantly as though I were in a position to be offended by any slur against Annette. 'Her face is the fairest I ever saw, didst not think so?'

'And you never saw her before?'

'No. I think not,' I said, puzzled.

'Oh, Fantom, Fantom. Think of those features. Do they not bring one to mind, one who you knew well of old?'

I thought, conjuring Annette's lovely face to my mind's eye. I regarded it in bafflement for a while wondering what the old fool could mean. Then gradually the hair shortened, the eyebrows thickened, a polished steel helmet domed above that fair white brow.

'Oh Christ,' I said, hardly believing. 'The beautiful boy. D'Amblève! Oh Christ! It is not true?'

'Ay, is it. As soon as I saw her, I knew. I have been to talk with various of her acquaintance and in particular with her maid, that French lassie. She was adamant, her mistress was not French, but Belge. From another I received her maiden name, Annette D'Amblève. I believe if we look closer we will find she was the boy prick's young sister.'

I still found it hard to believe.

'But even so! Why should she be so cunning in revenge against me? I did her no harm!'

'Recall how her brother pursued his revenges after you. He was so strong in hatred that your memory of it frightened you long after he himself was dead. What more natural than that he should describe his woes to his family and name the author of them? Did she not show interest in your German campaigns?'

'Aye, she did. She questioned me most closely,' I recalled.

'That would be her way to make certain you were the very man. For when you plan to set a rope round someone's neck, you will take care to find the right neck!'

'And all this? Her submission to me, her silence in my absence, this was part of her plot?'

Lauder shrugged.

'Who knows how carefully she plotted? May be she did not plot at all but, finding herself seduced and pregnant, and considering later by whom – the man who had ravished her brother's bride and poisoned his life, not to mention killing her own husband – she looked round for ways to take revenges and found this one. Most ironical!'

'Ironical?'

'Aye. That Fantom, who has committed so many ravishings scot-free, should die for one he did not commit.'

I walked round the room in agitation.

'She will not go so far,' I insisted. 'She will make me suffer but not so much.'

'She waited till you were unprotected before striking,' said Lauder.

'She is bearing my child!' I shouted.

'Well, as to that, like any poor wee married man, you have only the lady's word. Where the wolf has made a breach, the fox and ferret may easily go.'

The door opened before I could decide how I felt about this monstrous allegation. The court was reconvened.

I hardly bothered to listen to the court president as he declared me guilty and sentenced me to death. I was too busy looking for Annette but she had not stayed for her triumph. Perhaps her conscience would not let her. How could a woman so abuse a poor man?

It is strange what sinful traps our human hesitation can lead us into. Before, when I was merely arrested and awaiting trial, I could have escaped at the expense of one man's life only. Now that I was condemned, however, I would need to kill four or five in order to break free.

I protested again that the placing of such a large guard on my quarters was a slur on my honour, but this seemed only to amuse. I was waiting for the sentence to be confirmed – or quashed – and while normally Rupert would have been the one to do this, now it was for the King himself. I still had hopes of Rupert for all that. He was popular among the soldiers and though he had made some powerful enemies, he also had a large number of powerful friends. But his behaviour now (so I was told) was based on a sense of deep grievance rather than diplomacy and merely confirmed him in the

King's disfavour, who had already commissioned Lord George Digby as Lieutenant-General of his forces in the north. God help all poor soldiers!

Visitors, principally Lauder, kept me abreast of this news so it came as no surprise to have the sentence confirmed and to be told that a date had been set but five days distant for the ceremony. I made claim that, as an officer, I had the right to die by shooting, but so strong was their fear of my reputation as a hard-man that they would not countenance it. Indeed there were some (Lauder said) who would have liked me beaten to death with cudgels to make sure of the job, but such barbarisms disgusted the greater part.

You will understand how during this time I watched and waited for an opportunity to escape, but I was held so strait that for all my ingenuity none came. My guards always appeared to me in pairs and though in the last resort I was prepared to assault them both with my bare hands, I knew that this was but a fair way to be borne to the scaffold on a stretcher. I begged Lauder to smuggle in a weapon to me, but he refused, saying that he was closely searched at my door and to be found with a concealed weapon would but join him to me on the gallows. I have before noted this distressing tendency in Lauder to put his own well-being before that of his friends. The old virtues are fast disappearing from the earth.

Of Mistress Annette there was little news save that Lauder was now able to confirm absolutely what he had earlier surmized, that she was certainly the beautiful boy's young sister. Their mother, a noted beauty more French than Belge, had been in Queen Henrietta Marie's entourage till her marriage and had obtained a similar post for her daughter, during which service she had met young Matthias whose bones were now enriching the soil around Edgehill. The family fortunes had been in disrepair and D'Amblève's proposed marriage to the German girl had been based as much on her wealth as her beauty. Unfortunately in his obsession with taking vengeance on me, he had ignored his obligations to his family and, instead of adding to their store, had depleted it completely by the time of his death. I realized now the depth of Annette's feelings against me. It was not merely the family honour that I had hurt but the family purse.

I regretted Annette deeply. She was a girl after my own heart. I still had a deep-down hope that she would not let this matter go as far as the gallows. After all, she was carrying my child – that must count for something! But it was no use relying on such sentimentalities.

Lauder let himself be persuaded as far as this for me, that he would keep Petrarch saddled and provisioned for me each night of the four that now remained between me and the rope. As for money, once I could get to my Oxford cache I would be well provided, and a few days spent going from one city to another where I had left money hidden would see me a wealthy man.

But I still had to escape. Two more days passed and the vigilance and number of my guards seemed to increase daily. Any faint hope of Annette's interference disappeared when Lauder came to me that evening with the news that she had miscarried. Well, I daresay she was glad of it. How do you bring up a child to tell him that you had his father hanged?

My escape must be made now, I resolved. Tomorrow on the eve of my execution the guard's vigilance would be at its peak.

'Lauder,' I said. 'You will not bring me a weapon?'

'I have said so,' he answered, regarding me with something like sympathy in those wintry blue eyes. It filled me with an even greater sense of my own peril. Lauder dispensed sympathy like God dispensed manna, only in the case of utmost necessity.

'But the horses are ready?' I said, anxious lest his despair at my plight should have made him neglect this task.

'For what use it is, they're both ready,' he answered.

'Thanks for that, old friend,' I said. 'Now give me your hand for in this life we may not meet again.'

'I shall come tomorrow,' he protested.

'Nay,' I said, grasping his hand firm. 'Tomorrow I must make my peace with my Maker. I shall thank him sincerely that I had a friend like you.'

He squeezed my hand tight. I swear there were tears in his eyes. There certainly were next moment as I kneed him in the balls, and immediately, lest his eighty-odd years had rendered him insensitive in that area, brought my best silver sconce down on the back of his head.

I felt most virtuous as I let him fall gently to the floor and started removing his tunic. I was the nearest thing to a friend he had ever had and he would have suffered grievously later to think that selfish consideration of his own safety had prevented him from helping me.

By the time I had put on his tunic, cloak and hat, all of which were fortunately very distinguishable, if only by reason of their shabbiness, the old Scot was beginning to recover. I helped him to his feet, sat him at a table with his back to the door and gave him wine in the sconce I had hit him with. His grizzled pate was a giveaway, so I rammed on his head a long nightcap I used to wear against the cold which is very bitter in these draughty colleges. Then, dimming the lamp, I rapped on the door and as the guard cautiously opened it I said to Lauder in my best Scottish accent, 'Guid night to you, Fantom. Best say your prayers, man, and ask the Laird's forgiveness.'

Lauder, still dazed, drew deeply on the wine. From behind he looked the very picture of a man in some perturbation of spirit.

Now came the moment of crisis when I had to step out of the darkened room. There was no hope to continue the deceit. All my intention was to grab for Lauder's sword and pistol which he was made to put against the wall before entering, and hope to fight my way out. My room was at the head of a little staircase and I knew that besides the guard at the door, at least two others stood at the foot of the stairs. It was not a good prospect, but better than the rope.

Then Lauder did me a last service. The wine must have cleared his head a bit and he attempted to stand. That was too much. With a low moan he slumped sideways and crashed to the floor.

'He has taken poison!' I cried, forgetting my accent. But it didn't matter. Fearful of losing his prisoner to death, the guard rushed into the room and knelt over the twitching body. He realized his error just soon enough to turn his head round and receive my boot full in the face.

I buckled on Lauder's sword and spanned both the Scot's and the guard's pistols. Then, holding these beneath my cloak, I went down the staircase, moving sideways and slowly as an old man would in this narrow passage.

At the foot of the stairs an archway led into a cloister walk and here three more guards stood, warming themselves at a charcoal brazier. They were armed with pike and musket and their weapons presently stood against the cloister wall. They sprang to attention as I approached – Lauder would have been a stickler for military correctness on his visits – and I had no difficulty at all in planting a ball in each of the two nearest. But the third was a nimble devil and before I could get to him with my sword he had seized his pike and put the brazier between himself and me. I would have preferred that he had grabbed his musket for I would have taken my chance with a single ball, but this was a big strapping fellow, clearly trained to the pike, and though it was nearer ten than the sixteen feet a campaign pike ought to be, yet it was a great distancer of a man with a sword.

There was little time to spare. The shots would soon bring others. I attempted to circle round the brazier, meaning to run for it as soon as I got in the clear, but he was having none of that and with a couple of terrifyingly dextrous passes of his weapon kept me pinned in the archway.

'Fellow,' I said. 'Wouldst be rich?'

'Nay, sir,' he said in a very nasty kind of way. 'And how shall you repay me for a brother's life?'

'Brother? One of these?'

I looked at the two shot sentries, neither of whom was dead though soon like to be. One of them was cast in the same mould as the big pikeman.

'He still lives,' I said and bending down, I grasped him by the collar and pulled him upright.

'But not for long,' I continued. 'Soon he will burn.'

And I threw him across the brazier.

With a wild yell, the pikeman leapt forward to rescue his brother. I ran him through the shoulder and the two wounded men and the brazier fell in a heap on the stone flagged walk, scattering red-hot charcoal everywhere. Other men were approaching now, shouting and waving weapons. But they knew not what was amiss, and while they sought for an enemy, I in my quartermaster's insignia was able to stroll out of the college, mount Lauder's nag which was tied up by the porter's lodge and ride into the darkness.

Lauder had been as good as his word. The old bastard must have had some confidence in me after all. Petrarch and Athene were ready for departure and they neighed with pleasure to see me – and perhaps in protest at waiting so long. I embraced them, mounted and made my way swiftly through the dark streets to Sir Olwyn Matthias's house. A lesser man might have had thought of revenges but not I. All I wanted was the store of money which I had cached in his stable wall.

Leaving both my horses some yards from the house lest the inmates of Matthias's stable should call to them, I entered making soothing noises and went straight to my hiding place. The stone swun out easily. I reached in my hand and felt both therein and in my own stomach a great emptiness. My money had gone.

'Christ's fingers!' I snarled. 'The bitch has robbed me!'

Had my money been there, I should have taken it and gone. Time was short and though there were more important considerations for the garrison than my capture and execution, yet would all the guard-posts be alerted to my escape in very short time. But so enraged was I by this mean theft of a soldier's wages, honestly earned, that I went straight to the house, made short work of a small window on the ground floor and was on the stairs before I began to feel uneasy at my folly. But still I pressed on. Sir Olwyn was little to fear as my ball through his foot had lost him a couple of toes and turned him lame, though not to the improvement of his temper I guessed. The servants were far removed at the back of the house. Swiftly I made my way to Annette's quarters and entered.

She lay in her bed, her face lit only by the glow of the flames from the sweet-smelling wood burning in the grate. I suddenly recalled Lauder telling me that she had miscarried and strange to say I felt my conscience heavily smitten to trouble her at this time. But she was awake and had seen me. Sitting up with the sheet held tight against her neck, she said without surprise, 'You have come to kill me.'

'Nay, madam,' I said. 'More important business than your life fetches me here. I want my money.'

'Money? Which money?'

I approached with my sword drawn and thrust the point into her pillow.

'No trifling,' I said. 'The money which I hid in the stable. You have taken it. Come, madam, I know you for treacherous and vindictive, but I had not taken you for a thief.'

'I know nothing of your money! Nothing!' she cried. 'Except that it will have been dishonestly obtained by the greatest rogue the world has ever known.'

I began to believe her, but I was so enraged that I seized the sheet from her hands and dragged it away, as though she might have my wealth hidden beside her. But what I saw surprised me more. She was naked. I had seen her so but once before and even in my rage I admired once more the perfection of her body. And then something struck me. I am no medical man but when it comes to female physiology I have some expertise.

'Lady,' I said. 'What marvel is this? Was it but today that you miscarried of a six month child? You are marvellously recovered!'

She did not reply but made a grasp at the bell-pull which would summon her servant. I easily prevented her and brought my face close to hers.

'So,' I said. 'That too was a lie. A cushion up your skirt to give my judges the ocular proof of your slanders. What a long and cleverly planned malice this has been! And with me at the point of hanging, the "child" can go and Mistress Matthias can be herself again!'

She denied nothing. There was nothing she could deny.

She lay there, silent, expecting death. Instead I did to her what she had falsely accused me of and she did not resist but lay quiet all the time.

'There, madam,' I said afterwards. 'Go now to your chirurgeon and complain. Let him be as surprised as I have been! So now we have all had our revenges.'

'You still live,' she said coldly.

'And shall I die because your husband was a soldier and your brother was a fool?' I demanded.

'You have killed for slighter reason I do not doubt,' she answered.

'Ay, and wars have started for slighter reason, and kingdoms have been lost for slighter reason. But shall you and I and all manner of people living in peace under the law govern our lives by these slight accidents? Nay, lady. I have killed a man for killing my horse, which I loved more than that man. But if every woman in this land who has lost a husband or felt her family injured in this war should seek to hang one for it, why the forests would crack like muskets at the weight of the bodies. All of us may kill for rage, and some of us must kill for money, but only God should kill for revenge.'

'I shall pray for it,' she said.

'And I against it,' I said. 'Who knows how it shall end?'

Who indeed? At that moment the door burst open and Sir Olwyn appeared in his night-gown, his face puce, his sword brandished over his head. He hopped towards me, swinging his heavily bandaged left foot through the air. So I shot him in the other.

'You did not take my money?' I said to Annette.

She shook her head. She was extraordinarily lovely even though the features of her brother now showed strong in my eye. I might have gone to her again had not Sir Olwyn been rolling and groaning on the floor.

'Goodbye then,' I said. 'Think of me.'

Well, you've got to say something, haven't you?

1646
Bristol

It is a clear indication of how the war was going that getting into Bristol was ten times harder than getting out of Oxford. Why I should wish to get into Bristol at all requires some explanation.

After my escape I had found it fairly easy to make my way where I would in this troubled land. I avoided large groups from either army and stayed in no one place for any length of time. All I wished to do was collect the wealth I had hidden and leave the country. The disappearance of my Oxford cache I had put down to bad luck. Some ostler or stable-lad had chanced on my hiding-place and thought himself fortunate. Well, I had expected this in one or two cases.

But I soon discovered as I went from cache to cache that either ill fortune was pursuing me beyond the bounds of logical expectation or some more sinister force had been at work. They were all empty without exception. Bristol was the last place where I had laid up any store and my only hope was that this at least remained intact. Normally a man of my talents could easily have found provision in the countryside he passed through, but so often had all these towns and villages been scoured by successive armies that the people were suspicious, uncharitable, and ready to strike first and question afterwards. While my small store of ready cash lasted, all was well, but without the chink of coin all help was soon denied except to force – and that I wanted to avoid. A man who had survived my recent dangers would be foolish to end with some yokel's pitch-fork through his belly, and I recalled Lauder's emphasis that there had been *three* Queens of Spades.

So by the time I had reached Bristol, I was hungry, ragged

and altogether villainous in appearance, features which would not have drawn attention to me had it not been for my horses. Petrarch was an animal fit for a prince to ride, Athene, though not so striking as Petrarch was still a handsome beast, and ragamuffins like me did not normally own one, let alone two horses like these. I did not have it in me to neglect their grooming and their coats shone like polished wood. I might easily have relieved my financial plight by selling one of them, but this would have cut my survival chances by half and besides I could not sell any horse of mine to a stranger unless I was certain he was fit to own it.

Anyway, as I said, a losing army is a careless army and I had slipped out of Oxford with no trouble. But the garrison at Bristol were alert, confident, and eager to winkle out spies or spreaders of disaffection in this once Royalist city.

I had paused to stare up at the fort where only a few months previously Lauder and I had lain together, certain of death. My interest must have been noticed by one of the guard there, for soon afterwards a small party of troopers approached me and asked me my business. I claimed to be a Welsh horse-breeder, ruined by a series of attacks by marauding gangs of Cavaliers (whom I roundly cursed for their cruelty and irreligion) and looking for refuge in a loyal city with my only remaining mounts. I was extremely long-winded, as the Welsh so often are, in my description of the wrongs I had undergone and my cleverness in concealing the two horses, in the hope that I would bore them into accepting my tale. But I proved too clever for they became very sympathetic and, close examination confirming the quality of Petrarch and Athene, they assured me their own captain would give me the best price possible. I did all I could to get rid of them without risking suspicion but in the end I was obliged to accompany them into the city. Their captain was not available, however, and thankfully I took my leave, ostensibly to search out lodgings, promising them most faithfully that I would return that evening. But as I mounted to depart, the sergeant who had been most forward in urging the bargain said, 'Hold, for here comes Captain Hector now.'

I went cold at the name. The sergeant left me and went towards a party of officers who were riding down the street towards us. Sure enough, there in their midst I spied the long gangling figure of Hector. I looked around. The narrow street we were in ran right up against the city wall and there was no way out except past the officers. Pulling my hat over my brow, I set Petrarch walking gently towards the group with Athene behind. The sergeant looked round at my approach and pointed me out to Hector, imagining I was coming to display my livestock. As I drew alongside Hector's eyes flickered from the animals to me, back to the animals and then, puzzlement in his expression, to me once more. I let my jaw sag into an expression of semi-imbecility and kept on going. 'Stay!' cried the sergeant, seizing my reins. 'Here is the Captain.'

'Fantom?' queried Hector. Then, reaching for his pistol and in a voice loud with certainty, 'Fantom!'

I kicked the sergeant in the throat and drew my weapon. Hector swung wildly at me missing my cheek by a few inches while the other soldiers, surprised by the suddenness of the strife, looked on in amaze. I struck at his sword-arm, slicing the soft muscle below the shoulder so that he shrieked and dropped his sword. Petrarch responded to the pressure from my knees and broke into a gallop and as I went by I took another swipe at his throat this time thinking to still his tongue for ever, but his horse, badly trained as I would have expected any mount of his to be, reared in fright and I missed. It was a pity, for now the hunt would be up not for a lunatic Welsh horse-breeder, but for Carlo Fantom *in propria persona*. As it turned out, it was worse even than that, for on hearing the story, the governor of the city decided that I must be there on some official mission from the King to treat with disaffected persons in the walls with a view to plotting a local rising. Orders were sent out to all posts, urging my immediate capture, which no one would have bothered much over were my crime simply assault on a long streak of piss like Hector.

I lay low until nightfall, mercifully early at this time of year, and then went in search of my cache. My spirits were low now and I felt no surprise and even little dismay to find it as empty as the rest. Even the mystery had solved itself for my sight of the fort had put me in mind of Jem Croft's last words.

'I have wronged . . . forgive me. . . .'

They made sense now. Jem had, probably by accident, seen me hiding one of my sacks of booty at an early stage in our acquaintance. Thereafter he must have watched me most carefully after each share-out and as soon as I deposited my portion, he had removed it. No wonder the bastard begged forgiveness! I hoped his soul would rot in hell.

So here I was destitute in a city of enemies. Was this what all my fine schemes, my thriftiness, my plans for respectability and a settled family life, had brought me to?

But despair is the last sin, and I had hopes of committing many others before I reached that extreme. One chance still remained to me, one debt was yet unpaid. I led my horses down to the waterfront and searched among the ships moored there till I saw the leaky, warping old tub misnamed the *Albatross* which belonged to Captain Hugh Trengold. It appeared empty save for an old man who came up on deck momentarily to throw a bucket of slops over the side, and I settled to wait in a dark alley opposite. About an hour later I was frightened by a platoon of foot soldiers who marched by, stopping at each ship to talk with the watchman. I was too far away to hear what was said but my fears guessed they were searching for me.

Trengold did not appear till long past midnight by which time I was half frozen despite huddling between Petrarch and Athene for warmth. He looked drunk and when I reached out of the darkness and seized him by the throat, he was too surprised to struggle.

'Trengold,' I whispered. 'We have an agreement.'

'Who's there?' he asked screwing his eyes up as though he would bore through the dark.

'Carlo Fantom,' I said. 'You recall our arrangement?'

'Who? Fantom, is it? Nay, but the time is past, you did not come,' he said.

'Within a twelvemonth, I said. Had you forgotten that? Why then, you may have forgotten how the rest of the agreement ran. If you fail in your side of it, you are to die!'

I laid my sword against his drink-flushed cheek where the ice-cold metal must have felt like a bar of fire.

'Yes, yes I recall. You're right!' he gasped. 'Let us fix a time. Come, let us meet in the tavern tomorrow and fix a time.'

'The time is fixed. Tonight,' I said.

'Tonight! I cannot sail tonight! 'Tis madness to sail at this time of year. Besides I have no crew.'

'Tonight,' I repeated. 'I saw a man on deck just now.'

'Him!' he said scornfully. ' 'Tis but an old drunkard who watches the ship for me. He is no sailor.'

'He shall learn,' I said implacably. 'And I shall learn. For though we must row the *Albatross* across the entire Atlantic, still must we sail tonight.'

He was genuinely terrified at the prospect, but fortunately still more terrified of my sword, though he recovered sufficiently to protest when I told him my horses were coming. 'I carry no livestock!' he said. 'Hens, perhaps. But nothing larger.'

'They come!' I insisted. 'Else you remain here. For ever.'

Sobbing with fear he agreed. Petrarch had travelled on boats before, and Athene too, so we got them up the narrow gangplank with very little difficulty.

The old man when I roused him from his slumber turned out to be more valuable than I could have hoped. His name was Dickon Wells, an old sailor driven by age and alcohol to a dependence on the likes of Trengold. He agreed readily to help sail the *Albatross*, partly out of fear of my sword but most out of delight at the Captain's discomfiture.

'May three men sail this craft?' I enquired.

'Aye, sir. If the one at the helm be steady and true, and the others work like the devil. But let us hasten else we miss the tide without which here we must bide till the morrow.'

Our first task was to get the old lugger out into the stream and this required two of us to descend to the dinghy and row while the third manned the helm. I didn't trust Trengold alone on the ship and I have no seamanship, so I took him with me against his protests and left Dickon at the wheel.

The water which had looked still and polished from the shore now proved to be fast moving and rough, and my muscles cracked as I strained at this unfamiliar task. Slowly the lugger came out of its berth, following the tiny dinghy as sometimes a great stallion will follow the goat it has befriended. Suddenly there was a great deal of activity on the quayside behind us. Voices shouted I know not what, perhaps demanding why the *Albatross* was moving. Perhaps in the frosty light someone saw the two horses on deck, I cannot say, but now there came an outbreak of musket fire and as Dickon span the helm to turn the ship into the stream and we made haste to come alongside and clamber aboard, I saw another small boat push off from the quay, bright with moonlight glinting off metal.

'We are lost,' cried Trengold.

'Never say so, Captain,' said Dickon. 'Soon there'll be foul weather enough to hide a flotilla in.'

I glanced at the bright moon in disbelief. Such nights as this I had shivered through on many a field and never known storms to rise from them. But at sea the laws of nature do not apply, it seems, for as the boatful of soldiers heaved after us and I obeyed Dickon's instructions for hoisting some scraps of sail, I saw to the north east some traces of cloud come streaming across the sky and felt soon after the wind which drove them. We were now running fast down the broadening channel and behind us the labouring boat disappeared in darkness and spume. With a bit of luck the stupid bastards would all be tipped out and drowned. Soldiers who haven't got the sense to stay on dry land deserve no less.

'What now?' I yelled to Dickon. 'More sail?'

He shook his head and pointed upwards, at first I thought to indicate the bits of canvas we had laboriously hauled aloft.

'The sky, man,' he shouted. 'Any more sail and in half an hour there'd not be a stick left on her.'

I could not read weather as he could, but the sight of those frosty stars being eaten by great maws of black cloud made me feel a terrible unease. As we raced before the wind towards the open sea, the old lugger pitched and gibbed like an unbroken horse and strained old wood sighed and creaked at every turn. Trengold stood at the wheel, his pale face whipped by locks of his own lank hair.

'Is he all right?' I demanded, not knowing what I meant.

'Aye, sir. 'Tis terror makes a sailor of a man. He will shit his breeks, certes, but he's the man to care for this heap of coffin wood.'

Dickon laughed as he spoke and I saw his old eyes gleam madly. Perhaps he was still drunk, or perhaps this mad adventure came to him as a lightning before death. I knew not, nor cared long to think of it, but went aft to care for my horses.

How they cried out to see me, each vying with the other to come close. What I feared most was that a sudden movement might cause them to lose footing and crash to the deck, so I urged them to kneel, then lie down between two hatches, so that they were to some extent wedged against the rolling of the ship.

God bless the beasts, but they obeyed most trustingly and for a while I lay with them, an arm round either's neck, and prayed for their safety. Dickon joined me shortly and proffered a broken-necked jug of raw spirit which set my innards already disturbed by the violence of our progress in a turmoil.

'God's piss!' I said. 'Is this what sailor's drink?'

'If they can get it,' he replied. 'Otherwise they make do with unrefined stuff.'

'How think you, Dickon?' I asked. 'Will we be challenged by ships of the Parliament's navy?'

'Challenged? Tonight? What! on a night such as this promises, none but fools and rogues sail the seas! More liquor, sir?'

I sipped again, more cautiously, and this time felt my guts anaesthetized instead of provoked.

'So, we may make it safe to Ireland?'

'Ireland, is it? Well, sir, as to that, who can say? We shall go where this gale will take us, sir, and that may be to the Americas, or to the bed of the Bristol Channel.'

I did not like the sound of this.

'Can we not run for shelter on the Devon coast?' I asked.

'Fear not,' he reassured me genially. 'Our Captain fears enough for all and where it is safest, he will go.'

So we lay there and drank, while all around the night grew darker, and the wind wilder, and soon great waves began to run alongside the ship, rising like battlements above us, against which the ship's mast and rigging lay like puny assault ladders. Strange; I had thought of the ship as I stood on the fort at Bristol; now I thought of the fort as I lay on the ship. Both times I felt helpless and out of my element, but at least in the fort nothing was coming at me worse than men.

At first the horses screamed and tried to struggle to their feet as the icy water broke over the rails and rushed across the deck. With difficulty I calmed them and as the water came again and again they grew used, or perhaps numbed, through repetition.

Now the ship began to be hurled about as though it were a shuttle-cock on a court. Sometimes it seemed as though we went spinning through the air high above the water and at others as though the waves that towered over us would meet and blot out the skies for ever. All this time Trengold hung to the wheel and I began to admire the man for his tenacity, even though I knew it was fear for his own skin that inspired him. After a while Dickon went to assist him and I took this for a sign of increase in our peril. I would have gone myself but I did not dare leave Petrarch and Athene, who without my presence would certainly be washed overboard.

What time had passed, I did not know. Almost I began to wish myself safe in one of Bristol's gaols, for men and buildings I am skilled to escape from, but this ocean was beyond my cunning. There was naught to do but lie still and trust in the strength of a cowardly villain and a drunken old man, or so I thought, but there are weaker things in nature than the human spirit, and rotten worm-eaten ships are among them. I had thought our movement so erratic that no change would be perceptible but all at once the ship seemed to slew sideways and what I had before thought to be violence now by comparison seemed the smooth motion of a sleigh down a snowy bank. Peering through the mist of spray and spume which now perpetually shrouded us, I saw the wheel spinning free and thought for a moment that my two companions must have been carried away. Then their figures lurched along the deck and half slid, half crawled towards me.

'We are lost!' cried Trengold.

'What's amiss?' I demanded.

'The rudder has been carried away,' gasped Dickon. 'We lie broadside on and must soon turn turtle.'

I realized now how important their efforts must have been to preserve us thus far. Trengold, now that there was no physical task to keep his spirit upright, had collapsed completely and was sobbing out prayers and blasphemies in alternate breaths. Dickon was casting around for his jug but it had long since gone over the side and we were hard put not to follow it. Each wave lifted us up and threatened to tip us all out like chessmen from a box. Only the fact that our sails had long since gone and with them most of the spars and the best part of the mast gave us gravity enough to remain upright and that could not be for long.

'Where are we?' I cried. 'Are we near any shore?'

'Only of hell!' answered Trengold wildly. 'This is your doing, Fantom!'

He hurled himself at my throat in desperate haste to do the water's work for it. I wrestled madly with him while Dickon looked on and roared with laughter. Normally I would have broken him in two with ease but his insane fury seemed to have doubled his strength and he pinned me on my back, plucked a dagger from his side and raised it high. I ceased to struggle. Behind his arm I saw towering high above us a cliff of water which when it broke must surely crush us all. Perhaps the knife was the more merciful death. Dickon saw it too and yelled loud enough to be heard above the wind and waves. Trengold turned, the knife fell from nerveless fingers and he shrieked. I just had time to realize that what we were rushing towards was no cliff of water, but a real cliff of rock and stone, then we struck.

The *Albatross* fell apart like a whorehouse dream. One moment I was aboard a ship, next there was none. Dickon and Trengold went away from me like puff balls on the wind. I saw their white faces, Dickon's faintly puzzled, Trengold's wholly terrified, then they were gone. But I had no care for them. I was being sucked fathoms down, as though the devil himself were taking a draught and not giving over till he saw the bottom of the cup. Over and over I turned in pitch darkness, all the while thrashing and thrusting with legs and arms but with no sense of what was up or down. Still, a man does not go easily into the long darkness and while I had any vigour remaining I would fight. But my lungs could take no more, my struggles weakened, I had to breathe. My mouth gaped wide, I took one vile mouthful of water, then it turned to air and I was coughing and retching on the surface.

But it could not be for long. I was too weak and in any case it would have taken an immortal to swim for long against the mighty surges of those icy waters. Yet was I grateful for the air and though I could not see the sky, the knowledge that the stars still shone serene above that turbulence of cloud was a comfort to me. Almost I was resigned to slip beneath the surface once more and not come up again. Almost . . . but still was I Carlo Fantom, Soldier of Fortune and Hard-man, that had fought his way across a dozen countries and ravished his way across a dozen more. My being was precious to me no matter how little value it had to anyone else. No, they must drag me down, I would not go willingly.

Such is the empty rhetoric that buoys up a dying and desperate man. As though words should take shape and substance and float alongside him in the darkness. As though words should move and give back utterance, crying thinly from every side. As though . . .

'Petrarch!' I shouted 'Athene!'

And there they were. No delusion this, no dying vision, but my own two dear friends close by, striving towards me, their narrow handsome heads raised high from the water, neighing a greeting and an appeal.

With renewed strength I struck out to meet them. It seemed

as though the wind's strength was ebbing a little and the waters no longer beat so desperately against the side of that terrible cliff which was still visible but a handful of yards away. I was between my horses now, one arm draped over either's neck and as the water's surge carried us inexorably back towards the cliff I strained my eyes to find some break in its massy sweep wherein we might land. It seemed flawless, but reunited thus with my family, I could not believe fate had ordained my death that night. And I was no whit surprised when in these comparatively calmer waters a swirling side current caught us and took us spinning round the base of the cliff till the solid face began to break and corrugate into a series of inlets and coombs. Into one of these we finally paddled, half frozen and wholly exhausted, while above the storm as though tired of its game went scudding off to play havoc in some other quarter leaving the same cold untroubled sky that had watched my departure from Bristol.

To lie there and breathe the cold air and feel the frost begin to flower on my sodden skin seemed all the joy a man could ask. But my horses knew better and the wise beasts forced themselves awkwardly upright, their metalled hoofs clanging and slipping against slimy rock. So up I rose too, knowing they were right and that this sharp air could do just as well what the ocean had failed at.

It was a long struggle uphill, but we helped each other, and finally we found ourselves on a track which promised society to me, and Petrarch and Athene must have come across the scent of their own kind too, for they whinnied and walked forward the faster.

The boor who opened his cottage door to my knocking stood amazed as I pushed past him and led my two horses into his warm room. His wife shrieked and the four or five brats huddled beneath their squalid blankets and began to cry. But he knew better than to deny his superiors and instead threw a pile of dry logs on the embers of his fire and set his wife to heating some nauseating gruel.

'Is this Devon?' I asked through my chattering teeth.

'Nay, sire. This be Lundy island,' replied the oaf.

Lundy. I had heard of Lundy, but could not remember what. Surely it was still held for the King? But I must be careful.

'Who rules here, fellow?' I demanded dragging the blankets off the brats and draping one over Petrarch, the other over Athene.

'The King, master,' answered the fool.

Well, that answered my question more directly than I had meant. I settled down to getting dry and warm and making sure I had not got frostbite. I stripped myself naked and used some strips of sacking to towel myself down. God's sputum, but the water seemed to have got right beneath my skin and I doubted if I should ever be dry again. Yet the life was coming back to my fingers and toes and never have I been so pleased to feel pain. At the end of half an hour I began to think I might survive and when I found myself remarking that the woman of the house, though a smudge-faced slut, yet had large and well-formed breasts, I knew I was set to recover.

But her husband it seemed was not as stupid as he looked. He must have taken an opportunity to send one of his brood off for help, for as I tended to my steaming horses, the door burst open and a party of sturdy yeomen rushed in with swords in their hands. The sight of me standing there stark naked between two horses made them halt in amazement. Behind them in the doorway stood another figure, by his clothes and bearing a gentleman. Seeing that all was secure, he now stepped inside, a dignified ruddy-faced man of half a century or so, with a twinkling eye and a hawk-nose.

'Good morrow, sir,' he said courteously. 'In the King's name, welcome to Lundy. May I be permitted to know your business?'

I threw back my head and laughed. If this was the best Lauder's Queen of Spades could do, then I would sit at piquet with the devil.

'In faith, Mr Bushell,' I said, 'if you hope for more gold from me, you may plainly see I have none concealed about me. Nay, I am come here to judge how carefully you have managed my previous investment!'

1646–7
Lundy

I NEVER knew a man I admired so much as Thomas Bushell, for he went a-plundering with his tongue just as I went a-plundering with my sword, yet he gained every man's respect – as well as a hundred times more money than I. There was a kind of innocence about him which derived from his true belief in the feasibility of all his schemes. At one time he had a plan to tap Snowdon, a great hill in the Welsh wilderness which, when the local populace discovered it was like to flood the countryside, they resisted with force. 'Yet it would have made me rich. Aye, rich,' he assured me, puzzled that so good an argument for his plan should ever have met with opposition.

Politically he was no fool either. Regarded as one of the most loyal of His Majesty's supporters, he proved his loyalty by refortifying the semi-ruined castle of Lundy and occupying it in comfort, safe from the vicissitudes of the mainland war, for there was but one landing place on the island's cliff-secured coast and though a few boat loads of determined men might have overrun the weak defences, yet would the loss of life have been disproportionate to the winning of this small block of grass and stone.

I was well entertained and after a few days Thomas and I became very familiar. I told him most of my sad story which he heard with sympathy, only interrupting sometimes to reminisce of his own periods in gaol from which he had ever contrived to scape with much greater ease and less bloodshed than I. When I came to my financial losses at the hands of that treacherous bastard, Croft, he became grave, wished that he had the wherewithal to repay what I had invested with him, but confessed (as though it were a trifle) to owing a total of fifty or sixty thousand pounds. Yet even knowing this, when he came to talk of new projects for following the Welsh silver lode out beneath the sea, I would have supplied him with my last coin, had any remained to me!

It is to satisfy Sir Thomas, and to do I know not what for myself, that I have taken to setting down these accounts of my life. It was a laborious task to start with, but now, these many weeks later, I find it comes as easy as riding a well-schooled horse.

Sir Thomas is highly skilled in the theatrical arts of sound and light, and many an evening we have sat with a bottle of French wine between us (most of which I drank for he was extremely temperate) and watched some ingenious entertainment of his devising, with thunder-claps and lightnings, rainbows and water-spouts, and strange musics of all kinds.

It is a magical time and all the more precious to me for my awareness of the bitter fighting and the bitterer memories which lie behind me on the mainland. My only cause for concern has been Athene's health. Petrarch made a complete recovery from his ordeal after the shipwreck but Athene is plagued still with a cough and a lameness in her left fore-hoof which has been deeply gashed at some time, probably as she dragged herself ashore. Still, we have much to be thankful for.

I was called to the cliff-head one morning soon after my arrival by a group of the peasants who farmed on the island and, following their pointing fingers I saw far below lodged between two rocks which only appeared at low tide a human body. It was Hugh Trengold I was certain, though at this distance and after the work of fish and water little enough remained to make identification certain. These bucolic fools were bent on clambering down the cliff-face to retrieve the corpse. I assured them that they would find nothing of value. He wore no rings and most of his clothing had been dragged off by the sea. It was not worth the risk of a life. Then the boobies told me that it was to give him a Christian burial that they were willing to hazard themselves! This in my eyes put them beneath contempt so I said no more. However, noticing that my first host on the island was among those venturing himself, I made haste to his hovel where without preamble save to kick the brats and hens out. I tumbled his wife on the hearth. Do not misunderstand me, I had no fear of the fellow but why make even a peasant your enemy when there is no need? The wife took it all in silence with no false modesty or foolish resistance and when I heard later that her stupid man had slipped on the cliff-face and broken his ankle, I visited them again and left a silver coin I had won off one of Sir Thomas's retainers at dice. Why I did this, I know not. Perhaps I am developing a sense of responsibility.

Sir Thomas and I have found much in common besides our time in gaol. Though I know nothing of mining save that done by pioneers in a long siege and he knows nothing of warfare save how best to use explosives, yet at many points have our interests touched and from theory we have moved to practice, blowing large holes in the island rocks. I think I could bring down a castle wall with great ease now. Christmas Day we celebrated with a great feast and one of Sir Thomas's entertainments, at the height of which effigies of Cromwell and Fairfax were blown to pieces. This smacked rather much of paganism to me, but delighted the peasants.

There has been little news from the mainland during this long winter, but now the spring is here again, word begins to come of new disasters for the King. A Parliamentary ship approached our harbour the other day, a small vessel yet with cannon enough to do us harm. Fortunately Sir Thomas had devised a pair of floating petards which were kept in a house by the shore for dryness till a ship was sighted, then drifted on lines across the mouth of the little bay so that they bobbed in the water like the buoys used by fishermen to mark their lobster-traps. The petard priming was ignited by a pair of snaphanses connected to the shore by long cords. I had devised these myself, knowing full well the double dangers of all our modern firing devices, that they go off too early or not at all!

So the ship approached. Some of our men were for a parley, but I dissuaded them, pointing out that, once ashore, these trained fighters would make light work of the defenders. The ship was now nosing between the petards and to my dismay I saw that the bow wave was floating the buoys away from the hull. The knave operating the cords on the left hand petard must have seen this too, for now he pulled and with a great roar the bomb exploded. But alas, it was already too far to do any harm save send up a great spout of water to soak those on deck.

The helmsman however must have taken the explosion for a cannon-ball for suddenly he swung his wheel hard over to take them off the line along whicn he guessed our gun was firing, and in doing so brought the prow of the ship right against the other petard.

I pulled on the first cord and nothing happened; swearing foully, I pulled on the second. A short gap. The buoy seemed to have been forced right beneath the keel of the ship and I feared the powder must now be flooded.

Then it blew up.

I did not think a ship could sink so quickly. The deck was already awash before our rowing boats had reached it and all that remained was to slit the throats of those whose heavy arms had not already carried them to the bottom. Soon the water was reddish-brown like the lees of a bottle of claret and my peasants were looking at each other with the delight and horror and amazement of those who have just discovered the experience of killing.

One prisoner we took to learn the news and he told us most boldly that the King's cause was lost, Ralph Hopton had surrendered Falmouth to Fairfax and his soldiers had joined their conquerors, while but a week later the last of the King's forces large enough to be called an army had been broken at Stow-on-the-Wold. I think the fool was bold in his speech in the hope that certainty of the King's defeat might make us fearful to destroy him, but of course my brave peasants quickly realized that none save he knew of our part in the destruction of the ship and without more ado he was thrown over a cliff. The ship lying clearly visible in a few fathoms was then plundered by divers and afterwards dragged by a fleet of rowing boats into deeper water both for concealment and to prevent it becoming a hazard to navigation. I might make something of these fellows if I had the training of them.

The King has been taken by the Scots and Oxford has fallen. This is the news our fishermen have brought back after talking to their fellows from the mainland. It is a year since Naseby, Digby's battle to end all. I thought of Annette and of old Lauder. Had they both remained in Oxford till the end? There was none other I spared much thought for. Rupert and his brother Maurice are to leave the country. Did their mother still live? I wondered. And did she ever think of Fantom?

I grow tired of life on this island. The summer was well enough and the bad news seemed distant enough. But now the thought of another winter is a pain to me. Thomas smiles and says all will be well but, though I almost believe him when he is present, after he has left I know he speaks foolishly. I think the old rogue is now in debt to every native of Lundy too! In truth, there's scarce a family here that is not in debt to me or I to them, depending on how you regard my service to the womenfolk. The men are less friendly than before and I have taken care to let them see my prowess with sword and pistol to deter any rashness.

Essex is dead, God rest the man. He was a bore but he plucked me from the noose a couple of times. So: Essex dead, Rupert banished. Who shall protect me now? Yesterday I was caught with one of the local women and her stupid husband forgot his place and raised his hands against me in violence. I had to kill him and two others who came to the fellow's aid. Has this levelling philosophy reached even here?

Christmas has been a quiet cold time, far from our lively celebrations of a year ago. Supplies and spirits are equally low. Thomas is resolved to return to the mainland once the New Year brings in fair weather. Perhaps I shall go with him and rely on his golden tongue for my protection. Perhaps I shall go back to Germany and see if those stupid wars still hold employment for a man of my talents. I am now nearly fifty. God help me, I grow weak at the thought of a hard campaign.

Thomas has gone. He plans to sail up the Welsh coast and land near Chester where he believes his connection with the King will cause him least danger. I should have accompanied him but that Athene is too ill to travel. She has been in poor health since we were washed ashore on this cursed place. Besides, Thomas had scarcely money enough to pay for his own passage. He will land I fear with scarce a groat in his pocket. But the man carries his own light with him and has promised to send me news and gold as soon as ever he may! So here I sit, lord of the island, short of victuals and shorter of comfort. I scarcely dare venture out, the peasants regard me so threateningly. They have learnt to kill and men do not soon forget that lesson.

News both good and bad. Athene has died. I should be used to this by now but each loss touches my humanity. Later the same day I have been something relieved by the arrival of a small ship whose captain has brought a letter from Thomas and a purse of gold. What gullible ears has he been pouring his honeyed words into! The letter tells me of Cromwell and the King but I have no more interest in their stupid politics. More interestingly, he also says that those who remember me believe I was indeed hanged at Oxford. Somebody certainly was. Could it have been poor Lauder? Well, he had had a long life. Of Annette nothing is known. Perhaps she lives still on her brother-in-law's charity in some awful Welsh fastness. Or perhaps she has gone back to her native land. Perhaps the beautiful boy himself is not dead but jingles his way still across Europe in pursuit of Fantom.

But these are idle fantasies, unfit for a soldier.

The Captain tells me he sails on the evening tide. My passage is paid for. I have told him I will come.

Last night I dreamt of a green garden seen through a courtyard, with nectarines and roses and a fountain of crystal-water playing.

The peasants have guessed at my departure. I have heard them gathering on the road from the castle gate. Doubtless they are clutching their weapons won from the wrecked ship. They will not readily let me pass unscathed.

Petrarch is waiting too. He neighed joyfully as I saddled him up. He is keen to be on the move again. I thought of his mother, sweet Laura; of nimble Osman, noble Orfeo; of awkward, eager, loving Luke; of gentle Athene. What friends I have had.

Someone has discharged a musket-shot at the castle wall. Why do they hate me so? It is nearly evening. Time I must go. They fire again, growing bolder, calling on me to come out.

Fools! Do they not know I am a hard-man?